EVIL ENEMY

SAINT VIEW STRIP, #1

ELLE THORPE

WWW.ELLETHORPE.COM

For Sam.
Beta reader and candle maker extraordinaire. Thank you for
all the years of support.
Elle x

BLURB

Cops and strippers go together like…they don't.

I'm the ruling queen of Saint View Strip. After growing up poor, taking my clothes off and dancing for men is all I know. My thriving club and the people I employ are everything. They're my ride or die, and I'm theirs.

Nobody is taking them away from me.

So when a local politician announces plans to bulldoze everything I've spent the last ten years working for, I won't be silenced.

Not by some suit.

And not by the cops.

Joshua Boston can arrest me all he wants. He can come at me with strong arms and piercing eyes that make my insides tingle. He can push me up against the wall and cuff me all day long.

I'll still hate him.

I'll still want him.

In this town of gangs, shootings, and dangers around every corner, no one is safe. I'm no damsel in distress, but when a violent threat ups the stakes, it's Boston I'm forced to turn to.

We may hate each other, but the real enemy is the one neither of us will see coming.

Please note this story was first published in the Hate to Want You Anthology. It is dark M/F romance set in the Saint View world. It may contain scenes that trigger some readers.

Editing by Emmy at Studio ENP. Proofreading by Karen Hrdlicka at Barren Acres Editing.

ISBN: 978-1-922760-25-8

V:1

1

———

EVE

"Pretty sure I'm going to burst into Hell-spawned flame if I step one toe over that threshold, Eve." Augie stared at the quaint whitewashed church with the same sort of expression he had when it was his week to clean the bathrooms at the club. He crossed his arms over his broad chest, nose wrinkled as if the entire thing was offensive to his morals. If he'd had any.

Lyric stopped beside him, her long red hair flowing down her back in waves, and squinted past the crowds milling around us on the church lawn. "As much as I hate to agree with Augie about anything, I'm with him this time. What the hell?"

I rolled my eyes. "Don't be dramatic." Though dramatic was both Augie's and Lyric's middle name. Which was exactly why I hadn't told either of them where the press conference was taking place. Neither would have come. I actually hadn't told any of my crew where we were going. I'd just said I needed help with something, and the four of them had piled into my car willingly.

But now, even Phoenix's usually quiet demeanor felt more like he was waiting for an explanation, and Fawn who was usually all sunshine and rainbows, nibbled on a fingernail nervously.

I grabbed her hand, pulling Fawn's fingers away from her mouth. "Hey. You're not going to spontaneously combust because we're at a church."

"I know that." But she didn't look entirely convinced.

"You worried about being struck down by some almighty being, too?" I asked Phoenix.

His gaze raked over the milling crowd, who all edged around us as though we were a pond of alligators, ready to launch out of the water, snap our jaws around their ankles, and drag them down into the murky depths of our lair. One older lady, in her Sunday best, gaped up at Phoenix with his tattoos, scars, and scowl. He gave her a moment. At six foot five, and a wall of pure muscle, Phoenix was used to people staring at him. But when she made no move to carry on, he leaned down and whispered, "Boo."

The woman gasped and scuttled off deeper into the crowd, darting glances back at him as she went.

I sighed. "I can't take you guys anywhere."

"Not true," Lyric piped up. "Bar? Good. Beach? Good. Church?" She stuck both thumbs up then made a show of turning them upside down. "Seriously, though, what are we doing here?" Her gaze strayed to the young priest lingering in the doorway of the church. "I mean, he's hot for a guy dressed in a robe, but if you're hoping to save our souls, you probably should have told us to dress down a little."

Lyric's tiny shorts barely covered her perfect ass, and a low-cut top showed a healthy amount of her impressive cleavage. She wasn't wearing a bra, she had no need to, her boobs were courtesy of a great surgeon and sat high and proud without the assistance of an underwire.

"You look great," I told her. "But that's beside the point. We aren't here for some god to judge your clothes. Or your sins." If there was a God, He already knew our sins, and between the five of us, we had plenty. "And we aren't here to check out the priest."

"Did you see the tattoo peeking out beneath his sleeve though? I'm *so* intrigued."

I ignored her and passed over a creased piece of paper. "You're here for moral support."

Dragging her attention away from the apparently tatted up priest, she took the paper, running a long bright-pink fingernail beneath one of the corners to unfold it. She glanced over the neatly printed writing and then stared up at me with big eyes. "What the fuck?"

Heads turned around us, and Lyric glowered in their direction. "What? You never heard someone drop an F-bomb in your life? Get outta here."

Augie snatched the paper from her hand, and Phoenix and Fawn read over his shoulders. Augie was practically vibrating with anger by the time he got to the bottom of the page. "They're trying to shut us down?"

I took the notice back from him, tucking it inside my purse once more. "Yes."

"Unfuckingbelieveable," he swore, none too softly,

earning him more stares. "Who does this guy think he is?"

I pointed to one of the signs hammered into the grass. Right in the center, a middle-aged man stared out with an overly enthusiastic smile that showed off almost every single one of his pearly-white teeth. Lines crinkled at the corners of blue eyes, and a crisp white shirt, navy suit jacket, and matching tie completed the look. There was no mistaking a photo like that. They were reserved solely for real estate agents and politicians.

William Reed was definitely the latter.

"Speak of the devil..." I murmured, a sleek black limousine rolling up and stopping at the curb.

"And he shall appear," Lyric drawled.

William slid out of the fancy car, and the crowd around us cheered like he was some returning hero. They pushed forward, and the police appeared out of nowhere, calling for everyone to stay back and give them room.

William smiled widely, waving to his milling supporters, then eventually turned his attention back to the car, offering his wife a hand. She placed her fingers in his and allowed him to help her out. Two others followed, one a teenage girl and a slightly older guy.

"Who are they?"

I glanced up at Phoenix. "You mean, who is he?" His gaze was trained firmly on the mayoral candidate's son.

Phoenix shrugged and turned away.

I sidled closer. "His name is Dylan. He's twenty-one..."

"How do you know that?"

I shrugged. "I did my homework after I saw the notice about all this."

Phoenix didn't answer. But I didn't miss the way he

tracked Dylan through the crowd until he and his family reached the church steps. An assistant handed him a microphone, his family taking up spots behind in support.

"Imagine being the son of a politician," Augie mused. "Must be nice. All that money and tennis lessons and fancy houses."

None of us commented. At the microphone, William Reed cleared his throat, capturing the attention of his supporters. "Thank you all for coming out on this glorious day. Certainly does feel like summer is in the air, doesn't it?"

There were nods and murmurs of agreement.

"We're only weeks away from the local elections now, and so I want to delve into the real reason we're here today, gathered at our church. We all know Providence is a great area. Most of you probably grew up here and raised your families on these very streets surrounding us. Am I right?"

Lyric sniffed. "Oh yes," she mocked beneath her breath. "We all grew up in mansions with silver spoons in our mouths."

I shushed her, though I could have said the same thing. Internally, I resented the suit assuming everybody here was Providence born and bred. Never mind that Providence shared a border with Saint View, one of the poorest towns around.

And home for the five of us.

"We love our hometown. It's full of great schools, parks, and opportunities for our children to thrive. My own children grew up here, so Providence is in our blood."

"Gag me with that silver spoon." Augie scowled. "This guy is so smarmy."

"That's a big word for you," Lyric quipped back playfully.

He stuck his middle finger up at her with a grin.

"Shut up, would you?" I had to interrupt their squabbling, or they'd go on and on for hours. "I'm trying to listen."

William carried on like we weren't already attracting attention. "But we all know why we're here today. It's the one thing so many of you have brought up to me when I've seen you having coffee in our bakery, and the same thing you've told me right here on this lawn after Sunday morning mass. It's the elephant in every room, and the hot-button topic my esteemed opponent is too afraid to discuss. But I'm not."

He gazed out over the crowd, pausing for dramatic effect.

"Oh, for fuck's sake," I muttered. "Spit it out, old man. Some of us have better things to do. Just say the words. *Saint View*."

Fawn tittered beside me.

William, finally done with his meaningful stares, opened his mouth once more. "Saint View."

"Hallelujah," I huffed. "It's a miracle he actually got to the point before I went gray."

William's prewritten spiel carried on, despite my comments. "Saint View is the one problem our current mayor won't tackle. He sweeps it under the rug like it doesn't affect each and every one of us."

There were nods of approval all around, and I gaped

at their bobbing heads, stunned these people seemed to agree with him.

Though I really shouldn't have been. We were no strangers to residents of Providence looking at us like we were gum stuck to their shoe.

"Saint View drags our property prices down. The crime rate is high, and it spills over into Providence. The housing situation there is dire. Many areas need to be completely demolished and rebuilt, and I have plans for all of that. Starting with Saint View Strip, the main road that runs through the center of the town."

That was why I was here. That was why, instead of enjoying my day off and spending the unseasonably warm weather at the beach in a bikini, working on my tan, I was here, risking God shooting down a lightning bolt because a sinner like me dared step foot on His holy ground.

But some things were worth fighting for.

And the strip was one of them.

"What's wrong with the strip?" Augie yelled out.

William peered through the crowd, trying to find the source of the question. When his gaze landed on Augie, then slid to the rest of us standing shoulder to shoulder, his lip flickered in disgust.

It wasn't lost on any of us. Augie stiffened beside me, and Fawn put a hand on his arm.

He glanced down at her, relaxing visibly.

This was exactly why I'd brought her. She was an Augie muffler, and sometimes, the guy needed it.

William was completely unaware he'd set off Augie and his ticking time bomb, though. He scoffed into the microphone. "I think the question is what's right with it.

But I'm getting ahead of myself. Once you see what's beneath these cloths, I think you'll all be very excited for the changes ahead." He pulled the cloth off a large posterboard to one side with the flourish of a magician. "These are my plans for Saint View Strip."

A gasp ripped from my throat, but it was lost in the clapping of the crowd.

"My plans are to demolish every building and replace them with a new lineup of stores and services. I've already had interest from a yoga studio and a health food store, and we'll continue searching for other high-quality businesses that will service the entire area, both Providence and Saint View."

Lyric turned to me with wide eyes. "Is this guy for real? He wants to knock down the entire strip to put in yoga studios? He can't do that!"

Damn right he couldn't.

"Excuse me," I called.

William glanced quickly in my direction, took in what I was wearing and the people I stood with, and carried on like I hadn't spoken. "Once the construction is finished on the strip, we'll move into the residential areas. I have developers…"

I raised one eyebrow. I'd come here willing to be civil. Willing to put forward my objections calmly and professionally. But I hadn't come here to be looked down on. For my voice to be dismissed because I wasn't wearing a flowered dress with a fucking petticoat beneath.

I pushed my way through the crowd until I stood at the front. Without checking, I knew the others stood behind me. They always had my back. Just like I had theirs.

"I said, *excuse me*," I interrupted.

William finally glanced down at me from his spot on the podium. "Yes?"

"Have you actually asked the people who live in Saint View what they want?"

William was smooth as honey, and it dripped from his sickly sweet words. "Just like every other member of this community, Saint View residents have had the opportunity to express their needs and wants at town meetings."

"Town meetings held in Saint View?" I asked.

William's smile faltered an inch. "Well, no. The meetings were held here in Providence."

I nodded, like I completely understood his point. "Right, so all the members of the Saint View community, a large number of which don't have access to a vehicle, they were just supposed to walk here?"

He smiled tolerantly, though as close as I was, it was clear to me it was forced. "I can't be expected to personally chauffeur the entire community now, can I?' He chuckled, and his followers laughed right along with him, like the poor excuse for public transport in Saint View was something to laugh at.

It wasn't.

"Did you even tell anyone in Saint View about these meetings? Did you send letters to those families, the way you did here in Providence?"

His stare turned challenging. "You're here, aren't you?"

The insult was ingrained in his tone. The put-down. The clear, *I'm from Providence, you're from Saint View* line in the sand that had existed for as long as I could remember.

I wasn't playing into that. "Actually, I didn't receive any sort of notice about this meeting. I live in Saint View. I own two properties there, as well as a business on the strip. But not one of those properties received this flyer." I held up the notice about the meeting. "This, I got from my hairdresser, in Providence. It was pinned on her front desk, and when I walked back to my car after my appointment, I saw most of the businesses there had notices up about it, too. If I hadn't needed a haircut this week, I wouldn't have had a clue about any of this."

There was a titter of uncomfortable laughter that only riled me up more.

"Well, I'll have to look into that. But as I was saying—"

My blood boiled over. I would not be dismissed. Not by some privileged old white guy who had never roughed it a day in his life. He had no idea of what Saint View was like. He'd never lived in a tiny, government-owned house that was so derelict it should have been condemned. He'd never had to wonder where his next meal was coming from. Who was he to pretend he knew what the people of Saint View needed? He didn't know shit if he thought we needed yoga studios. There was no representation here. None except for me and the four people who stood at my side.

If we had to be Saint View's voice, then we would be.

"What about the businesses already on the strip? What happens to us? My business puts food in the mouths of my employees' families. It pays for clothing, education. What happens to them when you close us down?"

Augie, Fawn, Lyric, and Phoenix all shouted their

agreement. We might be outnumbered, but we would be loud if we had to be. We would be loud for all the people who didn't get to be here to have their say.

William held his hand up, calling for silence. "And who exactly are you, Miss..."

"Hawkins. Eve Hawkins."

A flash of recognition streaked across his face. He looked down at the piece of paper on his podium. "The same Eve Hawkins who owns Saint View Strip Club?"

An old woman to my left frowned, pursing her thin, wrinkled lips together. "Strip club? The Devil lives in those places. Shame on you."

I suppressed the urge to sneer in her face. They could try shaming me all they wanted. It wasn't anything I hadn't heard before. "Lady, your husband probably spends all his Friday nights at my club. Don't go acting like you're all high and mighty."

The woman gasped and turned away.

Augie chuckled his delight behind me.

"There's no need for language like that, Miss Hawkins. This is a peaceful discussion. If you can't keep your tongue in check, I suggest you go back where you came from." William nodded to the police officers at his side. At his command, the officers moved down in front of him, forming a barrier between me and the politician's family.

"*Where I came from?*" I seethed as the officers filed into place. "What is that supposed to mean?"

"Settle down."

My attention snapped to the police officer who had issued the warning. My gaze rolled up his solid chest only to be met with the most beautiful hazel eyes I'd ever seen.

I did a double take, absorbing the details of his face, partially obscured by his cap. A strong jaw covered by a light dusting of dark stubble, and full lips that were currently drawn into a frown.

He would have been hot if he weren't glaring at me.

It took me a second to compose myself long enough to glare back. "I'm sure you didn't just tell me to settle down, like I was some sort of overexcited dog. I have a right to be here and speak my mind."

"And I have the right to arrest you for making a public disturbance. I don't want to do that, which is why I politely asked you to settle down."

Anger bubbled up inside me. Another rich white dude trying to lord his power over me. "This is my business he's trying to destroy."

William huffed in my direction. "I'm not trying to destroy anything. I'm trying to make Saint View better. We need to attract wealthy investors and tourists. We cannot do that when the strip is overrun by prostitutes and sex clubs."

"Prostitutes!" Anger flushed through me, hot and raw.

"Oh no he didn't." Lyric stepped forward, fingers clenched into fists, only to come eye to eye with another police officer.

They tightened their ranks around us while the rest of the crowd backed away nervously.

"Oh yes he did." Augie's growl was menacing. He didn't even have a leg to stand on. I knew for a fact he took on personal clients, and there was a lot more than just dancing going on at those parties. But he wasn't doing that at my club. The man was a grown adult. He could do what he liked in his free time as far as I was concerned. So hypocrite or not, I was grateful for the backup.

"Nobody at my club is trading sex for money. We're dancers. Entertainers. Last I checked, there was nothing wrong with that. This is bullshit!" My voice came out shriller than I wanted it to, but screw them and their assumptions.

"Seriously," my cop said quietly. "You need to stop."

But I was beyond stopping. I was fired up, blood hot, and not going home without a fight. "Or what? We just want to be heard. We want to actually be consulted about what happens in our neighborhood. And instead we're here, in yours, being told that our livelihoods are being stripped away in favor of a yoga studio! Nobody in Saint View is doing any downward fucking dogs, cop!"

William sighed heavily into the microphone. "Officers, can we please remove the disturbance? There are other people who came here to be heard. I believe Ms. Hawkins has overstayed her welcome."

"Time to go." The cop stepped in closer, putting his hands on my bare arms.

A spark of electricity shot through my entire body at his touch. I jolted, my gaze slamming into his once more. For a moment he held it, while I drowned in his eyes. Damn, they were gorgeous.

But the real world came crashing back at a scream from Fawn as she was manhandled through the crowd. Augie launched himself after her, trying to get her away from the officers. Three more swarmed in, surrounding him, too.

The moment between me and the officer disintegrated.

His gaze narrowed into one of frustration. "Get your people under control, before we arrest the lot of you."

But anger, outrage, and healthy dose of lust swirled my blood. There was no backing down now. I grabbed one of William's campaign posters, ripping down the center in defiance.

William squawked from the podium. "That's destruction of property! I want her arrested."

I crossed my arms over my chest. "Oh, for fuck's sake. Shut up."

The cop's grip on my arms tightened and he hustled me through the crowd toward the squad cars in the parking lot.

"Are you really going to arrest me over ripping up a sign?"

"Are you going to leave quietly if I don't?"

I snorted. "I think we both know the answer to that is a big fat hell no, don't we?"

He pressed his lips together like I was impossible. "I hope you enjoy handcuffs then."

I almost told him I might have if we'd been in another setting.

He pushed me up against his squad car, his chest pressed to my back. But he was careful not to hurt me. His grip was tight but not punishing.

And when he slapped cuffs on my wrists it was the gentlest arrest I'd ever had.

2

BOSTON

*E*ve Hawkins was not only the most beautiful woman I'd ever had in the back of my squad car, but she was also the most beautiful woman I'd ever seen in my life. I drove her back to the station, darting little glances at her in the rearview mirror.

"You can quit looking at me," she deadpanned, halfway there. "I'm not going anywhere. I can't exactly bust out when I've got cuffs on, can I?"

"To be honest, I wouldn't put it past you. You kinda seem the type."

"The type to stage a breakout? You're driving fifty miles an hour. Even if I could get the cuffs off, I'd have to get past the locks, and then if I managed that, face-planting onto asphalt sounds painful. I don't want to get away from you that badly. We both know this is a bullshit charge."

"It didn't have to be a charge at all, if you'd just listened to me in the first place."

"Like when you told me to *settle down*?" Her voice dripped with disdain.

"You really have a problem with that term, don't you?"

"It's insulting. It implies I didn't have a reason to be pissed off with that old prude. He called me a fucking prostitute. Which would be fine if I were one. But I'm not. He just wants us out of town so he can line his own pockets with money. What a load of crap, having that meeting at the church. Like he's some sort of purer-than-white Christian man who can do no wrong. You think he hasn't been in my club? I bet you anything he has. Bet you have, too."

"Actually, I haven't." My gaze met hers in the rearview mirror.

"Huh. I actually believe you. What kind of stick do you have up your ass? You don't like naked women?" She cocked her head to one side, studying me. "Ah. Girls aren't your thing? We have guys, too. Augie and Phoenix are hot. You'd like them. Maybe they'll give you a freebie lap dance back at the police station since you probably arrested them, too."

Jesus Christ. This woman went from zero to one hundred in the space of seconds. "I like naked women just fine. I've just never been to your club."

We pulled up outside the police station, and I went to her door to let her out, trying not to notice her long tanned legs and the shapely curve of her bare thighs. Her miniskirt hugged her ass, her shirt showing a sliver of toned midriff. It took everything I had inside me to concentrate on actually getting her through the doors. We were the first to arrive, though I knew the other squad cars had her friends. We'd arrested the group of them at the request of the mayoral candidate, but nothing would come of it. We'd throw them into holding for a little while, let them think about what they'd done, and then let them go. Nobody had the time or the patience to fill out the paperwork for a minor disturbance when nobody even got hurt. I was pretty sure Eve knew it, too. She seemed completely unconcerned by the fact she was currently in handcuffs.

I bypassed the front desk, guiding her to the holding cells. At the doorway, we stopped, and I turned her to face me while I undid her restraints. I'd put them on carefully, but I didn't like the pink chafing they were causing around her wrists.

She didn't seem to notice, or care. She glanced up at me through her long, dark eyelashes. "We've been all up in each other's business today. You aren't going to buy me dinner, so you should probably at least tell me your name."

I paused, hand on the cell door. God. She was so fucking hot. If I'd met her in some other sort of circumstance, even in a crowded room she would have been the first woman to turn my head. I allowed myself a momentary fantasy, where we met at a club and I bought her a drink. She looked up at me the way she was staring at me now, but there, in my fantasy, I had the ability to do something about it. I had the ability to lean in, kiss her mouth, and take her home with me for the night.

Here, all I had the ability to do was walk away.

"Boston," I told her. "Joshua Boston. Have a nice day, Ms. Hawkins. I hope I don't see you again."

*A*fter leaving Eve in the cells, I went upstairs to my desk and waited for my partner to return.

Jayela wasn't far behind, slumping into her seat across from mine. "You want to hang out tonight? Mae will have something made for dinner, and we can invite Tori over, too."

I hesitated. Mae was Jayela's little sister, and I'd basically adopted her as my own sibling after years of hanging out in the apartment they shared. Tori, Mae's best friend, was often the fourth to our group, her husband, Will, sometimes bringing our hangouts to five.

Jayela raised an eyebrow when I didn't answer immediately. "You got better plans? Hot date?"

"Nah. Nothing like that. I was just going to stick around to release the church protestors."

"How long are we going to hold them for?"

I glanced at my watch. "What time does the politician's rally finish?"

The door to the station opened, admitting William Reed himself.

Jayela nodded in his direction. "It's done, I guess."

I groaned quietly. "What does he want now?"

The man was disheveled after Eve's little scene. His expensive navy suit was unbuttoned, and his tie had disappeared.

The chief came out of his office to shake hands with Reed. My gaze met his across the room, and he pointed at me, like we knew each other. The chief waved me over, and I got to my feet grudgingly.

Jayela chuckled behind me. "Have fun with that."

I peered over my shoulder at her. "Yeah, thanks. I

wonder what bullshit he wants to tout now. Let the Reed protestors go soon. Maybe keep Eve Hawkins an extra hour or two. She's the ringleader. Let her stew a little longer before you turn her out. Maybe it'll knock some sense into her."

I doubted it. But it was worth a shot.

"Sounds like a plan, partner. You better go, the chief and the politician are waiting. Hey, Boston. What do you get when a chief, a politician, and a cop walk into an office?"

I raised an eyebrow, waiting for her to answer her own joke.

"A really boring meeting. Better you than me!" She spun around on her chair with the sort of grin that only appeared when she amused herself.

"If it's possible, I think your jokes are actually getting worse." But she was right. Whatever the chief was calling me in for wasn't going to be anything exciting. I walked on slow feet across the station and into his office without knocking.

Both men lifted their heads, and the chief motioned for me to take the seat beside Reed.

I took it reluctantly. If I'd had my way, I probably would have been arrested right alongside Eve. This guy didn't know it, but I'd grown up in Saint View, too. And I didn't like his plans for my old stomping grounds any more than Eve did. Yes, there were problems there. Problems that needed addressing and money to fix. But everybody knew what he'd been doing by holding that town meeting in Providence and not in Saint View itself. The man was a coward and probably corrupt. Pretty typical of the politicians in this area. None of it sat well with me.

"Here he is, the man of the day." William held a hand out.

The fake compliment annoyed me, but I had enough manners to shake his hand. "Pretty sure you're the man of the day, aren't you?"

The chief shot me a look full of exasperation.

The question had come out kind of snappy. I tried to soften my expression into something a little more friendly. Or at least something more professional.

Reed slapped me on the shoulder and pumped my hand up and down. "So modest. I wanted to come in and thank you personally."

My eyebrows knit together. "For what?"

"You saved my life out there today. Those protesters were really getting out of hand, and you removed them quickly and calmly."

I blinked. What danger was he even talking about? Sure, Eve had two big guys with her, but neither had been interested in the politician. They only morphed into action once we'd started trying to move the women out. Nobody had even gone near Reed or his family.

But the chief was nodding at me with emphasis, obviously wanting me to take the man's praise.

I forced the words I knew he wanted to hear. "Of course. Just doing my job."

"Well, you do it well. I was very impressed today. And I'd like to request that you attend all my future public outings."

I frowned. "That's not really the sort of work—"

"Boston would be happy to do that for you, Candidate Reed. I'll make sure he's available anytime you need him.

If you just send me over your schedule, we'll get it handled."

The chief and I had a silent battle with our eyes across his desk. Mine saying, *"What the fuck, boss?"* His saying, *"Shut up and do as you're told."*

He won. But I wasn't happy about it.

"Good. And I want you all to investigate Eve Hawkins."

My head snapped up at the mention of Eve's name. I couldn't stop thinking about the fact she was downstairs in lockup. Every cell in my body itched to go down there and check on her, even though she was obviously more than capable of holding her own and really did need some time to cool off. "Why? We arrested her today, but we can't keep her. She ripped up a sign. That's not really a chargeable offence."

"The running of a sex club is."

"She runs a strip club, not a sex club."

"That's not what my sources tell me."

I folded my arms across my chest. "Reliable sources?"

"Firsthand sources."

"I'll need their names."

"Can't give you that. You have to do the grunt work yourself, Officer Boston. But just know, if you dig, you'll find the truth. Eve Hawkins' strip club is not above board. And neither is she."

The chief stood, offering his hand to William once more. "We'll make sure it's properly investigated. Don't you worry about that. And just send over a copy of your schedule so I can make sure Boston is available when you need him."

The two men shook hands, but I didn't bother getting

out of my chair. William left the office without either of us saying goodbye. The moment the door closed behind him, I pinned my boss with accusations.

"I'm his bodyguard now? Nothing even happened at that rally. He talked smack, and he got the same attitude back. His life was never in danger."

"William Reed is going to be the next mayor of this town. Have you seen the popularity polls? He's got this in the bag, Boston. Be smart. You think we don't need a man like that on our side?"

I ground my molars together. I knew he had a point. "I don't believe anything is happening at Eve Hawkins' club."

"Do you know that for sure, though? An accusation has been made."

"With no proof to back it up."

"Would it really hurt you to look into it, though? I'll get a search warrant."

"There's no grounds for one."

"Grounds are easily fabricated. Come on, you know this."

I might have known it, but it didn't mean I liked it. It didn't mean it was the way I played the game. But sometimes orders came from the top. I knew that better than anyone.

The chief eyed me. "You going to take this case, or do I need to assign it to someone else more willing to be a team player? We've spoken about this before."

My patience frayed. "Like when you forced me to accept bribes from the Saint View Sinners?"

The street gang was notorious in Saint View, and their dirty money had been lining my pockets for months. Never for long, because every time I took a payment, it went straight into an evidence bag that I then dumped on the chief's desk.

The chief narrowed his eyes. "Watch yourself. Those orders came from higher up than me. We needed someone on the inside, and you were the one they picked. You should be grateful for the honor."

"What honor is that exactly? You won't even let me tell my partner."

The older man shook his head. "We're all on a need-to-know basis. Bringing anyone else in could be dangerous. You want that sitting on your conscience if something happens to her?"

"So I'm just supposed to lie? Keep sitting beside her every time she has a gut feeling and wants to watch their hangouts?"

"I'll talk to her and tell her to stay out of their territory." He ran his hands through his graying hair. "You two are fucking killing me, you know that, right? Just follow the rules, would you? Quit questioning everything and you'll be a whole lot happier. Focus on the strip club case."

This is what I hated about being a cop. I so desperately wanted to do good. It was why I'd joined the force in the first place. But from day one, any good I did manage was always tainted by the bad, the corrupt, the dirty. And this operation reeked of foul play. I couldn't prove it, but there was no transparency. Everything was all, "Do as you're told. Don't ask why," and none of it sat well with me.

But I'd been outranked time and time again, and my questions always fell on deaf ears. This was the side of the department I tried to shield my partner from because I didn't want Jayela to know the true nature of the beast we found ourselves swallowed up by. Her ideals were still pure. And I wanted to keep them that way. Because she reminded me of why I'd started this job, and why I kept going even though the parts like this made it hard.

The chief was right. I needed to get my head in the game and just concentrate on the current case.

Eve's dark hair, tumbling in soft, pretty curls, floated through my mind. Her dark eyes staring up at me through long lashes.

I didn't want anyone else dealing with her.

"Fine." I snatched the paperwork from the chief's hands. "I'll look into Eve Hawkins' strip club and make sure there's nothing more than lap dances going on there."

EVE

I stomped inside the club, wishing I'd had the forethought to put on boots instead of flip-flops. Flip-flops thwacking against the concrete floors was not nearly as satisfying as a pair of heavy thumping boots would have been. I suspected I looked more like a duck than I wanted to. But I'd been too pissed off and short on time to really consider my choice of footwear.

"Eve!" Fawn flew out of the kitchen and across the main room, throwing herself at me. "Oh my God. You're out! I seriously thought they were going to charge you, they kept you so long."

"Tell me about it," I grumped. I'd spent hours in the holding cell at the police station this afternoon. They'd released Fawn first, then Lyric. I'd expected that I would get to leave soon after. But that hadn't been the case. I'd sat there for hours, twiddling my thumbs and staring at the ugly cinderblock wall. I'd glanced up every time a guard had walked past, but none of them had been the hot cop. Every minute that ticked by, my irritation grew. I knew the others would open the club and cover for me if I didn't make it into work. But it was hardly the point. It wasn't their responsibility to run the club. It was mine. And being stuck in this tiny cell, for no good reason, was preventing me from doing that. "They only let me out an hour ago. By the time I got through the paperwork, and got a taxi back to my car, I barely had time to go home and grab my stuff before I had to come here. I need a shower. I feel like a sewer pig."

Fawn giggled.

"What?"

"A sewer pig? Are they the cousins of those Ninja Turtles?"

I sniggered, and Fawn's grin grew. I slung an arm around her slim shoulders. "Funny, kid."

Fawn never failed to mellow me. She was like the daughter I was too young to have. At twenty-two, she was ten years my junior, and while I'd never wanted kids of my own, something about Fawn had woken up some dormant maternal part in me. Maybe it was her small stature that made her seem younger than she actually was. Or her quiet, timid nature. Or perhaps it was just the pure fact that she'd arrived on my doorstep, a disheveled mess, desperate for a job. I'd taken one look at her and known she was meant to be a part of the little family we'd created here.

Even Augie had a soft spot for her. And Augie didn't like anybody, so that was saying something.

The two of us walked out the back to the women's changing rooms, and I dumped my stuff in my locker.

Lyric was already sitting at one of the makeup tables, coating her eyelashes in thick black mascara.

Her gaze met mine in the mirror, and she jumped up with a squeal of excitement. "You're out!"

I smiled into her soft red hair, inhaling the familiar scent. "You can't get rid of me that easily."

She leaned back, her hands on her hips, and pouted at me. "Pity. Because I have actually planned something. I mean, somebody had to step in while you weren't here. They might have locked you up and thrown away the key."

I raised one eyebrow. "For ripping up a sign, Lyric? Really? You got your eye on my job?" But I was stifling a grin. Though I was technically their boss, that wasn't really how we rolled around here. They all knew their jobs, I didn't have to ride their asses. They wanted to make money, and so did I. We all worked as a team. And we respected each other like family.

"Nah. I've got my hands too full with Amelia. I don't need a day job, as well as a night job. But! I did sit here, stewing on the fact that you were still in jail, and brainstormed some revenge ideas." She strutted back to her table and pulled out a folded piece of paper from her purse.

I took the paper from her, unfolding it carefully, while glancing over the top at her. When I gazed down at the list, I had to stifle a laugh. "Good to see you used your time this afternoon productively." I started reading off the items. "Number one. Blowup William Reed's car."

"I like that one," Augie called out from the adjoining male dressing room. It was really all one big room, but when we brought the guys on, we'd separated into male and female areas with a curtain. Not that it really mattered. We all seen each other naked a thousand times. It kind of went with the territory at a strip club. None of us even batted an eyelash anymore. But it was a gesture of respect anyway.

"You would," I called back through the curtain. "We're not blowing up anyone's car."

Lyric went back to applying her makeup, picking up a brush and blending the foundation onto her cheeks. "I told you guys she'd never go for that one. We have alternatives. Keep reading."

"Number two. Find out a deep dark secret and share it with the world." I pondered that one for a moment. "I like it. But it sounds like a time-intensive project. And honestly? What are the odds of Mr. Vanilla, an upstanding Christian man, even having a deep dark secret? The guy had us arrested for ripping up a sign. He is the sort of man who probably never even got in a fist fight in high school."

"I never got in a fist fight in high school either," Fawn said.

I patted her on the shoulder. "Of course you didn't. Because you're a sweetheart. Lyric, how many have you been in?"

"Couldn't even count. You?"

"I grew up in Saint View. What do you think?"

"Okay, well now I feel left out. You're both badasses. And I'm a wimp. Who wants to fight? Come on, I'm twenty-two, and I apparently missed a rite of passage." She lifted her fists and danced around like a boxer.

Lyric and I both eyed her and cringed. I reached over

and raised Fawn's fists so they actually protected her face. "Sweetie, it would be like punching a kitten. And even Lyric isn't mean enough to punch a kitten."

Fawn dropped her fighter's stance. "Fine. But check out number three. That was my suggestion."

"Pin the Penis on the Politician party." I glanced up at her. "This was your idea?"

Her face dropped. "Yeah. Sorry. It's stupid, I know. Childish."

"Actually, I kind of love it."

Fawn lit up like she'd won the lottery. "Really?"

I leaned in and kissed her cheek. "It's the perfect revenge. Everybody around here hates politicians. Who wouldn't come for the chance to pin a penis on one? Or at least, a poster of one. I'm going to start practicing now, so I can get my dick right in the middle." I tapped Fawn in the same spot on her own forehead, and she grinned.

A warm feeling settled over me. I liked when she was happy. We all did. Lyric was smiling at her warmly in the mirror as well.

"We'll start promoting it immediately. I'll get some graphics made up, and we'll post them on Facebook, maybe even do a mass mailing. And unlike the mayoral candidate, we'll mail everyone. Including Providence. Including his house."

Phoenix's grumbling tone carried through from behind the curtain. "You sure that's a good idea, boss?"

I shrugged one shoulder. "It'll get us in trouble, for sure. But what's new? It's kind of my middle name."

I couldn't see Phoenix's reaction, but I could imagine that the big man was probably just shaking his head.

He'd worked here for over two years now. He was used to my troublemaking schemes.

I clapped my hands together. "Anyway, we need to finish getting ready. We're going to have to switch up the order. I need to go last tonight, I'm not even close to ready."

Lyric stood, adjusting her glitter-covered cleavage in a low-cut top and grabbed Fawn's hand on her way to the stage door. "We got your back. Take your time. We'll entertain the boys until you're ready."

I blew them both a kiss and then sank down into the chair Lyric had vacated. From out in the club, chatter had already picked up, so I knew that Terry, our bouncer, had started letting people in for the night. Our DJ, Lucinda, cranked up the volume on her speakers, and in a few minutes, once the club had started filling up a little, she'd play Fawn's opening song.

I hurried through my getting-ready rituals. Old makeup off and the quickest shower ever. I blew out my long dark hair into barrel curls. Heaped on the eyeliner and added fake lashes even though my regular lashes were fairly decent to begin with. I wasn't a huge fan, but guys seemed to like them. And happy customers equaled generous tips.

I slicked blood-red lipstick across my mouth, before pulling on a matching costume for the night. Red G-string, bikini top, hot pants, and a midriff shirt that I wouldn't be wearing for long. The guys' music had started up in their half of the club somewhere in the middle of me getting ready, and the women's cheers and screams had me wondering if the two guys were dancing together. The two of them on stage at once was always a crowd-pleaser. They put Magic Mike to shame.

I couldn't worry about them right now, though, other than to hope that they were making some good coin. I needed to get my own butt up on stage.

I added a pair of six-inch heels, strutted through to the backstage area, and gave Lucinda a fist bump. She was an eighteen-year-old from the hood and a damn talented DJ. She'd make it big someday, but for now we were lucky to have her, and she was happy to have a job.

"You ready to roll?" she asked me.

"Always."

Lucinda did what she did best, and within seconds my favorite song was pounding through the stereo. I took a moment to let the beat roll through me, let it pump me up, the adrenaline rising until I couldn't wait to get my ass out on that stage. I'd always love dancing. Even as a little kid music had called to me. I'd had stupid dreams of dancing on stages behind famous singers and traveling the world on their dime, doing what I loved.

Stupid childish dreams in a world that would crush them before I even turned sixteen.

But I found another way. School hadn't been my thing. I just wanted to move my body and make money. I'd been walking home from school one afternoon with some friends and had seen an ad in the club's window advertising for strippers, no experience necessary. One of my friends had dared me to apply. I hadn't needed much of a shove.

I'd always been attracted to trouble. Danger. The forbidden.

And Saint View Strip Club offered all those things as well as a hefty paycheck each night. The owner at the time, Sal, a short fat white guy with a beer belly that stretched his shirts, hadn't cared that I was underage. He'd asked if I was eighteen, even though he knew full well I wasn't. I lied and said I was. I told him I'd repeated a year because I wasn't big on the smarts and that's why I was still at school. He'd bought it, or at least pretended that he had. I'd started that night and had never gone back to school. I didn't regret a single minute of it. I'd bought the club from Sal a few years later with money I'd earned stripping, and never looked back.

Ten years later, nothing had changed. Did I have to dance? No. I could live off the cut I took from the others. But I loved it. So why stop doing something that brought me joy?

I grinned at the crowd getting riled up by Fawn and Lyric. And then I strutted onto the stage. A cheer went up as I swung around the nearest pole and waved at one of our regulars, sitting in his usual spot by the stage.

"Good day to you, Miss Eve," he called above the music, throwing a couple of bills onto the stage.

"How is my favorite guy?"

Simon grinned and nodded. "Real good, thank you."

And that was how more than half of our interactions in the club went, every single night. So many of these men were just sad and lonely, and wanting company. I couldn't even count the amount of times I'd been booked for a private room, only to find myself sitting on the couch, fully clothed, and listening to a man talk about his day. Or how his kids had grown up and left the nest. Or about his job that he hated. So many of them cared little for the actual act of stripping, and I was happy to provide what they needed. Within reason. I would get naked and dance, but that was as far as I went.

But they weren't the only sort of patron. And by the looks of it, there was a large group of college guys here tonight. We'd become popular with that crowd, despite the fact there was no college nearby. But with the rent as low as it was in Saint View, it allowed me to keep my prices down. So drinks were cheap. And Terry didn't check IDs as thoroughly as he probably should.

I kept it light and teasing to start with, a few swings on the pole, and some gyrating of my hips caught their attention. I waited until they started throwing money on the stage and then rewarded them by shimmying out of my shirt.

My tiny bikini top didn't cover much, and the guys let out a cheer.

"Shorts, too, baby girl."

I tried not to make a face at the 'baby girl' comment. They'd learn pretty quick that I controlled the show, not them. "Start putting money on the stage, and I'll see what I can do."

Maybe it should have bothered me, the way they were only here to see me naked. But it didn't. I had a body. Just like every other woman in this world. These guys had seen women naked before. Why was it a big deal? Nudity was never something I had a problem with. Dancing naked or dancing fully clothed, it made no difference to me. I just wanted to dance, make money, and live the life I chose for myself. Not a nine-to-five where I was chained to a desk all day, every day like my father. Not some diner job where I only made minimum wage like my mother. I knew I only had a certain number of stripping years in me. Until my tits sagged and my ass grew flat. Those years probably weren't far away. Despite my decision not to have kids, gravity would get me eventually. It was why I'd bought the joint from Sal when he'd decided to ship off to Europe. It was a business I could run for my entire life.

Lucinda changed the track to a bump-and-grind sorta song. All too soon, I was itching to get on that pole and really show this crowd what I was made of. I stripped off my booty shorts, flashing the guys an eyeful of my ass before I launched myself at the pole.

I inverted, spreading my legs wide as I twirled around. I saw every inch of the club from this angle. Lucinda cheering me on from her DJ booth. Lyric and Fawn working the room, Lyric already topless and giving a regular a lap dance, Fawn winding her way through the room with drinks in her hands, allowing men to put their tips in the elastic of her G-string.

And Joshua Boston, stopped dead two steps inside the club, his gaze pinned on me.

An instant flood of heat rushed my body, taking me by surprise. That was new. I never got turned on at work.

I maintained his gaze, until my rotation on the pole forced me to break it.

That seemed to snap him out of his trance as well.

"Shut it down," he shouted.

The music cut out, and I flipped myself upright. "Excuse me?"

He pushed his way through the tables of bewildered men who were starting to stand up, some, the ones who weren't twenty-one likely, edged toward the exit.

All I saw was money walking out the door.

"Hold up, nobody needs to leave." I stormed to the

edge of the stage and glared down at Boston. "What the hell are you doing?"

"We've got a warrant."

"For what? Harassment? You only just released me!"

"We've had a tip-off that there's illegal practices being played out here." His gaze strayed momentarily from my face, dipping once down my body.

My nipples hardened. Shit.

I crossed my arms over my chest, hoping he hadn't noticed the effect of his gaze on my body.

Boston turned away so quickly that I instantly knew my cover-up job hadn't been in time. He tapped the table nearest to him. "On your way, boys. Club is closed for the night."

"Hey!" I jumped down from the stage and put myself between him and the table of men. "You can't do that. You can't just close down my club in the middle of the show."

His gaze clashed with mine. This time it held no hint of the heat that had been there moments before.

"I just did."

To my dismay, the house lights came on, and one by one, the club patrons trickled out. Augie and Phoenix came in, pulling on robes, Augie shouting about the lights being on and the music cutting out. He stopped when he saw Boston and his partner and then turned to me for answers. "What the hell?"

I just shook my head, my irritation rising with every passing minute. But my number one concern was always my staff. "Don't," I told Augie, knowing how volatile he was. "Just chill, okay? Don't get arrested again."

"Good advice," Boston quipped. "You all need to take

a seat and stay there while we conduct a search. You may be questioned afterward."

Fawn sat quickly and obediently. Lyric, still topless, defiantly sitting down after her. Phoenix offered Lyric his robe, but she refused it, and the two men sat down as well.

All four looked to me for guidance.

"Sit, Eve." Boston's tone was no-nonsense.

"I'll sit when you learn to quit talking to me like I'm one of your German Shepherd dogs."

Boston's expression flickered, but he didn't apologize.

His partner, a smaller, dark-haired woman called out that she'd start in the front and he could start at the back. Boston nodded, and with a final glance in my direction, he swiveled, storming out of sight.

Lyric inched her seat closer to me, eyes trained on Boston's retreating figure. "I could just give him a freebie..." she whispered, a question in her tone. "Get him off our case..."

Jealousy stabbed through me, quick and fast and foreign.

I knew what Lyric was offering. And I loved her for it. These were the times where I really believed that these people I worked with were family. My true family. Not ones that shared my blood or my genetics. But a true family who loved each other. They'd do anything for me, just like I'd do anything for them.

But I wasn't going to let her do that with Boston. The thought of her naked body writhing all over his, his hands on her hips, guiding her movements as she gyrated over his lap, erection straining behind his work pants....

I slammed my eyes closed.

"It'll work," she insisted. "It always has in the past."

She was right. It was the way of things around here. Every so often, the cops came sniffing around for one reason or another.

I shook my head. "No. I'll do it."

They'd all been easily bribed. Boston would be no different.

4

BOSTON

In the locker room of Saint View Strip Club, I found myself lost in a maze of glittery bras, tiny miniskirts, and skimpy underwear. And it was my job to search through all of it.

Eve's name was written on a strip of tape across a beat-up metal locker that had perhaps once been white, but was now scratched and dented to the point the locker didn't even close properly.

I drew in a deep breath, pushing open the door, hating that I had to rifle through her personal belongings.

But this was my job. I wasn't here for pleasure.

Except the pleasure of seeing her curvy body wrapped around the pole, her legs spread wide, her gaze locked on mine.

Fuck.

She was a stunner. There was no doubt about that.

"Mind on the job. Mind on the job," I muttered, sorting through her belongings, feeling like the biggest sort of creep. I didn't even really know what the hell I was searching for. What signs were there that someone was selling sex? I doubted she kept receipt books with sexual positions and kinks in a nicely ordered list.

This was stupid and fraudulent, and I was really pretty pissed off that the chief was forcing this on me. It wasn't the first time he'd forced me into something I didn't agree with.

The longer I stayed on the police force, the more the corruption got to me.

Until I wasn't even sure I wanted to do this job anymore.

"If you told me what you were looking for, I could make this go a whole lot faster for you."

I spun around and drank in the sight of Eve's nearly naked body before I even realized what I was doing. High, perfect tits, barely covered by a glittery red bikini top, and a string bottom that seemed ready to fall to the floor with the tiniest of tugs. It was held up only by the ample curve of her hips, that my palms itched to run over. It was only a second, two at most, but it was a physical effort to drag my gaze back up to her eyes.

And then I berated myself silently for being so fucking unprofessional.

I ignored her question. "You shouldn't be back here."

"You're in a women's locker room, so neither should you."

I couldn't keep staring at her. I buried my head in her locker, pretending I was sorting through the clothes and shoes and God, packets of tampons. A blush heated my face.

"You won't find anything in there," she told me, moving in closer.

She was right. There was nothing of interest here. I doubted there was anything of interest in this entire club. William Reed's complaints were weak at best, and completely false at worst.

I shut the locker door, ready to agree with her, but the words dried on my lips.

Eve stood in front of me, completely and utterly, mind-blowingly naked.

I froze.

But there was no stopping the reaction my body had to her. My eyes drank in her luscious body, while my dick kicked to attention.

She moved in closer, putting one hand to my chest and pushed me back until I sat heavily on the bench seat.

I couldn't take my eyes off her as her hips swayed to a silent beat. Her tits were right there in my face, perfect and pert and round. And so fucking tempting. Her nipples just begged to be taken into my mouth and sucked and played with until she was crying out for more.

It all happened in seconds, a mere fraction of a minute, before I came to my senses. I shoved to my feet. "Shit, Eve! What the hell are you doing?" I grabbed a robe from a rack and pushed it in her direction.

She took a step back, confusion etched into the furrows of her forehead. It took her another long moment before she slowly pulled on the robe and tied the belt around her waist. She squinted at me. "I can get one of the guys for you instead if you prefer, but you seemed pretty determined that you were into women earlier, so I thought..."

"You thought you'd just offer sex?"

Her mouth dropped open. "What? Who said anything about sex?"

"You're bare-ass naked beneath that robe! You told me you weren't a hooker."

Fire flashed in her eyes. "I'm not, you asshole. Nobody said anything about sex. This was a dance. That's it. I get naked and grind all up on your lap. You get to touch my hips, and the outside of my thighs and that's it. You hear me? That. Is. All."

"What the hell made you think I would want that?"

She recoiled like I'd slapped her.

I immediately wanted to take the words back, because I was sure that even a blind man could have seen the sexual attraction I had to this woman.

"Fuck you, Boston. You don't have to be a prick about it. This is how things have always worked around here. You guys come in, we give you a couple of free lap dances, and you leave us alone for a few more months."

Now it was my turn to get annoyed. "You think I'm willing to take a bribe?"

That fire in her eyes turned into a challenge. "Haven't met one of you yet who isn't. Some just have a higher price than others." Her eyes narrowed. "But for the record, sex is too high a price. Despite what you seem to think of me, I do have a line drawn in the sand."

"I don't have a price. I can't be bought."

She threw one hand up in the air in complete and utter pissed-off frustration. "Fine. Then search the club. Search every nook and cranny for all I care. Because I've got nothing to hide."

We stood toe to toe, her chest heaving with her anger.

She was a wild animal, one I didn't have a hope in hell of controlling, no matter how much I might want to.

But fuck, did I want to. All I could think about was taming her. Pushing her back against those lockers with my hand to her throat while I ground my hips against hers and stole her breath with my kiss.

I backed away, right out of the club, dragging a protesting Jayela with me.

I knew a losing battle when I saw one. Eve Hawkins was so far out of my league she may as well have been in a different stratosphere.

5

BOSTON

*W*ith irritation, I straightened my shoulders, put on a professional front, and pushed William Reed's doorbell.

The chime rang out loudly, and there was a hum of activity from inside the house, but nobody actually opened the door.

I tried again.

"Would somebody please get that?" a deep voice bellowed from within.

The footsteps that eventually trudged to greet me were heavy and slow. The door finally swung open, and I instantly recognized William's eldest child, who really wasn't a child at all. The guy was young, early twenties, and taller than I was.

I smiled. "Dylan, right? I'm Officer Boston. I'm escorting your dad to his function this morning."

Dylan pulled the door open to admit me. "Sure. Come on into the madhouse."

I followed him inside and instantly understood what

he meant. There were people everywhere, half with their cell phones held to their ear, others banging away on their laptops. Dylan took up a seat at the breakfast counter beside his younger sister who didn't look up at my entrance. Her chunky black over-ear headphones probably kept her completely unaware of the chaos around her. The two of them ate cold cereal from a bowl while absently thumbing through their phones.

William stood at the center of the chaos, suit shirt only half buttoned, tie slung over his shoulder. His bare foot tapped impatiently at whatever was being said into his earpiece. He waved distractedly in my direction when he spotted me, then turned around and started barking orders at whoever was on the other end of the call.

Right. Guess we weren't leaving for the function anytime soon then, despite the fact I'd turned up right on time in the hopes of avoiding this exact situation.

"There's coffee in the pot over there." Dylan pointed farther along the huge island bench that could comfortably seat at least eight, judging by the number of stools tucked beneath it.

I thanked him gratefully and grabbed a mug from the stack piled up beside the machine. The coffee aroma wafted up, and I inhaled it greedily. I hadn't had my first cup yet, and I hoped it would be good. I had a feeling I was going to need it to get through a morning of listening to William's campaign speeches.

A high-pitched screech, sharp and shrill, cut through the monotone of business. Everybody in the room paused, then went back to whatever they'd been doing.

Everyone but me. I wasn't programmed to just ignore the scream of a woman.

"Don't worry about that," Dylan reassured me. "It's just my mother. She's dramatic. Her lipstick probably doesn't match her handbag or something."

I frowned but took his word for it, and in the next moment, Laura Reed swept into the room, her silky long robe flowing out behind her like she was some Hollywood movie star.

The scowl on her face ruined any pretense of that. "William! Have you seen this?" She held up her phone and thrust it in her husband's face.

He squinted at it, but it was so close to his nose he had to move back and take the phone from her hand. "No? What? An opinion poll?"

"Worse. A penis party."

I raised one eyebrow.

William stopped trying to make sense of the phone and focused on his wife instead. "Excuse me? A what now?"

"A penis party! That whore at the strip club is hosting a penis party!"

My ears pricked up at the mention of strip club. She had to be talking about Eve, though the word whore set me on edge. Eve was no whore. Even if I had sort of unintentionally accused her of being one the last time we'd seen each other. Heat crept up the back of my neck at the memory of her naked in front of me, hips swaying softly...

William let out a long-suffering sigh. "Why would I care about that?"

Laura shoved the phone in his face once more. "Because it's a Pin the Penis on the Politician party, and after your little showdown the other week, which politician do you think she'll use?"

Dylan let out a snort of laughter, and both his parents spun in his direction.

It was good they'd chosen to focus on him, because it gave me a minute to wipe the amusement off my own face.

"You think that's funny, Dylan?" Laura screeched at him. "This woman is targeting us. She's holding this disgusting event on the same night as the fundraising dinner I'm hosting. She can't do that!" She turned her steely gaze on me. "Can't you do something about it?"

I took a sip of my coffee before I answered, because, man, I needed it to deal with her. "On what grounds?"

"Defamation!"

I took the phone from Laura's hand and scrolled over the event page on Facebook, trying to hide my laughter. When I gave her back the phone, my face was schooled into something more professional. "They look like they're just having a bit of fun to me. Could even be good advertising if you roll with it."

"I'll do no such thing. I want this event shut down. William! Do you see how many likes this page has? Two thousand! Mine only has twenty!"

Dylan laughed into his cereal once more.

William whirled on him. "How about I send you down there to deal with those cheap sluts? You probably should, perhaps it would man you up a bit."

"Hey, watch your mouth," I snapped, only to be completely drowned out by Laura's screeches.

"William! Do not even say something like that. None of us are going anywhere near that filthy place. Officer Boston can take care of it."

My irritation with these people was reaching beyond 'bite my tongue' levels. Dylan had shrunk in on himself like a little kid who'd been scolded. And I was rapidly losing my patience. "Actually, I have real police work to do, you know, when I'm not here trailing around after you. If you want to make a complaint about this, you're going to have to go down to the station and fill out the appropriate paperwork." If they wanted to make a complaint about Eve then that was their right, but I wasn't going to make it easier for them. The chief was already kissing their asses. I wasn't about to join him.

Laura glared at her husband and then at me. I was positive steam would shoot out of her ears at any minute. Not finding support in either of us, she appealed to a man seated at the table who had just casually been minding his own business throughout the entire argument. "Easton? You can't possibly be okay with this?"

The man sighed heavily, getting to his feet. "I'm not. Will, I agree with Laura. You need to do something about this woman. You need the Saint View votes to win, and if this woman is tarnishing your name there, you need to fight back."

Laura glared at her husband triumphantly. "I told you so! Easton is your campaign manager. You might be able to ignore me, but you shouldn't be ignoring him."

William raked a hand through his hair, yanking out an earbud. He focused in on Easton, still sitting calmly at the table. "You're worried about this, too?"

"Yes, I am. I think you need to take it more seriously. Nobody in Saint View is going to vote for you if they only know your face because they spent a drunken night pinning illustrated genitals to your forehead."

I battled back laughter again. I kind of wanted to go and high-five Eve for this idea. It probably would get her in trouble. If William reported this, the captain would send someone out there to shut it down.

But it wasn't going to be me. Not this time.

"Well?" Laura prodded her husband. "Are you going to get it handled?"

He pinned her with a glare that silenced her instantly. "Don't I always?"

I wondered what the hell he meant by that.

6

EVE

Like always, I was early to the restaurant. But I'd made a reservation, and the place was fairly empty, so the waiter let me sit alone at the table while I waited for Fawn and Lyric to arrive. I ordered a glass of white wine, and with time to kill, pulled out my phone to check my social media.

A smile tugged at my lips when I checked in on the club's Facebook page, with a new barrage of likes that had come in overnight. I might have to hand over all the promotions planning to Fawn if this kept up. We ran them regularly, football and other sports-themed nights, casino, and Fourth of July. But nothing had ever brought the sort of attention Fawn's 'Pin the Penis on the Politician' party was drawing.

I scrolled through the comments, most of which were people tagging friends, or laughing emojis. I switched the view to newest first and frowned.

This is revolting. How dare you insult our mayoral candidate like this.

You should be ashamed. Devil worshippers.

Low brow and unclassy. Should be illegal to act in this way.

They went on and on. I was no stranger to trolls, but this was an odd number in a short space of time. All with no profile picture or history to help identify them.

Typical troll behavior and not worth any more of my time.

I shut down the app, deciding to focus on the hundreds of comments that did seem up for a fun night. I was looking forward to it. I planned to be first in line to stick a big old peen right between William Reed's eyes.

I might have still been holding a small grudge over him having us arrested at his church rally. And a bigger one over him wanting to tear down the strip.

The door opened, and Fawn and Lyric fell through it with an armful of shopping bags. Their laughter followed them inside, and when they paused to look around, I waved. Without checking in with the waiter, they beelined for where I sat, big smiles still stretching their mouths.

"No Amelia today?" I pouted at Lyric.

"Nope, daycare. You'll have to save your Aunty Eve hugs for another day."

"Damn. You need to bring her into the club sometime like you used to when she was little. I miss my Milly girl."

"She'd miss you, too, if she weren't so busy ruling the daycare. That kid works the place like a boss."

"She is your daughter."

Lyric smiled proudly. "Sure is."

I glanced between her and Fawn. "You two seem to be

in a good mood. Is it just a shopping high, or something more? Who got laid?"

"Not me." Fawn dumped her bags on the floor at our feet.

Lyric unhooked her purse and slung it over the back of her chair before she sat. "I wish. Amelia makes casual sex practically impossible."

"You could try relationship sex instead?" I offered.

Lyric laughed like the idea was completely crazy. "Or you could just babysit more often."

That was more likely. "Deal. What did you guys buy, anyway? Anything interesting?"

Fawn bounced on her chair like an excited puppy. "Actually, we got you something!"

"Yeah? A present? It's not even my birthday."

Lyric grinned. "We were in the sex shop—"

I rolled my eyes. "Of course you were. Because that's where everyone goes on a Tuesday morning."

Lyric shrugged. "You do when you're not getting any like us. Some of us have to take care of ourselves."

"Preaching to the choir, babe." I laughed. "It's just me and my hand at my place, too."

And my hand had been working overtime lately. As had my entire top drawer of toys. I was still pissed off as hell with Boston after what had happened at the club, and yet somehow, that only seemed to fuel my libido. Every time I thought of him, warmth flooded my body, and then I was counting the minutes until I could get home and be alone.

All while thinking about him. The chiseled cut of his jaw. His hazel eyes and stern expression. The way his chest filled out his uniform to perfection.

All I could think about was having nasty, dirty, throw-you-up-against-the-wall hate sex with the man.

I really needed to get laid. I was getting hot under the collar just thinking about it.

Fawn cocked her head to one side, then giggled at Lyric. "She's doing it again."

That snapped me back to attention. "Doing what?"

"Daydreaming about your hot cop."

I flushed pink, hating that I was that transparent. "Hardly. I was thinking about the bookkeeping I need to do when I get back to the club."

Lyric sniggered. "If bookkeeping truly got you as hot-and-bothered-looking as you are right now, I'd do it for you."

"And my course would be a whole lot more interesting," Fawn piped up. Then she immediately shot an apologetic glance at me. "Sorry. I don't mean that to sound like I don't enjoy the course. I do. It's just hard sometimes, but I'm so grateful—"

I held up a hand to stop her. "Shh. It's all good, I know."

I'd paid for the course Fawn was currently taking. She was young and excited and wanted to learn. And I wanted to provide her with something more than just a place to take her clothes off. Fawn had been so grateful she'd cried. And once again, I'd seen myself in her. Young, and lost, with no one to believe in her or support her dreams. No one to tell her she could be whatever the hell she wanted to be.

I didn't want to screw kids of my own up the way my mother had screwed me. I was destined to be a crazy cat lady. But Fawn had fallen in my lap, and I hadn't regretted it for a second. It was beneficial for me, too. She rented my investment property, a little house on the Saint View/Providence border that I'd bought with my club earnings. Fawn paid her rent on time every week and kept the lawn neat and tidy. She was the perfect tenant.

"Anyway," Lyric interrupted. "Like we said, we bought you something."

"Quit teasing me with it and show me then!"

Lyric grabbed a bag from the pile on the floor and rifled through it. "Funny you mention teasing…"

She pulled the item out of the bag like it was a game show prize and held it triumphantly in the air.

I blinked up it, clutched in her fingers.

A huge, ridged, bright-purple dildo.

"Surprise!" Fawn laughed.

Lyric waved the massive penis-shaped thing in my direction. "But wait, there's more! It's personalized!" She flipped it over to reveal letters printed down the side.

I snatched it from her grasp to read the letters.

Boston.

I gaped at her. "Really, Lyric? Why the hell am I holding a dildo with Boston written on it? Of all the names in the world!"

Lyric and Fawn burst into laughter and searched through their bags again, both producing dildos of their own. Fawn's was a fluorescent green, Lyric's a bright red that almost matched her hair.

"You both got one, too? Do yours have names as well?"

Fawn nodded eagerly.

I leaned forward, resting my elbows on the tabletop. "Let's see it then."

Fawn turned hers over with a small, shy smile.

My eyes widened. "You did not name your dildo Augie!"

She burst into laughter. "The guy at the shop said that he could personalize it with any name, but that most women chose names of men they had crushes on. You know, so you kinda have your crush inside you when you...you know."

"And you chose Augie? The guy is an asshole. Nobody likes him. I mean, we love him because he's family, but he's an ass."

She shrugged. "He's not to me. I like him."

"Jesus. That's a worry." But I didn't want to harp on about it. If she truly had a thing for Augie, there was nothing I could do about it. Except castrate the fucker if he ever hurt her.

I focused on Lyric. "What about you? If you have Phoenix's name down the side of your dildo, I'm going to be very concerned."

Lyric let out a scoff. "Nope." She twisted her dildo over to show off the letters imprinted in the side. *Lyric.* "Got my own name. Don't need no man in my life, or on my dildo. I'll leave that to the two of you."

"Hey! I don't need no man in my life either. You're the one who named my dildo Boston."

A hovering waiter gave us a dirty look. I shot one right back. The place was practically empty. He could quit being a prude.

Lyric picked up a menu and cast an eye over it, even though we all knew we'd order the exact same thing we did every week we met here for lunch. I'd get the Caesar salad. Lyric would get a burger and fries. Fawn would get pasta.

Lyric tapped a fingernail against her regular burger order, but her words were directed at me. "Please. You can lie to yourself all you want, but the chemistry between you and that cop? Freaking sizzling."

"The man arrested me. And then called me a hooker."

"So? How many times have you been arrested now? And he's hardly the first person to assume that stripping leads to more. The man is sexy as sin, Eve. Don't even pretend to me that you don't want to jump his bones. We could practically smell the pheromones pouring off you the other night."

My mouth dropped open. "Excuse me? There were no pheromones."

Fawn snorted. "Seriously, I got horny watching the two of you. It was like watching porn, but better because the acting wasn't fake."

I slapped her on the arm. "You've been hanging out with Lyric too long."

"Hey! Why say that like it's a bad thing? Our baby stripper here needed to be taught the ways of the world. So I taught her. She's my little protégé now." Lyric raised her chin proudly and patted Fawn on the head like she was a puppy.

I tossed my hair back with a grin and caught the eye of the waiter. "He's glaring at us again," I told the others. "Best put the evil sex toys away before he kicks us out. I really want that chicken Caesar salad."

Fawn side-eyed me. "So you're keeping your gift then?"

I threw the dildo inside my bag. It was big, thick, and yeah, I could definitely have a good time with it.

It had nothing to do with the fact it had Boston's name on it.

But the reminder of him while I was getting myself off probably wouldn't hurt.

7

EVE

I spent the rest of the afternoon running errands, both personal and things we needed at the club. I went home, did some laundry, cleaned my bathroom, and was just beginning to think about what to do for dinner when my phone rang.

I noted the unknown number but didn't think twice about answering it. "Hello?"

"Eve. It's William Reed."

"Bye."

"No, wait, please. I just want to talk. I'm trying to offer an olive branch. I'm just asking for one minute of your time."

I could be the bigger person when I wanted to be. "Fine. One minute."

"Actually, I wanted to use that one minute to invite you to my home. I felt terrible about what happened at the church, and I'd like to make it right. I really do want the input of people who live in Saint View and know the area the way you do. I'd like to talk to you about it, and how we can work better together."

I raised an eyebrow in surprise. That was a turn-around. And well overdue, but not an opportunity I was going to refuse. If I could just get in his ear, maybe I could convince him that his plans for the strip were misguided. There were so many other bigger, more pressing problems in Saint View that needed his attention. "Fine. When? Where?"

"Are you free now? Have you eaten? Come to my place for a late dinner, and we'll talk."

My stomach rumbled at the thought of food I didn't have to prepare and cook first. I'd bet William had people who did that for him. "Fine, text me your address and I'll be there in twenty."

"Great. Thank you, Eve. See you when you get here."

I tossed my phone onto my couch, marveling at the strange turn of events. "Didn't see that one coming," I mumbled to my empty house. Then sighed. It was so quiet here sometimes. It was why I spent so much time at the club. Maybe I should consider getting a dog. At least then I wouldn't be talking to myself. I did have a cat, but the animal barely tolerated me and had probably retreated to her favorite spot beneath the spare bed, where she didn't have to deal with me. Could hardly blame her.

A moment later my phone binged with an incoming message, and I grabbed my bag and keys from the hook by the door. I checked the message as I walked outside and got into my car. Of course, he lived on one of the fanciest streets in Providence. It was just around the corner from the church.

Without bothering to search it up on the map, I took the familiar back streets through Saint View and then crossed into Providence where the houses grew bigger and more lavish with every passing mile. I drove into William's driveway a few moments later, parking behind a Porsche, and stared up at his big house.

His big, completely dark house. "Geez. Thanks for the warm welcome. Could have left the front light on for me."

I got out, closing the door behind me, and fumbled through my purse for my phone. It was near pitch-black with only the stars and moon for light, and I was wearing heels. I wasn't interested in twisting an ankle. A busted-up leg would have me off the pole for weeks. I didn't need that. I switched on the flashlight function on my phone, and at least that gave me enough light to make sure I wasn't going to step in a hole and break my neck.

I passed a small, neat garden of roses and tried not to jump as my flashlight beam bounced over a creepy garden gnome. I shuddered. "Ugly little critter, aren't you?"

The gnome didn't reply.

"Rude bastard, just like your owners, huh?" Jesus. I was losing it. Was I seriously talking to a garden gnome?

I shone my light around the doorframe, searching for the bell, and put a finger to it.

Nothing happened. I didn't hear a ring, but perhaps this house was so big that the internal speaker was far away from the door. There were no footsteps, and no lights coming on. I pushed the button again and then shined my phone's light through the window. A beautiful sitting area, with couches, and an armchair atop a plush rug sat beyond the glass. But no owners in sight.

There was obviously no one home.

"Well, that's fucking great, isn't it? Invite me over, then don't show." I stuck my middle finger up at the door and swiveled on my heel, ready to march back down to my car and leave a nice black tire mark down the center of William's driveway as a parting present. "Prick."

I paused as headlights blinded me, another car pulling into the driveway behind mine. I put one arm up to cover my eyes, muttering, "Better late than never, I guess. Still fucking rude."

The lights turned off, bright splotches floating in front of my eyes while I blinked rapidly, trying to adjust to the darkness once more.

"Eve?"

I squinted. The deeper rumbling roll of his voice was one I'd been dreaming about for weeks now. "Boston? What are you doing here?"

He stopped a few feet away from me, flashlight of his own in hand but pointed at the ground. His was brighter than the one on my phone, so I tucked mine away and left the two of us standing in the dim glow with just enough light to make out his expression.

He wasn't happy.

Oh well. What else was new? Immediately defensive at his scowl, I crossed my arms beneath my breasts, squashing the strap of my bag slung across my chest.

He tapped the flashlight against his leg impatiently. "I think that's supposed to be my question. I had a report of a suspected break-in at this address."

My mouth dropped open. "A break-in? What? No, William called me. He asked me to come over here."

A muscle ticked in Boston's jaw. "The call said he'd

had an argument with a woman earlier in the evening and she'd threatened physical violence. He moved his family out of the house and then asked for the police intervention."

I couldn't have been more stunned if he'd punched me in the gut. "That isn't true! He called and asked me to come over here. He said he wanted me to be the voice of Saint View. He said we would try to work things through and work more harmoniously."

Boston sighed heavily.

"You don't believe me, do you? I can show you the message."

"I —"

A flash went off in the bushes behind Boston's squad car. We both spun around only to be flashed a bunch more times as a photographer came out of the bushes.

My anger flared. "What is this? Reed's personal pap squad?" I whirled on Boston. "Are you in on this, too? Is this just some big setup? Get Eve over here, call the cops, get her arrested again? Are you trying to destroy any sort of credibility I might have? Don't get me wrong, I don't mind being arrested for things I have actually done. But this is entrapment. As if I'd want to break in and steal anything here anyway. Look at their garden decorations! They're awful!"

My short temper got the better of me. I kicked over the ugly garden gnome, satisfied when it hit the concrete driveway and shattered.

The pap's camera flash went crazy again. "Destruction of property!" he shouted, like I'd just handed him a winning lottery ticket. "Excellent!"

Boston put a hand up in the direction of the photographer, blocking him from taking any more photos of me.

He groaned loudly. "Are you always this impulsive? For Christ's sake, Eve, and with a photographer watching and everything."

"He set me up!"

"Yeah. He set you up. How dumb do you think I am? You think I couldn't see that? You're wearing high heels. If you were planning on breaking into his house, I think you probably would have chosen more appropriate footwear."

"I'll have you know, I can run pretty fast in these."

He just stared at me. "Do you actually think before you open your mouth? I was trying to tell you I was on your side."

"I don't need you on my side!"

He threw up his hands in frustration. "You're impossible."

I couldn't blame him. I *was* impossible. And impulsive. I did run my mouth without thinking. They were my worst flaws, all right there for him to see. He'd called them, right off the bat.

Embarrassment heated my face. "What now then?"

"Get in the car."

I gaped at him. "For a garden gnome? You're arresting me over a two-dollar fucking lawn ornament?"

"Get. In. The. Car, Eve. Or is it *Evil*? I can never tell with you."

I was so frustrated and angry I could have stamped my foot like a toddler. But I wouldn't give Boston that sort of satisfaction.

The photographer was having a field day. "Where's the cuffs, Officer? Can we get a shot of you putting them on her?"

My blood boiled over. I launched myself in his direction, ready to smash his overpriced camera and his obnoxious face.

Strong arms caught me around my middle. I kicked and flailed, screaming for Boston to let me go.

"Do you ever actually listen to anyone?" he growled in my ear.

I went quiet in his arms. His voice sent a tremble down my spine, goosebumps spreading across my skin, his warm breath on my neck.

He had me in the back of his squad car before I even fully realized it.

The locks slammed down.

I shook my head. Boston played dirty. Whether he knew it or not, he'd used raw sex appeal to get his way. And now that I was stuck in the back of his car, under fucking arrest again, that just pissed me off more.

"Don't forget to take the evidence with you," the photographer called.

Boston paused half inside the car and then cursed. He leaned across the center console and grabbed a bag and gloves from somewhere on the passenger side. Then he got back out and collected the pieces of the broken gnome, putting them inside the brown bag. He shook it in the direction of the photographer. "Got the evidence. Happy?"

The photographer's only response was a flash of his camera.

Boston got back behind the wheel, tossing the evidence bag into the back seat beside me. He yanked his seat belt, shoving the metal piece into the clip.

"Dare you to run the guy over."

My gaze met Boston's in the rearview mirror. He just shook his head.

I rolled my eyes. "Can you at least put the radio on if you aren't going to talk to me." I flopped against the back seat and crossed my arms in a huff.

"Put your seat belt on and I'll consider it."

I did it, not because he told me to, but because it was the smart thing to do. Who knew what his night driving was like? I didn't fancy flying through a windshield if the man didn't know how to drive.

But Boston nodded like I was a good little girl and flicked the radio on.

I clenched my fingers into fists. I kind of wanted to throw one into his self-righteous face. Even though it would have been a pity to break his perfect nose.

He reversed out of the driveway and got us on the road, winding our way through the streets of Providence. It took me a moment to realize that I still had my bag. I rifled through it, looking for my phone to send a text off to Fawn and Lyric and let them know what was happening before Boston realized I still had it and confiscated it.

Instead of the phone, my fingers brushed against the solid rubber of the massive dildo Lyric and Fawn had bought me earlier.

I glanced at Boston, in the front seat. He was so straight. So good, right to his very core.

The guy could use a bit of a shakeup.

I pulled out the dildo and quietly tucked it inside the evidence bag. While I was sitting in a cell, he'd be putting a massive purple dildo with his name on it into evidence.

A wicked sense of satisfaction stole over me. And I smiled for the rest of the car ride.

8

BOSTON

Out in front of Saint View Strip Club, I killed my car's headlights and unlocked the doors, before opening Eve's for her.

She jumped, gaze snapping up from her phone, but her surprise was quickly replaced by a devious smile. It fell away, though, when she noticed we were on her home turf. Her perfect eyebrows knit together in confusion. "This isn't the police station."

"Last I checked, no, it's not."

When she made no move to get out of the car, I reached across and unbuckled her seat belt, trying not to breathe in her perfume.

She still didn't move. "I don't understand. I thought I was under arrest?"

I took her arm, guiding her gently. She followed, bewilderment etched into her expression.

"Did you really think I was going to arrest you over a garden gnome?"

"Well, you do kind of have a stick up your ass. So yes. I did."

I closed the door with a loud thud.

Eve looked back at the seat she'd just exited and cringed. "Um, what about the evidence? Are you going to log that?"

My boots crunched over the gravel parking area. "I only did that to keep the paparazzi off my back. And yours. I'll just throw it out when I get back to the station. That's not even a proper evidence bag. I brought my lunch in it this morning."

Pink tinged her cheeks. "Oh. I didn't realize that."

We walked side by side toward the club's entrance. I knew she was Saint View born and bred, and that she was probably used to walking the streets alone at night, but I wanted to walk her to the door anyway. "I'm not dumb, Eve. I know a bogus complaint when I see one."

"What about my car?"

"Don't worry about it. I've got a friend. He'll have it outside the club in an hour."

Her eyes went wide in mock surprise. "Are you telling me Mr. Vanilla has contacts who know how to hotwire a car?"

I frowned at that. "Though I suppose it doesn't help the vanilla tag, I actually know a guy who owns a tow truck. I already organized for him to get it for you. Because I don't think it's a very good idea that you go back to William's place right now. Do you?"

She chuckled softly. "I guess not."

We were at the doorway to the club. But it was quiet inside, and the closed sign was up. "Will you be okay here until your car arrives? I can give you a lift home, if you prefer."

She shook her head. Large hoop earrings with little sun charms dangling from the bottom jingled around her face. "No, that's okay. I've got plenty to do while I wait."

"Probably takes up a lot of your time, huh? Running a successful business?"

"You think my business is successful?" There was pure pride in her tone, and I wondered how many times she'd had to defend herself and what she did.

"Of course. I saw all the social media excitement about your penis party. Seems like it'll be a big night for you."

"Are you going to come?"

I smiled with a wry twist of my lip. "Don't think so. William has a fundraiser that same night. I'll be playing bodyguard."

"But you're a cop."

"Yeah. I thought so, too." This conversation was suddenly cutting a little too close to the quick. She could proudly defend her club, because she knew at her core that everything she did there, everything she'd built, was good and moral. Could I truly say the same for my own job? I was supposed to be a pillar of the community, and yet the chief had me babysitting politicians and taking bribes from local gangs. Every time I questioned any of it, it was always the same old story. Our orders came from higher up, and we needed to toe the line. I pulled my cap down on my forehead. "I should get back to it. I need to explain to my chief about the photos that are probably going to pop up online in the morning."

"Will you get in trouble?"

"Depends on what the photos are like, I guess. But that's not your problem. Sorry William was a dick. I'll talk to him about leaving you alone."

I turned on my heel before I could take in her expression. I went back to my car and got behind the wheel. The headlights lit Eve up, bouncing off her shiny dark hair, illuminating her like she was some sort of angel. My heart gave an unexpected little thump.

"Fuck," I muttered. I put the car in reverse and drove away before I could do anything stupid.

*B*ack at the station, I took all of my belongings out of my squad car and headed upstairs. The chief called me in the moment he saw me, motioning me over through the glass window.

With a heavy sigh, I stuck my head into his office. "What's up?"

"I heard there was a callout to the Reed's place. Anything going on out there?"

"Photographer." It wasn't a lie. It just wasn't the whole truth. Not something that sat entirely right with me, but neither did William trying to frame Eve for some sort of bullshit break and entry. But there was no point telling the chief any of that. He was obviously well and truly in Reed's pocket.

"Right." He flicked his head toward the door, dismissing me. "See you tomorrow then."

"See you."

I wandered back to my desk and dumped my things on top of it. Jayela and two of the other guys, Johnson—

an old dog cop—and his rookie partner, Stewart, looked up from their conversation. As usual, Johnson stood too close to Jayela, his crush on her clear for everyone to see. Everyone except Jayela, who laughed the notion off every time I'd brought it up. The man was a creep, a married creep at that, but Jayela had always been big enough to fight her own battles and didn't need me rescuing her from unwanted male attention.

"Where have you been?" Jayela asked. "I thought you were just getting dinner and then coming straight back?"

"Yeah. Me, too, but William called. Had to swing by his place."

She screwed her nose up. "I don't like that guy. He acts like you're his bitch."

I didn't say anything. But I didn't like it much either. I wasn't just William's bitch, I was the chief's as well, and it left a sour taste in my mouth.

Jayela nudged me toward my desk. "Anyway. Come out with us. Let's get a drink or something. Won't be too late. I want to check out the Sinner's hangouts again tomorrow so I don't want to be hungover.

I paused. "Did Chief talk to you about that?"

"He might have mentioned something about leaving them alone, but we'll stay well back. No one will even know we're there. I just have a gut feeling I can't shake."

"There's something going on with them for sure," Johnson agreed. "If I were a betting man, I'd put my money on guns and drugs."

Jayela nodded eagerly. "Yes! And we're going to nail them."

I could have killed Johnson for riling her up about it again. She was like a dog with a bone, and I should have known she'd ignore the chief's warnings to stay away. But there was no point arguing with her when she had her mind set on something. It was a problem for tomorrow. I'd try to come up with some excuse to keep her occupied. Maybe we'd have a rash of home invasions or some other interesting crime that would keep her mind off the Sinners. "Drinks sound good. Just let me put this stuff away."

I took off my badge and gun and locked them in the safe. One of the broken, sharp edges of the garden gnome protruded through the flimsy paper of my lunch bag, creating a jagged tear. I grabbed the top of the bag to throw it into the trashcan by my desk, when the entire thing split in two, the small rip becoming a big one. The bottom half of the bag hit the floor, contents spilling out everywhere.

A massive purple dildo bounced off my boot and rolled across the floor toward Jayela and the guys.

All four of us stared at it. It made a final rotation, displaying my name printed down the side.

The others burst into hysterical laughter. Johnson's snorts of amusement were so loud they drew the attention of the rest of the room. Heads swiveled in our direction, other officers pushing to their feet to see what the commotion was all about.

Jayela could barely compose herself enough to speak. "Is it April Fools' Day? What just happened here? Why do you have a ten-inch rubber dick in your lunch bag?"

Stewart poked at it with his toe, while tears rolled down his face. "The bigger question is, why does it have your name on it?"

I couldn't stop staring. My face flashed hot, mortification creeping up my neck, while the others howled their amusement. Slowly, the embarrassment turned to anger. I was so fucking sick of being everybody's punching bag. William. The chief. And now Eve. "Enough," I snapped. I stooped and grabbed the dildo from the floor, shoving it beneath my jacket as I stormed out of the station. Any desire to hang out with Jayela and the others was lost in their mocking.

Jayela's laughter trailed after me. "Don't be such a stick-in-the-mud, Boston! If you needed some alone time with your little friend, you could have just told us."

Without turning around, I stuck my middle finger up in the air. She only laughed harder, Johnson's snorts grating my last nerve to smithereens.

I had no idea why Eve had put it in my bag. But the fact it had my name on it felt like a pretty clear insult. I was a dick. Or maybe she'd just done it to embarrass me. Or to discredit me in front of my squad.

Either way, I heard her loud and clear.

Any enjoyment in talking to her earlier tonight disintegrated. She'd just declared a war.

9

EVE

I was tired the day after William had set me up and tried to have me arrested. Like he'd promised, Boston's friend had delivered my car to me, refusing to take payment for the tow, assuring me Boston had already covered it. Which only made me feel worse about what I'd done. I'd stayed at the club working on the books until my eyes had crossed, but once I'd gotten home and into bed, sleep had completely evaded me in favor of wondering if Boston had found the dildo.

The conversation after he'd dropped me off at the club had played over in my mind, and I'd lain there all night, regretting that I hadn't just come clean and confessed. But our talk had actually been kind of pleasant. He hadn't been a dick. I hadn't been a bitch. Nobody had arrested anyone. That was always a bonus. He'd caught me by surprise by actually being nice, and I'd had no idea how to admit my mistake.

Trouble had always been easier for me than truth.

I knew that said something about me.

"Okay. So, best-case scenario. He just threw the bag in the trash. He didn't see the dildo. Didn't see his name. Everything is fine. Maybe I can ask him to coffee?"

My cat, Lexi, just stared up at me with large, judgmental eyes.

I frowned at her. "What? You're on his side?"

She lifted one leg and began cleaning herself. I wasn't sure whether that was a confirmation or a denial. Rude cat.

"Fine. Perhaps I owe him an explanation."

Lexi eyed me, expression full of disdain.

"Fine! An apology then. Jesus, cat. So judgy. I bet a dog wouldn't come at me the way you are right now. It was just a joke."

But we both knew it hadn't been. I'd acted out in the heat of the moment, like I always did. But this time I actually regretted it. That was new.

"Okay," I mused. "What options do I have here? I can go down to the police station and apologize in person." I cringed, both at the thought of having to see Boston face-to-face, and at the thought I might have embarrassed him in front of his colleagues. I didn't want to embarrass him any further if that was the case.

My other option was the phone. But I didn't have the guy's number. But there were ways around that. I picked up my cell and dialed the number for my lawyer, Liam.

He answered on the third ring. "Eve? It's not late and you're ringing me from your phone, so I'm guessing you aren't in jail this time?"

"Hello to you, too. Why do you assume I'm in jail every time I call you?"

"Because you usually are."

"Maybe I'm trying to turn over a new leaf?"

He sniggered, like the idea was ridiculous. "I hope you do. Would certainly save me some time in getting you off these misdemeanors you seem to enjoy racking up."

"Shut up." I sniffed. "I'd never see you if you weren't bailing me out. You're always so busy working." Liam had grown up in the hood, his mom friends with mine. So he was like the annoying third brother I'd never wanted. Though unlike my biological brothers, at least Liam had a useful occupation.

Liam groaned into the earpiece. "Playing the guilt card, huh? Low."

"Truth hurts."

He grumbled something on the other end. "I'll stop by more, okay? You don't have to get arrested to get my attention. Just cook some of my favorite stew, and I'll be there with bells on."

"You know there is always a pot of it on the stove on family night."

"I know. I know. But I'm assuming that's not why you rang me. What's up?"

I sat heavily on my bed and played with the edge of my blanket, letting the silky material run through my fingers. "Do you have a way of getting me a cell phone number for somebody?"

"Legally or illegally?"

Despite the fact I'd just told him I was trying to turn over a new leaf, I wasn't actually all that bothered by how he came by the number. I just really wanted it. "I'll leave that to your discretion. I need the number for an Officer Boston. He's a cop in Providence."

"Joshua Boston?"

"That's the one."

"I know him. Worked a case with him a few years ago. Pretty sure I still have his number saved in my phone. Hold on." The phone beeped a few times as he scrolled through his contacts. "Yep. Still got it."

My breath hitched. "You do? Can you send it to me, please?"

He paused. "Are you going to use this number for nefarious purposes? Do you plan to stalk him? Write his name on bathroom stalls and tell people to call him for a good time?"

"Just give me the number, Liam. Don't forget I kicked your ass when we were kids, I'll do it again."

"I was five and you were ten. That's an unfair advantage."

"Want a rematch?"

He chuckled. "No way. You scare me. I'll text you the number. Bye, Eve."

I smiled smugly.

When the number came in, I quickly saved it to my phone. Then started a fresh text message. With trembling fingers, I tapped a few sentences.

EVE

> Hey, it's Eve. Just wanted to say thank you for driving me home. And for getting my car back to me. I appreciate it.

I hesitated, but it was a good, noncommittal, testing-the-waters sort of message. I pressed 'send' and waited.

The message receipt changed to 'read,' and I held my breath while the little bubbles that indicated he was typing popped up. They disappeared after a few moments, but no reply came through.

I frowned and tapped out a new message.

EVE

> Do you have time for a coffee tomorrow? I owe you one.

I considered adding a smiley face to the end of it but didn't want to be over the top. Plus, smiling emojis weren't really my thing. The one with the devil horns got a good workout, though.

Again the message changed to 'read' and little bubbles appeared. This time, his message pinged through almost instantly.

BOSTON

> Why? Did you want your dildo back? How did you even get this number?

I groaned and tossed my phone onto the bed in frustration. "Dammit."

I retrieved the phone again and held down the button to record a voice message. "Yeah, about that. I thought you were arresting me again. And I was kind of pissed off about it. Have you noticed that I'm somewhat impulsive? It's a problem. I'm working on it."

I sent the message through and got up to pace the room, unable to sit still.

He didn't reply.

I tried again.

EVE

> I'm sorry.

Still no reply.

EVE

> I'll make it up to you? Not with lap
> dances this time. I'll even wear clothes.
> Ha ha.

I tapped my foot on the thick carpet of my bedroom, hating that it was taking him so long to respond. Hating my own impatience. Why couldn't I be a normal woman, who could just let things go? Why had I brought up the attempted lap dance again? That had gone down like a sinking ship last time. God, I was an idiot around this man. I had no idea why he got me so frazzled.

I pounced on my phone when it finally buzzed.

BOSTON

> I'm at a stakeout, Eve. I don't have time
> for this.

I stared at that message for a long time. He had every right to dismiss me. But it still annoyed me. "Fine," I muttered to my cat. "I tried. That's all I can do."

But a sick sense of disappointment settled low in my belly. One I instinctively knew wouldn't disappear anytime soon.

***

*M*y day went from bad to worse. I obsessively checked my phone every hour for more texts from Boston, but it remained obnoxiously blank. About five, I got a message, but it was only my mother, summoning me to dinner at her place. My first instinct was to decline. To say I had to work or help friends or wash my hair. But I already knew no excuse would be good enough for her and then I'd just have to listen to her harp on about how I never made time for her. She loved nothing better than a guilt trip. Plus, I hadn't seen my brothers in weeks. And if I was being summoned, they likely were, too.

My mum's place in the center of Saint View was exactly as I remembered it from my childhood. Run-down and tiny. I hadn't lived here since I was sixteen when I started stripping, only coming back for the family dinners my mother insisted on.

I dragged in a deep breath, giving myself a mental pep talk. I could do this. My mother was toxic, but I was a grown-ass woman. I could get through a few hours in her presence.

I pushed through her front door with my head held high and my shoulders back. Not only because she'd criticize for hunching if I didn't, but because I wanted to.

She looked up from stirring something on the stove, steam floating off it as well as a delicious aroma. Her gray-flecked hair stuck to her damp forehead, wrinkles creasing the space between her brows. "You're late."

"Hello to you, too, Mama." I dropped an obligatory kiss on the shorter woman's weathered cheek.

She grabbed an apron from the drawer and tossed it in my direction, not returning my attempt at affection. "The vegetables need chopping. They should already be on in the oven. I was counting on you being here at six, but no, of course not. Eve runs on Eve time."

I dug my fingers into the fabric of the apron and

glanced in the direction of the living room. "Are Luca and Giles here? What about Papa?"

"Of course. They're always on time. Unlike you."

"And they couldn't have helped?"

She silenced me with a glare.

Of course not. Because she never expected my father or brothers to lift a finger. They never offered either, but even if they had, she would have shooed them away.

I pulled potatoes onto a chopping board and ran a knife through them, halving, then quartering, before tossing them into a bowl, ready for my mother. The knife thwacked against the board, louder than truly necessary.

I moved on to the carrots, popping a piece into my mouth to munch on. When I reached for another, my mother smacked my hand. "Stop snacking! You'll never find a man if you get fat!"

"Like your mama!" my father shouted from the living room.

I pinned him with a glare through the doorway. "Don't talk to her like that."

"Hush!" my mother snapped. "Do your work."

I gaped at her. "He just called you fat and you snap at me?"

She didn't say anything. The only sign that she was at all bothered by his comments was the vicious way she shook the salt into her pot.

"What's cooking, Mama?" Luca wandered in from the living room. "Hey, Eve."

I nodded at him, too annoyed with my parents. My father for being such a prick. My mother for not standing up for herself.

Luca leaned on the countertop and snuck a piece of

carrot from my pile. "Heard you got arrested at the mayoral candidate's rally the other week."

"What?" Mama gasped, spinning around. "Arrested?"

I glared at my brother. "Seriously?"

He cringed. "Ooh, sorry. You didn't tell the parentals?"

"Did you tell the parentals about the time Louisa Tepernath blew you in the church bathrooms after Sunday mass?"

The blood drained from my mother's face. "Eve! Luca!"

His mouth dropped open. "You're a bitch."

"Ooh, sorry," I mimicked, fighting back a laugh.

If looks could kill, I would have been dead on the spot. But typical of my mother, she ignored my brother's sins and focused on mine. "What does he mean you got arrested? Where? What for? How could you do this? What if my friends find out?"

I shrugged. "Please. We live in Saint View. Like Juliet's kids have never been arrested. They're thugs!"

She slapped my hand again like I was a naughty child.

I shot an annoyed glance at her. "I was just defending what's mine. William Reed wants to shut my club down. So I turned up at his rally and told him to take a hike. In return, he had me arrested."

"What?" Luca snapped. "He can't just close your business down."

It was too much to hope that my mother might react the same way.

She froze, too stunned for a moment to say anything while she stared at me with horrified eyes. "William Reed the politician?"

"Is there another? God, for the sake of humanity, I hope not."

"Eve! Stop it! He's a good man. A Christian with a beautiful wife and children. He's very smart and wealthy and handsome, and—"

"Jesus, Mama. Are you president of his fan club?" Luca asked before throwing another piece of carrot up into the air and catching it with his mouth.

My mother didn't admonish him the way she had with me.

I ground my teeth together. "William Reed called me a whore. Or was it a slut? I can't remember. He's trying to shut down a business I've spent a decade building. How Christian is that?"

Mama shook her head vehemently. "No, I don't believe that. You must have misunderstood."

"I understood perfectly. The man doesn't care what the people of Saint View want or need. He wants to turn my place into a freaking yoga studio or a juice bar or something."

"Well, a yoga studio does sound lovely. We don't have one of those around here."

I stared at the back of her head, disappointment coursing through me. "I employ ten people, Mama."

"Strippers," she muttered.

Hurt punched in. "And to you, strippers aren't people? Wow. Tell me what you really think."

Her silence only riled me up more. Luca gave me a 'sorry' pat on the arm but left the room, no more willing to back me up than he was to help me cook.

"Actually," I sniffed, fighting back hot, angry tears that pricked at the backs of my eyes. "Only four of them are strippers. The others work the bar and tend the door. But those strippers you look down your nose at? They are people, Mama. Just like I am. Fawn is in college, completing a course I paid for. And Lyric? Her stripping pays for her daughter's daycare. The best one in Providence."

She just kept on stirring her pot. "William Reed is a smart man. If he thinks we need new businesses in Saint View, then I believe him."

My hurt and irritation morphed into a sad acceptance. This was how she'd been with me ever since I'd left home. In her mind, I committed a mortal sin every time I took my clothes off for a man who wasn't my husband. Sure, she kept summoning me to her house for family dinner because she couldn't bear to lose face in front of her friends.

But there was no perfect family here. Nothing right, or good. It was one giant ball of hurt and guilt and shame.

One I didn't want anything to do with. Not anymore.

I took my apron off and placed it carefully on the countertop. "Bye, Mama."

When I walked out the door, no one tried to stop me.

10

BOSTON

The next day brought no new home invasions. No petty thefts at the shopping mall. There wasn't even a missing kid at the park which might have distracted Jayela for a little while. From the minute we came on shift, she'd had a single-minded focus on watching the Sinners.

Sitting in the car all day, knowing it wasn't going to lead anywhere, hadn't improved my mood any. Neither had the random text from Eve. For hours, Jayela left me to stew, silence thick in the air around us as we'd both stared steadfastly at the target. The sun was already beginning to sink when she finally let out a long-suffering sigh. "Shift will be finished soon. Are we going to talk about what's eating you, or not?"

"I'm fine."

"Bullshit. We embarrassed you yesterday."

I shook my head. "*You* didn't."

But Eve had. I could take a joke. But my job was important to me, and she'd crossed a line.

Jayela twisted in her seat to face me. "Nobody cares if you own a massive dildo, Josh."

She was the only person who called me that. And she generally saved it for when it was just the two of us, like right now. We'd been best friends since the first day of academy, when she'd waltzed right over, sized me up, and declared I could be her friend. My lips lifted a little at the memory. "I don't own a massive dildo. It's Eve's."

"Eve..."

"Hawkins."

Her eyes widened. "From the strip club?"

I nodded.

"Spill the freaking tea. Why does Eve Hawkins have a dildo with your name on it?" She let out a low whistle. "I mean, I could have cut the sexual tension between the two of you with a knife it was that thick, but fill me in on what I've missed. No, wait, just skip to the good bits. Did you sleep with her?"

"What? No! Of course not."

"All right, all right, settle down. Do you like her?"

I went quiet.

"She obviously likes you."

"How do you figure that? She tried to humiliate me with a dildo with my name on it. If that doesn't say she thinks I'm a dick, I don't know what does."

Jayela stared at me for a long moment then burst into laughter. "My God, men are so dumb. Did you ever name your car? When you were in high school or something?"

"Sure. Had a truck named Big Red."

She rolled her eyes. "Original. You ever named anything else?"

"Such as? I can tell you're fishing for something in particular here."

She grinned. "Ever named your dick?"

I laughed. "No. Have you?"

She tucked her hands behind her head and shifted back on her chair, spreading her legs wide. "Oh, Joshy. If I had a dick, it would have the manliest name around. Thor, maybe? Or... Henry."

I snorted. "Henry?"

She shrugged. "After Henry Cavill." She sat up straight again, resuming her normal position. "Anyway, point being, people name things. I don't think she named her dildo Boston because she thinks you're a dick. More likely because she's thinking of you when she *wants* some dick." She wriggled her eyebrows suggestively. "If you know what I'm saying."

"Subtle isn't exactly you're middle name. It would be hard to not know what you're saying."

I mulled over the idea, but it seemed incredibly arrogant to even consider she could be interested enough to name her sex toy after me.

But now Jayela had put it out there, the very idea made my balls ache. "At least it's a big dildo," I mused.

Jayela snorted. "A fitting tribute to Kong."

"Kong?"

She tilted her head quizzically. "You don't like that?" She glanced at my lap, then back up at my face with a wicked grin. "Ted? Rhino? Pointy?"

I shoved her in the shoulder as she dissolved into laughter. "Shut up. Quit trying to name my junk."

Her laughter cut off sharply as she leaned forward,

peering out the windshield. "Shit. Movement at the house. Where's my camera?"

A wave of guilt washed over me. Five hundred meters down the road, the Saint View Sinners home base sat like an ugly blip on the landscape, the run-down residence on the verge of being condemned.

I couldn't tell her that while I shared her same gut feeling that the Sinners were up to something, no amount of watching this house was going to get us anywhere. Knowing the chief would have my head if I compromised the bigger operation in any way, I'd shot off a text message to my contact in the gang hours ago, telling them we'd be watching.

Some days, I really hated my job.

Jayela put her camera up to her eye. "It's Hayden and that weedy little guy we haven't identified." Her camera clicked half a dozen times, capturing images in the low light of the fading sun. "Shifty fucks. They're getting something out of the trunk."

She always did this. Commentated our stakeouts like I wasn't sitting right beside her, watching the exact same thing. It was one of the things I enjoyed about her. She loved this job more than life itself. More than food. More than sex. More than breathing. Her enthusiasm had pumped up my own, until I'd thought we were equal.

But it was clear to me at times like this, why the chief had picked me to be the inside guy. At first, I'd thought it was a respect thing. That he thought I was a good cop, worthy of being in the know, and involved in tasks beyond my pay grade.

But as the months had worn on, I'd seen it for what it really was.

I was the one more easily swayed.

Jayela's morals were too strong. She never would have agreed to the things I had. Even if they'd promised her a raise, a promotion—hell, they could have offered Jayela a yacht and she still wouldn't have accepted bribes from a gang, even if it was for some greater good. She would have found another way.

I couldn't see one that didn't involve me compromising everything I believed in.

"They're getting something out of the back," Jayela whispered, dropping her camera to her lap.

I leaned forward, resting my elbows on the steering wheel. We were several houses down the street, with cars parked all around us. We didn't exactly stick out, but if the dumbasses had ignored my warnings and gone ahead and accepted a shipment of guns or drugs, or hell, bodies for all I knew, then the chief was going to have a coronary. My instructions from the get-go were that we needed these guys working with us to catch the bigger fish. They couldn't go down.

"Pass me the camera." I grasped it by the strap, pulling the body up to my eye. Peering through the lens and feeling like an asshole, I made sure my next few shots were blurry.

"Shit, Josh. They're getting something out of the back. What is that? Are you getting this?"

"Yeah, of course."

I wasn't.

Hayden, a big guy, covered in colorful tattoos, slammed down the trunk, hoisting something wrapped in black plastic over his shoulder.

Jesus Christ.

"Please tell me that's not a dead body in that plastic," Jayela whispered.

"It's not." It couldn't be.

"Are you sure?"

No. "Yes."

Hayden hoisted his parcel a little higher on his shoulder and darted a glance to his left and then his right.

Then raised one hand and waved.

Jayela slumped back in her seat as Hayden waltzed down the street toward us like he didn't have a care in the world. He stopped outside Jayela's door and rapped his knuckles across the glass.

With a heavy sigh, Jayela put her window down.

Hayden ducked down, resting one elbow on the door-frame. "Evening, Officers. Enjoying your shift?"

Jayela didn't bother answering his question. "What's in the bag?"

"Wouldn't you like to know?"

"I would actually."

He grinned and dropped it from his shoulder and down into his arms, yanking the black plastic back with one hand. "Ta da!"

Jayela recoiled so far she almost headbutted me. "Oh my God."

A dead pig stared at us with unseeing eyes.

"Got him from a friend who's a butcher. Going to spit roast him overnight, then have a party tomorrow. Want to come?"

"Pass."

"Food will be good. Drinks will be free. Many illegal goings-on to keep someone like you entertained, I'm sure.

Sex, drugs, rock and roll. Name your poison." He winked at Jayela.

She stared him down. "While I appreciate the invite, I think I have to be literally anywhere else that night."

Hayden chuckled. "Like that, is it?" He patted the pig's rump. "Guess it's just me and Wilbur then. See you next time, Officers."

With a mock salute and a lingering look in my direction, he straightened and strutted down the street, no fucks given.

"I hate that guy." Which was the truth, but I was also a tiny bit relieved we could leave. "Want to get some food on the way back to the station? Is it too early for Chinese? I think the place on Lewis Street might open early..."

I glanced over at Jayela. Her jaw was set tight as she stared out the windshield. She didn't say a word for the entire drive back to the station. And when we got there, she stormed right inside the chief's office.

I followed behind at a much slower pace.

The chief sat behind his desk, peering up at us. "Can I help you two with something?"

Jayela kicked the door shut behind me and folded her arms over her chest, glaring at me. "Why doesn't this bother you?"

I blinked. "Hayden? He does."

She shook her head. "No, I mean the fact that the last three stakeouts we've been on in relation to this gang have been complete and utter busts."

"Maybe they actually aren't doing anything illegal..." My excuses were lame, and I knew it.

Jayela shot a death look in my direction. "They're as crooked as a dog's hind leg, Boston!"

I glanced at the chief, praying he'd give me the green light to tell her everything. But his steely expression gave nothing away. There was no permission coming. We'd been through this. And he'd already made his mind up.

I sighed, turning back to Jayela and trying to be diplomatic in the hopes of calming her down. "I get it. I'm frustrated, too. But this is the nature of stakeouts. You know that. Most of the time they don't produce the goods. We just have to be okay with it."

I jumped at the slam of her hand coming down on the chief's desk. "Bullshit! There's something more going on here, and you know it."

Shit. "Jaye, I—"

"Someone is tipping them off. They have to be."

Someone. Not you.

But I couldn't do this anymore. Lie to her. We were supposed to be partners, and I wasn't acting like one. My resolve to keep her in the dark under the guise of keeping her safe and following orders crumbled with every second she stared me down. I couldn't stand it. I opened my mouth to confess it all. She needed to know what was going on.

The chief cut me off with a glare, though his words were directed at Jaye. "I've told you before to stop worrying about Hayden and his crew."

Jayela blinked at the harshness in the chief's tone. She was a favorite of his, and she was such a good cop, he'd never had much reason to come down hard on her.

But he was coming like a ton of bricks on this.

"There's something going on there, boss. I can just feel it."

"And you?" The chief demanded, turning to me. "You share this same gut feeling?"

It was a question loaded with unspoken intent. I heard it in every syllable. A clear warning to end this now.

But not in the way I wanted to. Not with me telling Jayela everything.

Going against the chief would end my career.

"No," I said reluctantly, giving him what he wanted. "I don't."

Jayela's eyes flashed with hurt.

"Well, with Boston's observations, and the lack of evidence so far, I think it's fair to say they aren't worth watching anymore."

"Jaye..." I reached for her hand.

She stepped away, dodging my touch. "No, that's fine. Would have been good to know before now that you didn't share my suspicions." She bit out the words harshly. "I thought we were working as a team."

"We were. We are."

She shook her head sadly. "Doesn't feel like it."

She spun on her heel and let herself out of the office, the door slamming closed behind her again.

I watched her storm away, not back to her desk, but straight out of the building.

I glared at the chief, anger swirling inside me. "Happy now?"

He narrowed his eyes at me. "Watch your tone."

I heard the command loud and clear.

Drop it.

The chief sighed. "When are you going to realize this is how the job is? You either learn to fall in line, or you enjoy being a beat cop for the rest of your career. If your superiors can't trust you to follow instructions, you're nothing. Donovan is a beat cop. That's all she'll ever be."

"She's the best cop we have!"

"That's where you're wrong. The best cops we have are the ones who know how to be team players. Who know how to toe the line. That's you, Boston. Donovan's a loose cannon, waiting to explode. She can't mold the way we need her to. But you have. You've shown that. There's a promotion in the works. Just keep your eye on the prize."

I didn't say anything. Once upon a time, just the mere mention of a promotion would have had me chomping at the bit, ready and eager to do whatever needed doing.

But that was when I'd thought Jayela would be by my side.

The chief had just blown that concept out of the water.

"Are we good here?" he asked finally.

I needed time to think. Time to breathe and process.

"We're good."

We weren't. But if I voiced those thoughts, I wasn't sure I'd have a job to come to in the morning.

11

EVE

I went straight from my mother's place to the club where the doors were flung wide, a reggae beat floating through the warm night air. We had an hour until the doors opened to the public, and nobody was actually required to be here until fifteen minutes before showtime, but I wasn't surprised to find my entire staff inside, all seated around a large table with beers in their hands.

"Eve's here!" Lyric shouted, her shoulders moving in time to the beat.

At their smiling faces, a little of the tension ebbed out of my body.

This is where I should have been tonight. Here, with my people. Not feeling guilty over Boston and being disappointed by my family. Who needed all of that when I had this?

But I mustn't have had much of a poker face, because while the others went back to their beers and conversation, Fawn stood and trailed me through the club to the little office in the back where I had a desk. I didn't spend much time in here because administration duties weren't my favorite, but sometimes, shutting myself off from the rest of the club was the only way to get any work done.

She shut the door quietly behind her, closing the two of us inside the windowless room. "What happened?"

I forced a smile, not wanting to burden her with my troubles. "Nothing. All set for tonight?"

"Of course. But there's something wrong."

"Really, I'm fine." I knew she didn't believe me.

"Lyric and I can cover your dances tonight if you aren't in the mood and just want to hide back here or something."

Fawn was the newest member of my staff. She'd only been here two years, and yet somehow, she was the one who knew me best. She saw through the front I put up for the others. I knew they cared about me, just like I cared about them, but Fawn had gotten deep under my skin and into my soul.

That didn't mean I wanted her worrying about me. "Thanks, but I'll be fine. I'll be out soon to get ready. I just want to pay a couple of bills first."

Fawn hovered uncertainly for a moment but then nodded and left me alone. The music was muffled back here, in my tiny room, and I threw my phone and keys down on the desk before slumping into my chair. It was barely nine, and I felt like I could sleep for a month, despite not doing anything physical all day. I really did need to pay some bills, but that felt like an overwhelming task. As did working for the rest of the night. Maybe I should take the night off and just hang out in here.

My phone buzzed, and I leaned over to retrieve it. I sat

a little straighter when I recognized the number, suddenly not so tired.

> Boston
>
> What are you doing?

Why did just the sight of his name send a thrill straight down low between my legs?

EVE

> You ignore me all day and now you message me at nine? Is this a booty call?

I cringed after I sent it. It was a joke, but from the little I knew about Boston, there was a good chance the man couldn't take one.

BOSTON

> I would have waited 'til ten for that.

Well, well. What do you know? Mr. Straight and Narrow did have a sense of humor.

EVE

> Just as well. I would have turned you down.

BOSTON

> You don't do booty calls, huh? Is that why you need a massive dildo with my name on it?

I blew out a breath and realized I was smiling. Touché, Officer Boston. Touché.

EVE

It was just a gag gift my friends got me. I really am sorry about that.

BOSTON

Don't be. Sorry I was short with you earlier. Shit day.

EVE

Me, too. Want to tell me about it?

BOSTON

You ever feel like you're having a midlife crisis?

EVE

I'm only thirty, so I hope not.

BOSTON

Same. But somedays I feel like I am.

EVE

You gonna spend your life savings on a flashy car and start dating an eighteen-year-old?

BOSTON

I'm a cop. My life savings total about three dollars.

I sniggered.

EVE

Want a stripping gig? Pay is good, and I know someone who could hook you up.

There was a long pause before he finally wrote back.

BOSTON

Is that your way of saying you want to
see me naked?

I raised an eyebrow. Okayyyy. Well, that took a turn I wasn't expecting. It almost read like flirting.

EVE

Seems fair. You've seen me naked
after all.

BOSTON

Yeah, but you look better than I do
without clothes on.

I flushed hot at the compliment. Though I was pretty sure it was a lie. I'd seen the way his shoulders filled out his shirt, and the way his pants hugged his ass. He was a beat cop, and that required a fairly high level of fitness. Without him even removing a stitch of clothing, I was sure Joshua Boston's body was nothing short of exceptional.

BOSTON

Sorry. Inappropriate.

I typed back quickly.

EVE

Not inappropriate. Do you always do the
right thing?

There was a pause, and then...

BOSTON

No.

I stared at that no for a long time.

Too long apparently.

BOSTON

Did you keel over from shock?

I grinned.

EVE

No, I'm just thinking about you being bad and I kinda can't picture it.

BOSTON

I've never been arrested if that's what you're thinking.

That was so not what I was thinking. My mind had gone straight to the gutter. I typed out a response with the hugest grin on my face.

EVE

Actually, I was still thinking about you naked.

I tapped long fingernails on the tabletop, knowing I should cut this off and go get ready for the show. I was still in the denim shorts and T-shirt I'd worn to my parents' place. It wasn't exactly stripping attire. But I knew the girls would cover me for as long as I needed.

And right now, I needed this. It had been a shitastic day, and flirting with Boston was a nice distraction from it.

BOSTON

Funny that. I haven't been able to stop thinking about you naked, either.

EVE

> Seems unfair you've actually seen the real deal, though. I have nothing to base my daydreams on. I could be picturing you all wrong.

BOSTON

> Tell me what you're seeing in your head, and I'll tell you if you're right.

Heat flushed the back of my neck. This was rapidly moving in the direction of sexting. I hadn't been expecting it, but I certainly wasn't going to turn it down. Not with Boston. I got up off my chair and locked the door before I replied.

EVE

> Hairy back, bit of a hump, possibly a few scales...

BOSTON

> I just spit my Coke out laughing.

I liked the idea of him smiling at my messages. I imagined him stretched out on his couch in a pair of gray sweats, one hand tucked behind his head while the other worked his phone. He was hot when he was scowling, I could only imagine how a smile would transform his face.

EVE

> So, no scales?

BOSTON

> No scales or humps. No hairy back either, for the record.

EVE

I don't believe you.

The next message that pinged in was an image.

I've never come so close to falling off my chair. "Jesus fuck," I whispered.

It was a selfie in his bathroom. His back turned, one hand up, holding the phone to take the photo in a mirror's reflection. It didn't show his face, but it did show every inch of delicious, sculpted back.

No hair, scales, or bumps in sight.

I swallowed hard.

EVE

Okay, so your back is good. But now I'm thinking you're hiding something on your chest, since you conveniently left that out of the photo.

I went back to admiring the photo of his back, in particular, the lower half that narrowed into his hips and ass.

His ass looked damn good. And I knew he was a gray sweatpants sorta guy.

When my phone binged again, it was another bathroom selfie.

His body was more perfect than I could have even imagined. Any daydream I might have had about defined pecs and ripped abs was blown away by the real thing. For an insane moment, I considered licking the screen. That was how hot the man was.

EVE

Jesus Christ. Do you live at the gym?

BOSTON

Only every other week.

He lied. Nobody got a body like that by working out intermittently. His sweatpants hung low on his hips. So low they showed off his V lines and a tiny sliver of dark hair that disappeared beneath the waistband.

Perv that I was, I tried zooming in to check out what he had going on beneath it, but he was hidden behind the bathroom sink.

A flash of disappointment joined the heat coursing through my body. Did I dare carry on the game? Just how far could I push the man before he said stop?

I really wanted to find out. "Ah, fuck it. We've come this far, might as well push my luck a little more."

EVE

Photo stops at your waist? Shame. I'd hate to think it was your dick that is your problem area.

BOSTON

Did you just ask me for a dick pic? I thought girls hated those?

EVE

We hate the unsolicited ones... Different story if we asked for one.

BOSTON

Are you asking for one, Eve?

Fuck. I think I was.

EVE

Yes.

I held my breath, gripping my phone tighter with every passing second. "Come on, come on." I took a sip of water, trying to drown the sudden dryness in my throat.

BOSTON

Soft or hard?

I spat the water everywhere, coughing as half of it went down into my lungs.

EVE

You've never sent a dick pic before, have you?

BOSTON

No.

EVE

Hard. Always hard.

BOSTON

Give me a minute.

My nipples stiffened beneath my bra, and an insistent ache rose from between my thighs. I leaned back in my chair, imagining Boston slipping his hand beneath his sweatpants and stroking himself.

The ache between my legs became a pulse.

EVE

You need any help?

BOSTON

You going to send me a photo to jack off to, Eve?

Tempting. I had a couple of naked selfies on my phone, locked away in a private folder. But we were trying to even the score here, and besides, I was saving those photos for someone I truly trusted.

Boston and I weren't there yet.

EVE

No. But does it help if I tell you the thought of you getting yourself hard is really turning me on? I'm in the office at work, with a club full of people outside, and yet I'm seriously considering joining you.

BOSTON

Do it. Fuck. What are you wearing?

EVE

T-shirt and cutoffs.

BOSTON

Take your shorts off.

EVE

I thought I was supposed to be getting you hard?

BOSTON

Oh, trust me. It is. Did you do it?

I shot a glance at the clock and then at the door. I was definitely late for my shift, but I couldn't go out there like this. Arousal pooled at my core, coating my panties. I'd slip right off the freaking pole if I went out there as wet and needy as I was right now.

Wouldn't that be a fucking show.

All my staff was out doing their thing. Nobody was going to know what I was doing in here.

I flicked the button on my pants and tugged them down, lifting my ass until they pooled around my ankles.

EVE

Yes. I did it.

BOSTON

And? What do you want?

What did I want? I squeezed my thighs together. I wanted to call him and hear his voice grumble down the line. I wanted him to be here right now. I wanted to come.

I only told him the last bit.

BOSTON

Fuck.

My phone binged again with a video. Holy shit.

I moaned quietly and slipped my fingers inside my panties while I watched the video.

Boston's dick was huge. And the noises he made in the background of his video while he ran his palm up and down his shaft had my breath coming in pants.

I rolled my clit beneath my fingertips, making tight, rapid circles, going hard right from the very beginning. Normally when I did this, I started slow and easy, but I was already on the edge of coming, I didn't need slow and easy tonight.

I needed hot and fast. I needed hard and strong. I needed Boston, but my own fingers would have to do.

I set the phone down on the desktop, knowing I was too close now to continue texting or watching his video.

At the last moment, I hit 'record' with the camera pointed in my direction.

I thought about him. About sending him the video. About him watching as I brought myself to the brink while I thought about him. I pushed my fingers up inside myself, stretching my tight cunt, and worked my clit with my other hand.

Tiny moans escaped my mouth and I threw my head back, rocking on my chair while the pleasure spiraled out of control.

"Oh!" My internal walls clamped down around my fingers and pulsed, riding out my orgasm.

I shuddered with the release that had been so very needed. Stress and tension melted away, along with every problem I had riding on my shoulders. All of them replaced with complete bliss and relaxation.

My phone binged again, and I straightened, wiping my fingers on some tissues. I stopped the recording and checked the message.

BOSTON

No good?

He meant his dick video. I hadn't finished watching it. Or responded to him.

Shit, poor guy. Sends his first dick pic, a video at that, and I don't even respond?

Blowing caution to the wind, I attached my own video. Then typed out a message.

EVE

Too good.

I waited a minute for him to watch, anxiously waiting on his reply.

BOSTON

And now I'm hard again. Fuck, Eve.
You're beautiful.

Many men had called me beautiful. In the club, at bars, during sex.

And yet somehow, those two words on a text message from Boston meant more to me than any of the others.

I brought up his video again, watching while he made himself come.

I moaned at the erotic sight. And then put my fingers back down my panties and started all over.

Because something about Boston had me instinctively knowing that once was never going to be enough.

12

———

BOSTON

I lay in bed for hours, alternating between staring at the ceiling with a stupid big grin on my face and watching the video Eve had sent as she made herself come.

Fucking hell. What a firecracker she'd turned out to be. The video was only from her shoulders up, but I didn't need to see anything more than that. I could use my imagination.

She'd captured my complete attention anyway. The relaxed set of her shoulders, her head thrown back, her long dark hair swept up in a ponytail, loose tendrils framing her face. Watching her expression change from one of enjoyment to one of pure and complete abandonment as she'd come, had me hard every time I thought about it. And the noises she made...fuck. I wanted to be the one drawing those sounds from her mouth.

I'd jacked off so many times tonight it was surprising there was any lift left in my dick at all. Then I'd fallen asleep and slept more solidly than I had in a long time.

And that was why I didn't hear my phone the first two times. It was only on the third try that the incessant ringing woke me. I didn't even check the number. I probably couldn't have read it with my eyes as bleary as they were anyway. "Hello?"

There was a rush of words my sleepy brain couldn't work out. I sat up and looked at the phone, then held it back to my ear. "Chief?"

"Dammit, Boston. Wake up and listen."

That got my attention. "What's going on?"

His silence on the other end sent fear trickling down my spine. It was the heavy pause of a man who had been sent to deliver bad news. "Chief?"

"We just got a call in from Johnson and Stewart. There's been a stabbing."

Relief rushed through me. "Right, okay. Text me the address and I'll go pick up Jayela now. Give us twenty."

I went to hang up but I stopped at a shout from him.

"Jayela's place is the address, Boston. There was a stabbing in her apartment."

The fear punched through me once more, this time bringing nausea with it. Jayela and Mae both lived in that apartment. I cared about Mae in the exact same way that Jayela did—as a sister. But Jaye was my best friend. My other half for the past decade. Neither of us were any good at relationships. We'd joked more than once that perhaps we were each other's soul mates and that one day, we'd end up old and retired somewhere together. Not together-together, because I'd never thought of her like that, and the feeling was mutual, but could I have been happy living out my days with my best friend by my side? Absolutely.

And for that reason, that wholeheartedly selfish reason, I began praying that it wasn't Jaye. I prayed it was Mae who was hurt. And even though I was ashamed to even think it, I let the question loose. "Who is it?"

I already knew the answer before he even uttered a word. I knew from the sullen tone of his voice. "Jayela, Boston. And it's bad. She's..."

There was a choked noise from the other end of the line.

My blood ran cold.

"She's what?" I yelled. "Tell me!"

My fingers clenched around the phone so tightly my knuckles ached.

"She's dead."

The room spun around me in dizzying flashes of light until I squeezed my eyes closed. "No!"

"I'm so sorry."

I didn't reply. I cancelled the call and hauled myself out of bed, yanking on jeans and a T-shirt as I ran down the stairs of my townhouse. At the door, I shoved my feet in a pair of Converse, and at the last moment, grabbed my badge from the entryway table.

Jayela and Mae's place was only a few miles from mine, both of us on the outskirts of Providence in more affordable housing than the center, where all the really big residences were. I fought to keep my focus on driving. Foot on the gas. Turn the wheel. Stop at red lights. I forced my attention to all those things I normally did automatically. And when that didn't fully occupy a mind that wanted to scream in agony, I brought my focus inward.

Breathe in, breathe out.

Eyes forward.

Don't think.

The swarm of cop cars was expected but still out of place, and I pulled in so haphazardly one tire ended up on the sidewalk.

Jayela would have given me shit for that.

Blindly, I stumbled out of the car toward the lobby of her apartment building. I couldn't take in their faces, but the officers stationed at the door stepped aside once they saw me coming, so I must have known them. The elevator to her apartment was always slow, so I took the stairs two at a time, my heavy footstep echoing around the empty stairwell until I burst out onto Jayela's floor.

More people. Officers. Civilians. I passed them all in a blur until a hand reached out and grabbed me.

"Boston! Wait, what's going on?"

I looked down at the small woman and then at the taller man beside her. I took me a second to realize I knew them. Tori and Will, Mae's best friends. My friends, too.

Fear turned Tori's eyes wide, and her fingers trembled around my arm. She looked at me like civilians often did, searching for reassurance that everything was going to be okay.

I couldn't give her that.

I shook her off and pushed my way inside the apartment.

"Boston…" The officer who stood in the middle of Jayela's neat living room didn't fit. He wasn't one of the people we hung out with, drinking and playing stupid card games until the early hours of the morning around the low coffee table. He was the sort of friend we said hi to at the station, then didn't really think about until the next time we ran into him.

"Where?" I demanded.

He bit his lip. "Bedroom. But wait, I don't think—"

A scream cut him off.

I didn't think. I just pounded down the hall and burst into Jayela's bedroom, stopping dead in the doorway.

My knees buckled. Bile rose in my throat, threatening to choke me. I almost wished it would because I would have welcomed the chance to pass out.

I'd seen dead bodies many a time. It was a staple of my job, especially in an area like this, where rich met poor and crime was high.

But those bodies were never people I knew. Never people I loved.

Jayela hadn't just been stabbed. The red gash across her throat and the pool of blood her body lay in were all telltale signs of the brutality she'd endured in her last moments.

Agony rushed my system, as strong and swift as a raging current, bringing the guilt and shame and horror right along with it. Pain pierced my chest, my gut, my heart. A thousand stabbing spears that mimicked Jayela's wounds.

Another scream caught my attention.

"We're going to have to sedate her," someone murmured, backing away from the huddled ball of a person in the corner.

Mae. She had her arms tucked tight around her knees, rocking back and forth, staring at her sister with unfocused eyes.

"Nobody is sedating her," I snapped.

"We need to get her out of here, but she keeps thrashing out every time anyone goes near her." The cop stared at Mae like she was some sort of science experiment.

Did he expect her to be turning cartwheels? Idiot. "Wouldn't you? That's her sister."

The man had the sense not to say anything.

I squatted, grateful for something else to focus on. Because I couldn't keep looking at Jayela. If I did, it might all sink in, and I couldn't afford to break down. Not here.

"Mae." I reached out to touch her.

Her head jerked my direction, and she threw her arms out, kicking and screaming and clawing at me. I jumped back.

The other cop gave me a 'I told you so' stare.

I'd never wanted to punch someone so much in my life. "You don't touch her, you hear me?"

I waited for him to agree, then stormed back out through the hall and living area and stuck my head out the main door. "Tori. Will."

Tears streamed down Tori's face. "I can hear Mae's screams, and they won't let me in."

"She's hysterical. They want to call in paramedics to sedate her."

"What? No, let me in. Let me talk to her first."

I didn't give a shit that I was breaking every protocol. It was what Jayela would have done. "My thoughts exactly." Tori and Will both pressed forward, but at the last second, I grabbed Tori's arm. I knew she was close with both Mae and Jayela. "Hey. Can you handle this? It's… bad." I couldn't bring myself to explain exactly how bad it was. I could barely begin to process that myself.

Another scream from Mae came from deep inside the apartment, and determination hardened Tori's eyes. "Let me in, Boston."

I stepped back and then followed the two of them down to Jayela's bedroom.

Tori flew to her best friend's side, only a slight fumble and a muffled cry giving away that she'd noticed Jayela's body. Will dropped down beside them, wrapping his arms around Mae, lifting her from the floor. Her screams cut off when she realized who they were, and she allowed the two of them to usher her out of the room.

But when the bedroom door closed behind them, that left me with nothing to focus on but the cold hard truth of what had happened.

I stared at my best friend. And all I could think about was the last words we'd said to each other. She'd been mad at me. Disappointed in the fact I hadn't backed her up. She'd walked away angry.

That was how things would finish with us. There'd be no chance for apologies. No chance for explaining. This was the end.

A lump rose in my throat that made it hard to breathe. I wanted to bend over, put my head between my knees, and ward off the impending breakdown that was coming.

But I didn't get to do that. Because I was a cop, and it was my job to find her killer.

So I took every raw edge, every frayed nerve, every choking breath, and let myself feel them. I stared at Jayela's blood soaking into the mattress and let the anger come. I couldn't fall apart. That wasn't going to help Jayela. That wasn't going to show her that I was still the same cop I'd been when I left the academy. The one she'd been proud of. So I let the rage stitch together the broken parts of me and made a silent promise to my best friend.

I'd fix this.

In the living room, Mae sat on the couch, surrounded by her friends.

"You need to leave," I told Tori and Will. "We need to question her." The words came out gruff and short, but sharp words that got straight to the point were all I had to give if I wanted to remain standing.

I couldn't find a killer if I couldn't get off the ground.

I should have known Tori wouldn't listen. She went straight into protective best friend mode.

"We aren't leaving. You can question her all you want when she's had medical attention. Can't you see that she's not in a state to do anything right now?" The anger in her eyes was belied by the crack in her voice. "God, Boston. What's wrong with you?" A sob cut off the last of her words, her grief finally overcoming everything else.

Her husband wrapped his arms around her small frame, drawing her into his chest and murmuring words of comfort in her ear.

"It's okay. I can do it." Mae's quiet voice broke the standoff between Tori and me.

I dropped to my knees in front of her. "I need you to get it together and talk to me."

Frustration rose when she didn't immediately answer. Every muscle in my body was coiled too tight, and my heart thumped overtime, a ticking time bomb just waiting to go off. I needed action. I needed to move. I needed to get the hell out of this apartment where all I could smell and see and think about was the deep crimson of Jayela's blood.

My patience snapped. "Do you want whoever did this to get away with it? Come on, Mae. I need you to tell me everything. Any little detail, and I need you to tell me now. There's no sign of forced entry, so this is probably someone you know. The longer you take, the bigger the chance we never catch this guy." I lowered my gaze to the floor, my head too heavy to hold up any longer, and silently begged her to have seen something. I needed something to go on, a name of who'd done this, or at the very least, an idea. Around here, murders got solved quickly, or not at all.

I refused to let Jayela's death be the latter.

"I don't know what happened," she said finally. "We got drunk last night, and when I woke up this morning it was to Heath yelling my name—"

I glanced up sharply. "We? Who's Heath? There was someone else here?" It took me a minute to realize why the name sounded familiar. "Heath? As in Jayela's ex-boyfriend Heath? What the hell were you doing with him?"

"Yes. That Heath. I met up with him in a bar last night, and we came back here afterward."

Tori's eyes went wide.

"We had drinks. A lot of them." She glanced toward her bedroom.

I followed her line of sight. Mae's bedroom was right off the living room. The open door revealed a neat and tidy space, apart from an unmade bed and a mostly finished bottle of tequila discarded on the floor.

I swallowed hard, putting the pieces together. "You had sex with your sister's boyfriend?"

"What? No! I mean, I don't think so. We had some

shots and we flirted. But then Jayela came home. We passed out. Or at least I did. I don't know what happened after that. All I know is when I woke up this morning, Heath was in Jaye's room, covered in blood..."

More pieces slammed together. Heath and Jayela had broken up on bad terms. I'd never really gotten the full story from her, not wanting to upset her further after their breakup, but now I wished I'd pushed her harder for it.

So instead, I pushed Mae, whose incessant babbling was only fueling the frustration and anger inside me. What on earth would have possessed her to bring her sister's ex here? She knew that never would have been okay with Jayela. And the longer she babbled, the longer this guy had to get away. That wouldn't happen on my watch.

"He was trying to save her, Boston. He had his hand on her throat, trying to stop the blood..."

"You think that means anything?" I snapped. "He wouldn't be the first jealous lover who had instant regret. You're going to have to give me more." I racked my brain but I couldn't even remember the guy's surname. It had been years since I'd last seen him. "Tell me his full name. Quick, Mae. If I can get a team out over to his house now, before he does a runner, we might actually be able to nail him."

"Wait. Nail him? You don't know he did anything." She turned to Tori and Will, looking for some sort of support, but thank God, they had the sense to back me up. Both of them nodded at her, encouraging her to tell me everything.

"Michaelson," she said slowly. "Heath Michaelson. He has an apartment in Saint View. But I—"

That'd do. I could get the rest of the story from her later. I grabbed a walkie-talkie and barked an order into it. "Somebody find this guy's apartment and get a team over there now. Restrain him, but you do not talk to him until I get there. Is that clear?"

A garbled response crackled across the radio in agreement.

I stared down at Mae. "Did you hear anything during the night?"

"No, I swear. Heath and I... And then nothing. Nothing until this morning when I woke up and heard him yelling for me."

"Did you see him with the knife?"

She blinked up at him. "What knife?"

I waved at one of the officers, and they moved into Jayela's bedroom, emerging a second later with a knife in an evidence bag. He passed it to me, and I held it up for Mae to see.

She cringed away from the blood-coated steel. I wanted to do the same, but I held my ground, knowing that I needed every piece of information.

She hesitated, then reluctantly admitted it. "I did see him with that knife but—"

"Son of a bitch," I muttered.

"That's all I saw, though." She grabbed my hand. "He used it to cut up lemons for tequila shots last night. That's all."

I couldn't stand her touching me. It felt too much like a comfort I didn't deserve. What had I been doing last night while this had all been going on? Sexting with Eve.

I shouldn't have let Jayela walk away angry. I should have gone after her and told her everything that was going on. Why didn't I know everything about Heath? I'd called myself her best friend, but in fact, I'd actually known almost nothing about their relationship. Guilt pressed down hard on my shoulders. "What do you know about him?" I urged Mae. "Is he violent?"

"Heath? No, never."

"Has he got a temper?"

"I've never even heard him raise his voice. And he dated Jayela. You know how she is, she loves to argue. Loved... Oh God."

Fury rose inside me.

I didn't want to hear it. Not even from Mae. Jayela was good, and pure. The perfect cop. If she argued with anyone it was only because she was passionate.

Mae's face crumpled, and she ran for the bathroom, Tori following after. It took her too long to come back, my irritation growing with every passing second. I paced the room, waiting for someone to buzz back and tell me they'd gone to this guy's house and arrested him.

"Is there any news about Heath?" Mae asked when she finally returned.

I stared at her, suspicions going haywire in my brain. "Why are you so concerned about him?"

"Because he's my friend!"

Was she for real? Had she not seen her sister's body in there? When the man had murdered her, he'd done it viciously and brutally. "Your friend? You said yourself that the man was covered in your sister's blood. She's lying dead in there, and you're worried about *him*? Your friend probably killed his ex in a jealous rage, Mae! Don't fucking ask me how he is!"

She recoiled, stumbling back a few steps. "He was trying to save her! What reason would he have to kill her now, four years after they broke up?"

"Opportunity?" I spat, voice filled with a venom I couldn't control. I couldn't stop the swirl of emotions now. They were consuming me, one by one. "You opened the door to your apartment when you opened your legs for him and let the man back in. You admitted yourself that you were passed out, too drunk to hear a thing. You gave him the opportunity."

Mae's mouth dropped open, her cheeks flaming pink.

Tori gasped. "Boston!"

Will stepped in front of her, his anger clear in the pinched tone of his voice. "I know you're hurting right now, man. But you're out of line. You're too close to this. Back off."

The pain was all-consuming. I rose to my feet, going chest to chest with Will.

Mae yelped, pushing between the two of us. "Stop it!" She whirled on Will. "Thank you, but you don't need to defend my honor."

Then she spun back and cracked her palm across my cheek.

A roar went up from the other officers, one launching himself across the room and grabbing her by the arm.

But nothing was going to stop Mae from speaking her piece. "How dare you," she seethed at me. "How dare you imply even for a second that I am in any way involved in what happened to Jayela. You can go to Hell, Boston."

It was the wake-up call I needed. My cheek stung

where Mae's palm had made contact, but I welcomed it. I let this new pain clear my head of all emotions, making way for rational thought.

Mae wasn't the enemy here. The enemy was still out there somewhere, walking around the streets a free man.

The officer yanked Mae tighter and withdrew a set of handcuffs from a holder on the side of his pants. "You're under arrest for the assault of a police officer—"

I shook my head. "Stop. Let her go."

The officer glanced up in surprise. "But she—"

"I don't fucking care what she did!" I yelled. "I said let her go!"

Both the officer and Mae took a step back, and the cuff disappeared from her wrist, as did the officer's grip. He scuttled out of the apartment and hightailed it down the hallway. Probably terrified of me. I couldn't blame him. I was as up and down as a roller coaster. But the one thing I knew for certain was that I'd stepped over the line, and I needed to apologize to Mae.

"Sorry," I murmured, running a hand through my hair. "I was out of line."

Mae wasn't as quick to forgive. Her gaze still flashed with anger. "I don't believe Heath did this, Boston. I don't. You need to listen to me. It looks bad, I know. I thought that, too. But now that I've had a minute to think about it—"

My phone binged with an incoming message, and I edged away to open it. I swallowed hard as I read the message, and then turned to Mae. "It doesn't matter what you think. Or what I think. Heath Michaelson just admitted to murder."

13

BOSTON

Halfway to Heath Michaelson's place in Saint View, I found myself trailing the other cop cars and an ambulance. Four vehicles, all headed to the same destination, but none of them had skin in the game the same way that I did. So even though I was the last one to park my vehicle, I was the first one out and racing through the doors of the shabby apartment building.

The chief's shouts splintered through the quiet morning, but I wasn't stopping for anyone. He could try to take me off this case all he wanted, but I wasn't listening. The man who had killed my best friend was inside this apartment. I'd be the one who spoke to him. I'd be there when he admitted what he'd done. And I'd be the one to make sure a lethal injection was put in his arm.

I stopped dead in the lobby.

Johnson and Stewart dragged a near lifeless body out between them. The man's hands were cuffed behind his back, and his feet trailing along the ground. His head hung limply, bloodied hair plastered to his forehead, and one eye swollen so tight it was completely closed.

Nausea rose in my gut at the sickening sight of damaged flesh and open wounds. "What the hell happened?"

The older cop gave me a hard stare. "He confessed. You can thank me later."

I glanced over at Stewart, younger by probably twenty years and not long out of the academy. He refused to meet my gaze.

"His confession is no good if you beat the shit out of him to get it," I snapped. "For fuck's sake, is he even alive?" I rushed forward to pull Heath's head back and pressed my fingers to his neck, checking for a pulse. I breathed a sigh of relief when there was a steady thump.

This wasn't right. Jayela never would have stood for torturing someone into a confession. Instinctively I knew that even in her own murder investigation, she would have wanted everything above board. What these two cops had done to this man was so low, the board wasn't even close.

Johnson narrowed his eyes at me. "Do you know what the scumbag did? Did you see? He's an animal. And Jayela was one of us. We did what we had to do to restrain him."

Anger boiled up. "If what you did isn't legal—if you threatened, and coerced, or beat him until he said what you wanted him to say—none of it will stand up in court."

"It'll stand up. He'll go down for this."

I shook my head slowly. If they'd screwed this up because of Johnson's fucking crush on Jayela, then there'd be a good chance of me fighting murder charges right alongside Heath. "If this man walks free because of your negligence, it's you I'm coming for." I pointed a finger in the older cop's face. "You hear me? Get him to a fucking ambulance. He looks like shit."

He scowled at me, and it was so fucking tempting to punch the old coot in the head. But Michaelson seemed to be getting worse by the minute, the color draining from his face. There was no way he was dying on my watch. He would stand trial, and then he would spend his life rotting in jail, paying for what he did. If not worse.

A heavy hand clamped down on my shoulder, and I flinched beneath the touch.

Chief frowned at me. "You know what I'm going to say. You can't be in on this case, son. We both know that."

I hung my head, some of the fight going out of me. He was right. If those other two cops hadn't beaten the shit out of Heath, I might have. That only made me as bad as them.

Chief glanced at me with pity in his gaze. "It's over. We got the guy. There's no need for you to be at work and involved in the details. Take some time off. See a counselor."

I didn't even try to argue. The adrenaline was wearing off, and shock was setting in. My head was a mass of confusion and exhaustion. It was barely nine in the morning, and yet I felt like I'd lived a thousand lives in the space of a few hours.

"Come on. Go home. That's an order."

He was right. With a shake in my hand I couldn't ignore, I managed to make it back to my townhouse, though it took several tries with the keys before my hand was steady enough to get the door open.

Right there in the entryway, on the little table that I threw my keys on every night, was a photo of me and Jayela. We both grinned out from the image, our arms slung around each other as best friends do. I realized with a start it had been taken during the time she was with Heath. We'd gone out with him, Mae, Tori, and Will, to see a band that Jaye and I both loved.

I picked the photo up, trying to remember what Heath had been like that night. Had there been signs I'd overlooked? Something that gave away that deep inside, the man was capable of taking a life?

I should have known. I should have seen something. Instead, I'd gotten drunk and sung along with the band.

I hurled the photo frame across the room. It hit the wall, glass exploding and raining down over the floor. And then I slid down beside it, an empty scream of pain hollowing out my lungs.

I spent most of the day there on the floor, too numb to feel the pins and needles in my legs. Too tired to try walking up the stairs to my bed. By the time night fell, the emptiness in my stomach from lack of food and water became a grumble I couldn't ignore.

But it was more than just those basic bodily needs. When I got in my car with the intent of just heading to a fast-food restaurant to grab a burger and fries, I found myself driving to Saint View Strip.

I stared up at the neon-pink sign for a long moment,

trying to decipher why I'd driven here. With no answers, I decided to just go with my gut.

It was still early, though a blasting beat thumped through the walls and out into the parking lot. There was no bouncer on the door yet, but it was unlocked, so I let myself inside. The dark interior grew lighter as I wandered down the hall until it opened up into the main room. Tables and chairs were scattered around the lower level, and a wide stage with several dancers' poles took up one side of the room.

"Get fucked. What the hell are you doing here?"

I recognized the woman with flaming-red hair. She'd been arrested at the church rally, and she'd been here the night Jayela and I had searched the club. She glared at me now, eyes narrowed with hate.

Her accusation caught the attention of the big blond guy.

He looked up from his conversation with the DJ and came storming across the room. "Get the hell out. We're sick of this bullshit. You think you can just walk in here and mess the place up whenever you feel like it? How many times have we gotta tell you? We aren't doing anything illegal. This is harassment. So like I said. Get the hell out."

They were right. I was out of line being here. Of course they hated my guts. We'd arrested them, searched the club, and accused them of things when there was no proof. I didn't have a leg to stand on. I'd gone along with the search, even though I'd known that warrant wasn't legally obtained.

Coming here tonight had been a mistake. I held my

hands up, trying to show I meant no harm. "You're right. I'm sorry. I'll go."

He crossed his arms over his broad chest. He was a brick wall of a man, completely blocking me from getting any farther into the club. "Good. Adios. Don't come back."

I turned away, feeling like a fool. What the hell had I been thinking?

"Boston?"

The sound of Eve's voice was an instant balm to the ache in my chest. It was like throwing water over a fire, then enjoying the slow, rolling rise of the smoke. It wrapped around me, a blanket warding off the chill that had been threatening to engulf me all day.

And that was why I'd come. I might not have known it in the moment, but something deep inside me had sought her out.

There wasn't the same venom in her tone. Only curiosity.

"The pig was just leaving. Oink oink. On your way."

Eve shoved the guy out of the way. "Shut up, Augie." She pushed past him, coming to a stop by my side. She peered up at me, her big brown eyes full of questions.

A rush of emotion threatened to take me down. The kindness there, the concern. I didn't deserve any of it. "I was just going."

"I'm more interested in knowing why you're here in the first place?"

I couldn't tell her I'd subconsciously sought her out because I was broken and she felt like a healing balm. "I just want to drink."

She must have seen something in my eyes. "I'm

working tonight. But you can drink at the bar. Plenty of alcohol there."

Augie whirled on her. "Eve! Are you serious? Have you forgotten that the last time this prick was here he trashed the place trying to prove we're running a sex club?"

Eve fixed him with a hard glare. "Last I checked, I own this club. If I say he can drink at the bar, he can drink at the bar."

Augie's jaw went hard. "This is a mistake." Then he stomped out, disappearing into the backstage area.

We watched him go, and then I turned back to Eve. "I can leave. I don't want to cause any problems for you."

She shook her head hard and indicated to the bar, empty stools lined up beneath it. I took the one in the farthest corner, a spot that was darker than the rest of the seats which caught the glow from the bar lights.

I sat heavily, resting my arms on the countertop. I'd kind of half expected a sticky residue, but the bar was squeaky clean and smooth.

Eve motioned to the woman behind the bar, one I hadn't seen before. "Echo. This is Boston. Get him whatever he wants tonight. On the house. Food, drinks, whatever."

"I can pay," I protested weakly.

Echo acted like I hadn't even spoken. "You got it. What's your poison, cop?"

"Rum."

She turned back to Eve. "I've got him. You go."

With a final glance at me, Eve nodded. "I'll check in with you later."

The ache inside me started up again the moment she

walked away. Echo pushed a glass across the bar, and when I knocked that back in one, she sent me another.

The alcohol warmed its way through my system, and Echo kept the drinks coming, as well as a hearty bowl of rich stew that tasted as amazing as it smelled. Every bite tasted better than the last. Around me, the music ratcheted up, and bodies filled the other seats along the bar. It rapidly became a crowd, their chatter a low hum beneath the music, and slowly I began to relax.

Echo pushed another drink in my direction, then cocked her head to one side, studying me. She was a tall black woman, with big eyes rimmed in heavy eyeliner. "You aren't watching the show?"

The bar was opposite the stage. It wasn't an ideal setup because I had to swivel on my seat to watch. But I hadn't come here to watch women dance, so I was happy with my corner, food, and drinks. "No."

"Eve is up in a minute."

The temptation to watch Eve on the stage was great. A niggling curiosity in some very male part of me was definitely interested in watching her do her thing.

But a bigger part of me didn't feel good about it. It wasn't what I'd come here for. And despite what we'd done together last night, and the venue, I didn't feel I had that right. "Is there any more stew, please?"

Echo nodded and left through doors I knew led to the kitchen.

Minutes disappeared into hours. Hours that I sat alone, drinking at the bar, watching Echo work while the rhythmic music regulated my heart and my breaths. The people around me came and went, none of them paying me any attention. The alcohol buzzed through my system pleasantly, and I was happy to be around people without actually interacting with them.

"How you doing?" Eve slid onto the stool beside me, her voice like honey.

She was different. Instantly I leaned in her direction, hoping she'd talk some more. "I don't know," I answered honestly.

She looked different tonight. Heavy makeup accentuated her eyes and cheekbones. Glitter sparkled in a thick slash across her eyelids, and her neck and cleavage were misted with sweat. A tiny t-shirt covered her breasts, leaving her belly bare, but whatever she wore beneath that was lost to the darkness that crept up from beneath the bar.

She stared hard. "Echo said you're drinking to get drunk."

"I am."

"Do you do that often?"

I shook my head sadly. "No. Not at all. I'm normally a two or three beers sort of guy."

She nodded. "So what's different about tonight then?"

A lump rose in my throat so fast it took me by surprise. I'd been doing good since I got here. The alcohol helped drown out everything I'd seen and heard and done today. It helped bury the pain. But the kindness in Eve's voice nearly undid hours of drinking.

I glanced over at her. "My partner was murdered today."

Eve recoiled, her hand coming up to cover the gasp that punched from her lips. "The woman you were here with the other night?"

I swallowed down the lump in my throat. "Yes."

"Jesus, Boston. I'm so sorry."

I stared down at my hands, wrapped around my glass, and nodded. "Thanks." I had to force the word out. My throat was too tight.

Eve's fingers crept across the bar top and wrapped around mine, prying them from the glass until she held my hand.

I stared at her fingers between mine for the longest time, fighting back waves of emotion.

"Boston…"

I couldn't face her. I knew if I did, I'd fall apart.

She inched closer until her bare arm pressed against mine.

I closed my eyes. Last night with her—talking dirty, getting myself off, watching her video—that had all been hot and fun. But it had been a means to an end. Talk the talk. Flirt it up. Get her off. Find a release.

None of it compared to the way she touched me now. I leaned heavily against her, needing that contact. Needing her to fill the void.

She turned her head and pressed her lips to the top of my arm.

I glanced over at her, and her dark-eyed gaze met mine. She squeezed my fingers. "I don't like seeing you like this," she whispered.

"I don't like feeling like this," I admitted, voice cracking in the middle. "Shit." I turned away, tears pricking at the backs of my eyes. I hadn't cried in years. I didn't want now to be the time I started again.

The music blared on around us, other people danced and yelled and sang. And then Eve reached out, put one palm against the side of my face, and twisted it so I faced her.

It all disappeared. The noise. The other people.

I drowned in her sad gaze.

Then she drew me down and pressed her lips softly to mine.

I closed my eyes and sank into her, abandoning my glass to hold her instead. I wrapped my arms around her smaller body and held her tight, as if she were a lifeboat in a stormy sea.

In that moment, she was. She was all I had to cling to in an ocean that threatened to end me.

Her kiss was gentle and slow, her lips parting, tongue seeking. And I accepted her without hesitation. I greedily hauled her in, her knees bumping against mine beneath the bar top but neither of us really noticing, all concentration on our mouths, our tongues, and a kiss that had become a lifeline.

My heart pounded, and I snaked my hands up into her hair, holding her face and deepening the kiss until the entire fucking room spun.

Until I could breathe again.

Until a flash of light so bright went off the two of us jerked apart in surprise.

I held Eve close, not willing to let her go, even as several more flashes went off, leaving behind giant white spots to blind me. I moved between Eve and the flash, pulling her closer, cradling her face to my chest until the light stopped.

Then she pushed me away.

"Well, well, well. What do we have here? Copper getting it on with a stripper in a sex club." Augie glanced up at me. "Your term, not mine." He leaned against the bar, scrolling through a series of photos on his phone. "Good work, Eve. Using those feminine charms like a pro."

Shock punched through my gut. "What?"

Augie held up his phone, an image of Eve and I wrapped around each other on the screen, our lips locked in a passionate embrace.

Heat crept up the back of my neck. Even on such a tiny screen, I could see the desperation in the clinch. My hold on her needy.

The heat turned into full-fledged embarrassment. I barely knew this woman, and yet here I was, throwing myself at her like some stupid teenager with a crush.

Augie chuckled. "Don't worry, cop. Just a little bit of insurance. You leave us alone, and this photo never has to see the light of day. You keep harassing us and I'll send it to every email inbox within the police department. And the local newspapers for good measure."

Cold seeped through all other emotions. I gaped at Eve. But when she didn't immediately respond, I turned my attention on Augie. "Are you blackmailing me?"

That finally spurred Eve into action. "What? Blackmailing?"

Augie waved the phone in my face. "Blackmail. Motivation. Whatever you want to call it. Whatever keeps you out of this club."

Anger reared its ugly head. It had been there all day, held at bay by my sadness and pain. But now it came roaring to the surface, desperate for a release. "Give me your phone. Delete those photos. Now."

Augie taunted me. "Nuh ah. Where's your badge

tonight, copper? You haven't got it, do you? No uniform, no badge, no cuffs. As far as I can see, you have no power here."

The anger swelled, and I pushed to my feet, lunging for the phone.

Augie danced out of my way.

But he was right. I couldn't force him to give me the phone or delete the incriminating photo. A heavy disappointment stole through the anger.

I'd thought that kiss had been real. I thought I'd felt something in it, something beyond a physical attraction. The disappointment stirred the anger up until it was all I could see. I pinned Eve with a hard glare. "You set me up? Who does that? Today of all days, and after what I told you. This is my career, Eve! Messing with that's fucking evil."

It wasn't lost on me that Eve and Evil sounded really similar.

Her head snapped away from Augie and toward me. Her mouth dropped open. Then closed. Then opened again. She shot off her stool and put herself right between me and Augie.

But it was me she stared at with shimmering eyes. Me she stared at with fire in her gaze.

She slammed one hand into my chest. "I set you up? How the hell would I have set you up, Boston? You came in here tonight. You! I didn't invite you. I didn't trick you or coerce you into coming here. I opened my fucking bar to you. Fed you. And yeah, maybe I kissed you."

The fire in her eyes flickered, showing a raw vulnerability. It was only a flash. But it was there.

I saw it.

But Eve didn't give me time to comment.

"The real question here isn't whether I set you up, but why a photo of you kissing me would be such a problem for you. Great to know that kissing me would have such devastating effects on your career. What about my career? You're the one who waltzed in here and accused me of running a sex club! You're the one who trashed my place. Who's ruining whose career, again? But I was willing to overlook all that. To be the bigger fucking person."

Her chest heaved, fingers balled into fists at her sides. Her gaze raked over me, head to toe in a long, sweeping look that somehow tore me right open.

She saw me for who I truly was.

And I saw her.

"I don't know why I thought you were something different. You're just like all the rest. Get out of my club," she seethed.

Augie smirked at me and held the phone up again, the photo still displayed. It was way too fucking tempting to punch him in his smug face. But Eve still stood between us, and even though I was pissed, I wasn't going to risk taking a swing at Augie while she was anywhere near him.

I walked out of the club, leaving Augie, Eve, and the photo behind.

14

EVE

I watched Boston walk out of the club with a red haze clouding my vision. Fuck him for last night and turning me on like no other guy ever had. Fuck him for walking in here tonight, soft and vulnerable and sad. Fuck him for kissing me back.

Fuck him for being so damn good at it.

I clenched my fingers into fists at my sides, spun on Augie, and slammed one right into his stomach.

My knuckles met hard abs with a jolt, but the satisfaction I got from Augie doubled over and winded outweighed any ache in my hand.

He coughed and spluttered, clutching his midsection. "What the hell, Eve! What was that for?"

I snatched his phone from his hand and found the photos he'd taken of me and Boston. The one of us kissing gave me the tiniest moment of pause. I'd been into that kiss. I'd felt it right down to my toes. It wasn't a typical first kiss, that was full of heat and passion and a promise to rip the other person's clothes off.

He'd been so full of pain, I'd just wanted to take some of it away. Something deep inside me called out to comfort him, protect him. And he'd sunk into that kiss like he needed it to keep going.

Ha. What a fucking lie.

I hit the 'delete' icon and thrust the phone back at Augie. He wasn't in my good books either. "Who asked you to do that?"

"I was just trying to help!"

"I don't need your help, Augie! I'm perfectly capable of handling Boston and the cops without your interference. Got it? I know we're friends, but don't forget, I was doing this way before you came along, and I'll be doing it way after you've lost interest and moved on to something else."

Suitably chastised, he nodded once. "Understood."

A little of the fight went out of me. This was Augie to a T. He was such a prick, pissing off almost everyone, never letting people see that there was actually a nice guy inside him. The good inside was almost always misguided, as it was tonight. But it was there if you searched deep enough.

Most people didn't look beyond the surface. But I did. So I blew out a long breath and patted him on his solid shoulder. "How's your gut?"

"Sore. Who taught you to punch like that?"

"You don't work at a strip club as long as I have and not know how to take care of yourself."

He nodded and shuffled away without an apology.

I wouldn't have expected one. That was part of why Augie and I got along. We understood each other.

Needing some fresh air, I shuffled to the doors. It was

close enough to closing time that there was no line waiting to get in, and Terry, our bouncer, sat on his stool staring off into the dark night. I stopped beside him and leaned against the side of the building, breathing in deep, warm, almost summer air.

He glanced over at me with a fatherly smile. Terry was a big guy. Huge, really. Almost a foot taller than me, and probably twice as wide. He was also ten years older, married to a lovely, tiny woman, and the two of them had a couple of preteen kids. He'd worked the door at the club longer than even I'd been around. I'd inherited him from Sal when I bought the place.

"Wanna tell me what that was all about? I stuck my head in when I heard the commotion, but you had it under control."

I grinned up at him. "Augie asked me who taught me how to throw a punch."

Terry smiled softly and gazed down at his lap. "When I taught you that, you were barely older than my kids are now."

"I know. Time flies, huh?"

"Sure does."

He eyed me, and I could tell there was more he wanted to say. But I gave a tiny shake of my head, and that was enough. Terry nodded, accepting that I didn't want to talk about Boston and what had happened between us. None of them knew about what he and I had done on the phone last night. So me suddenly kissing him was highly likely the hot topic of gossip floating around the club right now.

I sighed and pushed off the wall. "I suppose I should get back to it."

"Wait. I nearly forgot. Someone gave me this for you." Terry took an envelope from the pocket of his jeans and passed it over to me. "I shoved it in my pocket to give to you after the show, but since you're here now, you might as well take it."

I peered at it in the dim light. "Who's it from?"

Terry shrugged. "No idea. Some guy. Never seen him before. I told him he could give you his fan mail himself, but he said he didn't know which one you were."

I frowned. "Why is he writing me letters if he doesn't know who I am?" I dragged a nail beneath the seal, ripping open the envelope. There was a single piece of paper inside, folded neatly several times. I took it out and smoothed over the creases with my palm so I could read it. Terry flicked on his flashlight and trained it on the paper so I'd have enough light to read by.

Whores in the whorehouse. I see you.

"Oh, hell no," Terry grunted, getting off his stool. "Fuck that shit. Give me that."

He grabbed the paper before I could protest and stormed through the club, searching the tables one by one. "There." He pointed to a lanky man whose red hair flopped in his eyes. His cheeks were a ruddy pink, probably from too much alcohol. He looked up as Terry pushed his way around the table, the man's eyes widening when he was hauled to his feet by the back of his shirt.

Terry had him up against the wall in seconds. And though I'd just punched Augie in the stomach and told him off for trying to handle my business, I let Terry go at it now, knowing he knew me well enough to let me have my say.

"Want to explain this letter you left me?" I asked.

Terry shoved the piece of paper in the guy's face.

The redhead held his hands up in surrender. "I didn't!"

I didn't recognize him. He wasn't one of our regulars, but that didn't mean he hadn't been in here before. We had a lot of patrons who came once or twice on a bucks night, then not again for months or even years. "My man Terry here says you did." I glanced at Terry for confirmation.

He nodded. "Definitely him, boss."

Half the club was staring at us. I couldn't blame them. It had been an eventful night.

The man reached out to me, then thought better of it when Terry let out a low growl. He went with a verbal explanation instead. "No, I mean, I did give it to him. But it's not from me. Some woman gave it to me while I was standing in line outside. Asked me to give it to the stripper."

I narrowed my eyes at him. "Who was the woman? Which stripper did she mean?"

"No idea. Never seen her before. She didn't say which of you."

I waited for Terry to confirm or deny the plausibility of the man's story.

He shrugged. "I just assumed he meant you because you were on stage at the time he came in."

"You believe this guy?"

Redhead jumped in with a shaking voice. The guy

looked like he was about to piss his pants. "I swear, I've never even been in here before. I'm not even from around here, just visiting a friend."

"It's true," one of the guy's friends interrupted. "Some woman pulled up in a Porsche and told us to give it to you."

"You get a plate number?" I asked.

The young guy shrugged. "No, sorry. It didn't even cross my mind. I just thought she was delivering mail."

"In a Porsche? At nearly midnight?" I demanded.

The guy shrugged again.

Terry let him go, and the two of us walked away. "Jesus Christ," he muttered. "Twenty-somethings are fucking stupid."

I glanced up at him and grinned. "Spoken like a true old man. Though I won't take insult since I'm thirty. You believe him?"

Terry nodded. "Yeah. You?"

I nodded.

Terry handed over the paper. "You worried about this?"

"Not worried. Pissed off."

"Got any ideas who it's from? If you hadn't just run your cop buddy out of the club, I might have suggested you tell him about it."

I scoffed. "That won't be happening. I've got a pretty good idea who it's from anyway."

"Want to share your theory?"

"There was a Porsche parked in William Reed's driveway when I was there the other night."

Terry raised an eyebrow. "You think it's from him?"

"Or his old lady maybe. She's hosting that fundraiser

the same night as our penis politician party, and her thing is getting no love on social media."

"While ours is getting a ton of attention."

"Yep. Just sour grapes."

Terry rubbed a hand across his forehead, his worry lines deep. "If you're sure... The police might—"

"I'm sure." The police might nothing. I wasn't going down there. Not tonight, or any other night. That ship had sailed off into the darkness, caught fire, and sank. That's how done Boston and I were before we'd even really started.

And I was balling up the anonymous letter and throwing it right into the flames as well.

15

BOSTON

stared up at the police headquarters and contemplated how the hell I could possibly walk inside, knowing the Jayela was never going to again. Her desk would still be exactly as she'd left it, with an empty coffee mug, and chewed-on pens in the holder. Her jacket would probably be hanging over the back of her chair because it was warm enough now to not need it outside, but the air-conditioning at the station was intense. Hurt panged through my chest, and my head throbbed in sympathy. Though the headache was more about how much rum I'd drunk last night. It had taken me a long time to get off the couch this morning and drag myself into a shower. I had no idea how I'd gotten home or what time I'd passed out.

But I did remember every single second of the fight with Eve.

I closed my eyes. I was still angry. Not just with her and Augie. I was angry at everyone, myself most of all.

And that was eventually what got me off the couch. I

couldn't do another day of lying in this house, completely shut down and nursing my own misery. It wasn't what Jaye would have wanted.

I got out of my car and took the elevator to my floor. There were pats on the shoulder and sympathetic smiles, but I ignored them all. I walked straight into the chief's office and pinned him with a glare. "Don't tell me to go home."

He looked up from his morning coffee. Slowly, he put it down on the table. "Fine. I won't. But you're riding a desk."

"I want in on the Heath Michaelson case."

"You know that's not going to happen. And besides, there's no point. It's open-and-shut. He had means, motive, and opportunity. His prints are all over the murder weapon. And he confessed. We've got video. He's in jail waiting for a trial where they'll sentence him to life. Or worse."

The memory of Heath's unconscious body being dragged out between two officers sat heavily in my mind. "I want to see the confession."

"Camera got knocked over during the scuffle. It's just audio."

"I want to hear it then."

Chief tapped his stumpy fingers against the side of his mug. "If I let you listen to it, will it ease your mind any?"

"Yes. It has to." It couldn't possibly make it any worse. I needed Jayela's killer to be off the streets. I needed him to stand trial for what he did, and I'd be right there, watching when they sentenced him to life. If Johnson and Stewart had fucked this up in any way, I wanted to know now, not when it was in front of a jury.

"We're just about to go into a meeting about it anyway. You might as well come along."

The chief stood, and I followed the shorter man out of his office, through the bullpen, and down the hall to a large room full of chairs facing various screens and whiteboards. Most of our briefings took place here, and there were already multiple people milling about, helping themselves to a pot of coffee that had been brought in and set up by the window.

I wasn't interested in caffeine. I sat myself in the front row without saying hello to anyone and waited for the briefing to begin. The room filled, slowly, like everybody had better things to do. My impatience mounted by the second. My right leg bounced uncontrollably, jitters coursing through my body.

After what seemed like a lifetime, the chief got up. "Good morning, everybody." He shot small glances in my direction while he talked about the current open cases, like I was a loose cannon about to erupt.

He was right to be worried. As he walked through the events of the past forty-eight hours, detailing Jayela's murder in graphic detail, my head swam.

He didn't ask if I was okay. It was probably clear I wasn't. But I'd come this far. And I wasn't going to back down now.

Finally, he called Johnson and Stewart up to talk through Heath Michaelson's arrest. There were claps and cheers as they stood and made their way to the front of the room. They were patted on the back, and a piercing wolf whistle came from somewhere behind me.

Johnson smiled proudly, like he'd just been awarded a first-place ribbon. The kid next to him smiled, but there was a stiffness to him. The smile didn't reach his eyes, and when he shot a glance in my direction, he looked downright worried.

Johnson droned on, talking himself up, until I couldn't stand it a minute longer.

"Just play the fucking recording already," I snapped.

All eyes turned to me, their gazes judgmental. I could practically read their minds. *He's losing it. He shouldn't be here.*

Chief frowned at my impatience, but he hit a button, and the recording played through speakers mounted to the walls.

"*Admit what you did, you prick. Give her the respect she deserves.*" That was Johnson's voice, hoarse and terse.

"*I didn't do it.*" The deep rumble of Heath Michaelson's voice was a blast from the past. I remembered it from back when we'd been friends. But here it sounded strained and full of pain.

"*You're covered in her blood. They found the murder weapon. How long do you think it'll be before they find your fingerprints on it?*"

"*They won't because I didn't fucking do—*"

"*They will,*" Johnson taunted. "*They will. So admit it. Open your mouth and let the words free. Maybe it'll ease some of that guilt sitting on your soul.*"

There were two thumping noises and then coughing.

I'd punched enough people, and been on the receiving end of a fist to the gut, enough times to know what it sounded like. But Johnson's smug smile didn't leave his face, and no one around me commented on the fact the man had obviously crossed a line.

Heath's voice was a wheeze while he tried to talk and

suck air in all at once. *"Ease my guilt? Or ease your guilt over your fucking hard-on for her? Ease your guilt that you wanted in her panties, but she wouldn't look twice at a man like you? Your jealousy reeks. You're the one who should feel guilty. Did you tell your wife that while you fuck her with your tiny dick, you're thinking of some hot piece of ass from the station?"*

All eyes in the room turned to Johnson.

His smile wasn't quite as smug anymore. I suspected he'd forgotten about this part of his 'interrogation.' He waved it off casually, though the tips of his ears turned pink. "He would have said anything at that point. He knew we had him."

There was a crash and scuffle, and the audio went muffled. But not muffled enough to cover the smacking of flesh against flesh and the grunts of a man being beaten.

"Admit what you did to her. Admit what you took from me."

My head snapped to Johnson who now looked like he might want the floor to open him up and swallow him whole. "Took from you?" I snarled.

Choking noises echoed around the room, and my eyes went big. I gaped at the chief, but his face was expressionless.

"Admit it. Admit it!" Johnson bellowed.

"I did it. Is that what you want to hear? I did it. You fucking happy?"

A cheer went up around the room, and Johnson's smarmy confidence returned.

I just gaped at all of them. "You are not seriously giving this man a pat on the back for beating the shit out of a man until he confessed?"

"It was nothing more than a scuffle—"

"A scuffle? You can hear your fist laying into his skin, Johnson! Were you choking him? Because it sure as hell sounded like it. I saw what he looked like when you dragged him out. He wasn't even fucking conscious. None of this is going to hold up in a courtroom." I gripped the seat of my chair either side of my thighs to stop myself from launching across the room at him. "I told you to wait for me. I told you! And you went ahead and did it yourself because you wanted to be a fucking hero and now you've fucked the entire thing up."

The chief put himself between me and Johnson and held up a hand for calm. "I'll admit, some of this is a bit on the rough side. But we'll trim it down to the confession and that'll be enough."

There were nods and murmurs of agreement all around me.

Was I truly the only one who was going to speak up? Jayela never would have stood for this if the shoe was on the other foot. She was so by the book, so pure and determined and driven by a need for every person—cop or civilian—to be given a fair go.

Nothing about Heath Michaelson's interrogation and confession was fair. And now we were going to try to doctor the evidence to make it sound like it was? "You can't do that!"

The chief levelled me with a hard gaze. "You're only here as a courtesy, Boston. You have no say in how this investigation is run, or in how the evidence is presented. We have a lot more than just his confession. His prints on the murder weapon for one. And a motive, being that he was her ex. We don't even need this confession in the grand scheme of things, so if we take some of it out to save one of our own some embarrassment, then that's what we do for family."

That was what he was worried about? That Johnson might be embarrassed? Johnson fucking should be embarrassed. Not of the things Heath had said about his crush on Jayela. Everybody knew about that anyway. He should be embarrassed over the way he'd completely lost it and beat the shit out of a suspect.

He'd had a position of power and he'd abused it.

So had the chief.

So had I.

I got up and left the room without a word, disgusted with all of us.

16

EVE

"Eve, you need to come look at this."

I stopped in the doorway to my office and peered over the top of my monitor to where Fawn sat behind my desk. "What's up?"

I didn't enter the room. I'd kind of been avoiding it ever since my argument with Boston. Every time I'd tried to sit in here and get some work done, I started thinking about texts, and then I started thinking about the videos we'd sent each other, and that was a one-way ticket to horny town. I just didn't need that right now.

So I'd handed off some of the admin work to Fawn, pretending I had other things to fill my time.

I didn't. It just gave me more time to think about him, and how he was coping after losing his partner, and how I still kinda wanted to punch him in the throat. Asshole.

Fawn motioned me around to her side of the desk and tapped one fake fingernail against the monitor. "Trolls."

She had one of our social media pages pulled up, where we were advertising our upcoming Pin the Penis on the Politician party. Or the Triple P Party as we'd taken to calling it. I leaned in and squinted at the screen. We had hundreds of comments and tags. We'd been monitoring them fairly closely, knowing we'd probably get some hate, too, but then the Boston thing had happened and I'd lost focus. Now there was a ton of troll-like comments.

I heard they have rats. And herpes.

Someone I know got food poisoning there and spent a week in the hospital.

This is so tasteless. If you have any class at all you'll show your support for Mayoral Candidate William Reed by attending his fundraising gala that night and donating generously.

I grew increasingly pissed off as I read through each one. But it was the last one that really ate at me. I commandeered the mouse from Fawn, recognizing the poster's name. "Is this woman for real?" I searched Laura Reed's profile, scrolling through her friends list and matching names up with the troll comments on my page. "She's got all her friends posting shit on my event. What is this, high school?"

"You could post some stuff on hers. Not that her page is getting much traffic so nobody will see it but her."

"Not my style." I grabbed my keys from the desktop.

"Uh-oh."

"What?"

Fawn folded her arms across her chest and leaned back in the chair. "I know what your style is. You're going to go confront her in person, aren't you? Don't do it. We can just delete the comments."

"It's not just the comments. There was a letter, too.

And like you said, it's not my style to hide behind a keyboard. Plus, I have a beef with William Reed that hasn't been settled. Perhaps I can kill two birds with one stone."

Fawn gaped at me. "You aren't really going to kill..."

I cocked my head to one side. "Really?"

Fawn shrugged with a small smile. "You never know with you. You're a bit of a loose cannon."

I winked. "If anyone's looking for me, I'll be back in an hour. Now get off social media and get that book-keeping done before I get back."

She nodded seriously. "Got it. All books will be balanced within the hour. Unless I screw it up."

The woman had no faith in herself. I hated whoever it was who had made her feel like that. "You won't. You totally got it. See you soon."

I left her in the club, locking the main doors behind me so nobody could wander in hoping for a midday lap dance and terrify Fawn. It only took fifteen minutes to drive across Saint View and into Providence, and then I was pulling into William and Laura's neatly paved driveway and parking behind their Porsche.

Ugly fucking car. So pretentious. The devil on my shoulder whispered that running my keys along its shiny paint job might be fun. But I didn't listen to her anymore.

Well, not as often.

Laura's shiny paint remained intact.

I bypassed the bell and banged on the door with a closed fist instead. When nobody came, I banged again. "Reed! I know you're in there. I think we need to have a conversation." I didn't even know which Reed I was addressing. It didn't really matter. I had bones to pick with both of them.

When the door finally opened, I was ready with a mouthful of accusations.

They all dried on my tongue.

"Eve? What are you doing here?" Boston stepped outside, closing the door behind him.

God, he looked good in uniform. His fitted shirt tucked into his pants, showing off his tapered waist. The stubble across his jaw was thicker than it had been a few days ago, but it suited him.

"I'm here to see Laura."

"Did you have an appointment?"

I blinked. "Does she have a secretary to organize her busy days of lunching and tennis? Silly me, I didn't realize."

Boston narrowed his eyes at me. "Don't be a jerk."

"I'm not the one whose been trolling all over social media and sending threatening letters."

Boston opened his mouth to reply, but Laura came storming outside, cutting him off.

"What are you doing here?" she demanded. "This is private property."

"And so is my club. So stay away from it. Both online, and in person."

She screwed up her nose in disgust. "Why would I go anywhere near that place? I heard there's rats..." She gave a small, smug smile.

That just confirmed her guilt.

"You'd know all about rats, wouldn't you? Considering you married one."

Movement flickered at the corner of my eye, but I didn't have time to investigate what it was.

"You watch your mouth, you whore." Laura stepped forward, getting in my face. "You think you can come around here, into my home, accusing me and my family? I'll have you arrested. Again. You and all your slut friends. And when William is elected, the first thing we'll do is bulldoze your dirty club to the ground. Let's see where that leaves you." She jabbed a sharp fingernail into my sternum.

On autopilot, everything Terry had taught me as a teenager kicked in. I grabbed the woman's wrist, gripping it tightly, preventing her from jabbing me again.

Laura's eyes widened. Then she launched herself at me, going straight for my hair and yanking it hard. "Get off my property, you bitch!"

Sharp pain prickled across my scalp, and I let out a startled yelp. "What the hell?"

I dug my fingers into the pressure point above her thumb, and she screamed. The bloodcurdling noise nearly deafened me before Boston jumped in the middle of us. His arms came around me, lifting me straight off my feet, and walking ten paces down the driveway.

Laura was still screaming obscenities at me from her front steps.

"Now who's not being classy?" I called. "Do you talk to your children with that mouth, too?"

Boston tightened his grip on me. "Enough, Eve."

Laura whirled around and slammed the front door behind her.

I shoved at Boston's chest. "Since when do you get to tell me what's enough? They harass me, attack me, and yet it's me who's being too much? I wouldn't have to be here at all if she didn't spend all of her time trolling my Facebook page and sending me threatening letters."

His mouth pulled into a tight line. "Everybody gets social media trolls. They don't go to the person's house and get in fist fights with them!"

"I didn't start any sort of fight. I was trying to defend myself."

Boston let go of me and stepped back, pinching the bridge of his nose and screwing up his face. "Social media posts aside, what are you talking about with the threatening letter business?"

I shoved the letter in his face. He read it without touching it. And then he stared at me. "Why didn't you report this?"

"To who? You? You proved the other day you're just as useless as the rest of your damn department. Why would I bother? We deal with things our own way in Saint View, Boston. That's how it's always been, that's how it always will be."

"Jesus fucking Christ, Eve. Why do you make everything so difficult? If you brought me this, I would have done something about it myself. We could have avoided this entire scene."

"Or you could have ignored it. You could have told me it was nothing. You could have told me I was overreacting. All things I've heard it from your department in the past. Your track record when it comes to actually helping people in Saint View? Pathetic."

Boston shook his head slowly. "I can't help you if you don't want to help yourself."

"Like I said, I don't want your help." I spun on my

heel and marched down the driveway to my car and threw myself behind the wheel. I paused with my fingers clenched and watched Boston storm away, back inside the house, the door slamming behind him once more.

I jumped as the noise echoed back.

I was pretty sure the entire house shook with the force of that slam.

I punched the side of my fist against my door. "Dammit!" I didn't know whether to scream in frustration or let the hot, angry tears pricking at the backs of my eyes loose.

A tapping at the passenger-side window caught my attention.

Reed's son motioned for me to wind down the window.

I cracked it an inch. "What? If you're here to deliver some message from your mother or father, I don't want to hear it."

But he shook his head quickly. "Can you open the door? I need to show you something."

He didn't have the same aggressive anger in his eyes his mother did. Or the same calculating gleam of his father. He just looked young. And lost. He kind of reminded me of Fawn.

I would probably regret it, but I unlocked the door anyway. "What's your name again?"

"Dylan." He slid inside the car and motioned for me to start the engine. "Can we just drive around the block? I don't need my mother seeing me with you and stomping out here again."

I didn't need that either. I was more than ready to get

out of here and leave the Reeds, and Boston, in my review mirror. "Put your seat belt on."

I gunned the engine, louder than I would have normally, and peeled out of the driveway.

Dylan didn't talk until we were out on the road, the house disappearing behind us. "I've got everything that happened between you and my mom on video."

Anger flared through me, hot and fast. I slammed on the brakes, not caring I was in the middle of a suburban street. "You're here to blackmail me? For real? Get the fuck out."

Dylan's eyes went wide, and he held his hands up in a stop motion. "No, no. I swear. I actually wanted to offer the video to you."

"What for?"

He shrugged. "For whatever you want it for. Post it online. Take it to the cops. Sue, get yourself some money. I don't know."

I stared at him. "Why would you give me that? Where's your loyalty to your mother?"

He laughed a hard, bitter sound. "I can't stand either of my parents. They're the biggest hypocrites I've ever met. And I'm sick of playing the dutiful son because that's what's expected of a candidate's family. I'm supposed to stand there, behind a man I despise, wearing my Sunday best and smiling like all is right in the world."

I couldn't stand his parents either. So I could hardly blame him. "So what? You give me this video, and that's your revenge?"

He looked down at the phone clutched in his hands. "I don't know. I hadn't really thought it through."

I let out a sigh. "Pass me my purse. It's down there at your feet."

"Yes, ma'am."

I couldn't help but smile at him. Nobody ever called me ma'am. I rifled through my bag and pulled out my business card, holding it out to him.

He took it, eyeing the details. "You want me to email you the video?"

I shook my head. "No. I've said my piece. If your mother leaves me alone, I won't have to come back."

"But she attacked you. Called you all those names. This could really hurt my father's campaign, and then maybe your business would be safe."

"It's not really my style, kid. I'm always happy for a confrontation, a one-on-one discussion, if you will, when someone's wronged me. But I can be the bigger person when I need to be. It's not in me to run a smear campaign. I'm not like your mother."

"Why are you giving me a card then?"

I shrugged. I couldn't explain to this kid that he reminded me of Fawn. And that Fawn reminded me of me, ten years ago. "If your parents get too much, and you need somewhere to go, call me."

He turned the card over in his hands. "I'm gay. I can't tell them. We go to church every Sunday morning. They'll never accept it."

I still remembered the way he and Phoenix had looked at each other at the church rally. It had been barely a moment, but it had been so loaded with attraction that I doubted anyone could have missed it. Even his parents, with their heads stuck in the sand. "You should try them. Maybe they'll surprise you."

He scoffed at that. I couldn't blame him. I didn't think for a second that his parents would accept that sort of news. But the poor kid seemed like he still cared what they thought.

I knew how that felt.

"You know I'm a stripper, right?"

Dylan nodded.

"I started stripping when I was younger than you are now. A lot younger. I was only sixteen. I hid it from my parents for a really long time, pretending I was still going to school every day, when really I was going to the club, taking my clothes off, and dancing for men more than twice my age."

"Shit. That's huge."

I nodded. "It was. But I never regretted a second of it. I like this job. I like the money, and the people. I like the freedom it gives me. And sure, I shouldn't have started that young. But I've always been kind of stubborn."

"When did your parents find out?"

"I told them the week before I turned eighteen. I had to come clean when they thought they'd be attending my high school graduation."

"How did that go down?"

I almost didn't want to tell him the truth. Because it had been one of the worst days of my life. "You know those names your mother just called me?"

Dylan cringed, but nodded.

"Imagine hearing them from your own mother's mouth. Then multiply it."

He sighed heavily. "Did she ever come around to accepting it?"

He stared at me with hopeful eyes. He was putting himself in my shoes.

My mother had never come around. Sure, I'd been invited back for family dinner, but things had never been the same between us. Some words, once spoken out loud, couldn't be taken back. But I couldn't bear to break Dylan's heart. I couldn't be the one to tell him that leopards didn't change their spots. I doubted with every fiber of my being that his parents would ever accept him the way he wanted them to.

"Sure. She came around. Everything is good now."

Dylan settled back against the seat, relief etched into his expression. I could only hope that for him, it wouldn't be a lie.

17

───────

EVE

On Tuesday nights, the club was closed to the public so a couple of friends and I could use the space to jam in. They played. I sang. None of us wanted to chase a career in music, but our hangouts had been fun, and over the years, it had turned into something more. It had become a family night, where the four of us put on a show that didn't involve nudity. I made a pot of my famous stew, baked some crusty bread rolls, and fed whoever turned up. I never really knew who would appear from one week to the next. Fawn, Augie, Phoenix, and Lyric were all regulars. Lyric brought her tiny daughter sometimes, and her sweet laughter echoed around the room as she ran about, being chased by Phoenix or Fawn. My brothers dropped in from time to time, and other friends and family were always welcome.

I always cooked early in the day, so the stew had time to get tender, but also so I could enjoy my friends. There was nothing I liked better than standing at the head of the stage, with a microphone in my hand, and taking in the family I'd created for myself. I belted out lyrics, watching over them all. Fawn and Augie, flirting in a corner. Echo and Lucinda deep in conversation at the bar. Terry spun his wife around the dance floor, making her laugh while their two kids sat at a table watching their phones, pretending their parents didn't exist.

This was my happy place. Nobody was going to tear it down or run me out of town. I owed it to these people to keep my doors open. I was the matriarch, the one who provided them with jobs, and food, and this sense of family that most of them didn't have anywhere else. They relied on me, and this club was home.

I closed my eyes and let the music wash over me. But every time I did, I saw Boston. All the different versions of him. The smiling version, when I did something that amused him. The scowling version, that I'd gotten the last time we'd met. The sexy-as-fuck version, who kissed me like no other man had, and sent me videos that had me aching with need.

A big part of me wanted him here. I could see him fitting in with my family, with my life.

The logical part of my brain knew it would never happen, and that I had to stop fixating on him if I was going to get over whatever it was between him and me.

So I concentrated on singing. The band and I practiced until, one by one, the rest of my crew waved goodbye and headed out. Fawn and Augie left together, arm in arm, probably off to another bar where there was more action. Phoenix carried a sleeping Amelia to the car for Lyric, and the others followed, until the club was empty of everyone but me and the band.

I wasn't ready to be done yet, though. I wasn't ready to

go home to my empty house and think some more about Boston. "Twenty minutes more? And then I'll send you home with the leftover stew?" I asked the guys, who all nodded, indulging me.

We launched into a cover of "Come Together" by the Beatles, which was one of my favorites. I was only two lines into the first chorus when the doors opened again. I blinked through the darkness, recognizing one of the two people who entered. "Well, well, well. Look what the cat dragged in, will you? What are you doing here? Shit, am I being sued again?"

Liam grinned. "I was in the neighborhood, and hungry. You know I won't eat anywhere else around here."

I stepped down off the stage to stand in front of my old childhood friend and current lawyer.

He gave me one of his charming grins. "Please, Eve. Feed us. We don't want to go somewhere else and get food poisoning."

"Damn straight you don't. The only other place open at this time would be Ugly Joe's."

I made a face, and Liam made a gagging noise, both of us grinning.

I turned to the woman he was with, casting an eye over her. She was gorgeous. A curvy blonde and not at all Liam's usual type. I would have killed to get her up on stage, though. She had a similar build to me. Not overweight, but not super skinny either. I had hips and boobs and a booty. This woman did, too. "Who's this?"

She didn't wait for Liam to introduce her. "Hey, I'm Mae."

"You here for a job?"

She frowned. "A job? No, no. I have one. Actually, I have two. Definitely don't need a job."

I raised one shoulder in a shrug. "Pity. You'd do well with that face and body. If you change your mind..."

She blinked. "Sorry?" She glanced around the room in confusion, like she had no idea where she was, before her gaze came to rest on Liam.

He was barely containing his laughter. He put his arm around her shoulders, his heavy biceps weighing her down. "Oh, Mae. Sweet, sweet, innocent Mae. You really haven't changed all that much from high school."

I chuckled. Liam was such a dick. "Stop being a jack-ass. She's obviously not from around here." I turned back to her. "You're at a strip club, sweetie. I actually thought that was why Liam had brought you here. It wouldn't be the first time he'd asked me for a job for a friend."

The woman gaped at me. Then elbowed Liam sharply. "That better not be why you brought me here." Then she glanced at me. "I'm sorry. I didn't mean to imply that it wouldn't be a very, um, nice job. I'm sure you're a very good employer. But like I said, I'm pretty full up on the employment side." Pink flushed her cheeks. She looked ready to kill Liam.

I couldn't help chuckling as he led her to a table, holding a seat out for her.

"Don't think that gentlemanly manners are going to save you from this one, buddy," she muttered.

Liam grinned at her. "I swear, we're only here for the food. I happen to know that Eve makes the very best stew around, and that she always has a pot of it on the stove on Tuesdays when they're rehearsing. The club isn't open to the public Monday or Tuesday, though, so no strip show for you, unfortunately."

"You're welcome to come back on Friday night, though. We go all out on the weekends," I called.

"Um. Thanks. That sounds nice," Mae answered politely.

I nodded. I hoped the two of them would come back. Liam hadn't stopped by in ages, and I'd missed him. We'd spent a lot of time together as kids. He'd played more with my brothers, them being closer in age, and I'd just bossed them all around. "I'll bring you both stew, yes?"

"Yes, please. With bread?" Liam asked.

I messed up his hair affectionately. He was always so perfectly put together now. Nothing like the kid I remembered from the block. "Fine. Bread, too. But you owe me a free consultation next time someone tries to sue me, got it?" I strode across the room, heading for the kitchen.

"She hasn't paid me for a single consultation yet," Liam told Mae. "And she's been sued a lot."

No matter how big he got, he was always a shithead. "I heard that."

I got two clean bowls out of the dishwasher and filled them with the still-warm stew. Then added some crusty bread rolls to plates and took them to their table.

Liam thanked me, groaning with delight as he inhaled the aroma coming from the bowls.

I smiled to myself. I liked when people enjoyed my cooking. "Welcome. We're done with practice for the night. But Liam knows how to lock up. Wash your plates."

Liam stood and kissed me on the cheek. "Thanks. Catch you later?"

I nodded. I'd known Liam my entire life. I didn't even

think twice about leaving him to lock the place up. I knew he'd take good care of my baby.

I handed the guys in the band their takeout containers and promised to see them again next week.

"Thanks, Eve. The Mrs. would have my hide if I came home empty-handed."

"Can't have that. I don't need to be searching for a new guitar player. Should bring her down sometime. We haven't seen her for ages."

"I will. Night."

"Night, guys."

I watched them drive away, and then with a heavy sigh, got into my car. I drove home alone, to my empty house. Sometimes it got to me, that everybody seemed to have someone. The guys in the band had their wives and kids. So did Terry. Lyric had Amelia to keep her company at night. And lately, Fawn and Augie had been spending time together, so she wasn't around much either.

"I need to get a puppy," I mumbled as I trudged up the stairs to my bedroom. My cat was nowhere in sight, probably mad at me for reasons known only to her. But deep down, I knew it wasn't really a puppy I needed. An animal wasn't going to be there to ask me how my day was or hold me close in the night and press kisses to my forehead. It wasn't going to walk into my life in a policeman's uniform and make me want things I'd thought I was just fine without.

I stared at myself in the mirror above my chest of drawers. "You're an idiot. It's attraction. Nothing more. You've been fine on your own this long, there is nothing you need from a man that you can't do yourself."

With a determined nod, I rifled through my drawers,

looking for something to sleep in. I immediately went for a soft cotton nightshirt, but then my fingers brushed a sexy, low-cut black teddy, and I paused. How long had it been since I'd worn it?

I took it out, smoothing my fingers over the lacy bodice. And my immediate thought was that I would have loved to have worn this for Boston. If we'd been on speaking terms right now, I would have pulled it on and sent him a photo.

Tingles started deep between my legs. Fuck him. I'd put it on for myself, then I'd take a sexy photo and save it for someone who deserved it.

I shimmied out of the dress I'd worn to the club, unsnapped my bra, and took it from my shoulders, before tugging my panties down my legs. I swapped them for the lacy one-piece, lifting my boobs and fitting them into the material so they sat nicely. The lace brushed against my bare pussy, the need inside me growing. I let my hair down and fluffed it up in the mirror. At the last second, I touched up my bright-red lipstick. I studied my reflection in the mirror, twisting to the back to check out my ass.

"His loss," I determined. I looked hot. Too bad for Boston.

I held up my phone, taking a few selfies of myself staring seductively into the camera. And then I flicked off the lights and crawled into bed. I scrolled through the phone, checking each photo and deleting the ones that weren't as flattering, leaving me with one I loved. My lips were full and pouty, my cleavage on display, the barest hint of nipple showing through the sheer material. My hair had a sex tussled appearance, and my cheeks were flushed pink.

My finger hovered over the photo. I wanted to send it to him. There was no denying that I wanted him to see me like this. Instead, I scrolled back to the video he'd sent me, back when we'd actually been speaking to each other. I watched him jerk off for maybe the hundredth time, and I reached between my legs.

My phone let out an obnoxious ring, Liam's smiling face popping up on the screen. I let out a frustrated groan. "Shit timing, Liam," I muttered. But I hit the 'answer' button. "What's up?"

Liam's voice was solemn. "Hey. You need to come back to the club. There's been a shooting."

BOSTON

I hated my new partner. To be fair, the guy was probably okay, but he could have been the nicest person on the planet, and I still would have hated him just because he wasn't Jayela. Even worse was the fact the chief had forbidden me from actually working. When I complained about desk duty, he'd allowed me to go out in the squad car with Richards, under the guise of getting to know each other.

I wasn't interested in making small talk. But it was better than sitting at a desk or babysitting William Reed.

At least I thought it had been. Until Richards started firing questions at me as we drove around the hood. Everything from my favorite color, to where I'd vacationed as a kid. At some point, I tuned out completely and stopped answering. So the car was dead silent when the call came in.

"Shooting at Saint View Strip Club. All available units please respond. Address..."

I jerked upright in my seat and grabbed the walkie-talkie from its holder. "Did you say Saint View Strip Club?"

When the affirmative came in, I cut them off again. I didn't need the damn address. "Squad car nineteen responding. Estimated time of arrival, two minutes."

Without any instruction from me, Richards switched on the siren and put his foot down on the gas.

Maybe I did like something about him after all. At least the guy could drive.

The Saint View streets blurred outside my window, and my heart rate picked up with every passing mile. "Come on, come on," I mumbled.

Eve would be inside. The call hadn't mentioned any injured parties, but that didn't necessarily mean we weren't about to pull up to a club full of injured people.

Or worse. Dead ones.

The thought of Eve lying dead in a pool of blood the same way Jayela had been stole the breath from my lungs, leaving behind a terror I now knew all too well.

I couldn't breathe.

Richards bumped up the curb, stopping with a screech of tires in the club's parking lot. I jumped out, not even waiting for him to put it in park. Recklessly, I slammed my way through the front doors and inside the club.

No bodies. No blood. And the woman standing in the middle of the room was not the one I'd expected.

"Mae? What the hell?" I stormed over to Jayela's sister and grabbed her by the tops of her arms. "What are you doing here? Were you here during the shooting?"

She nodded. "I was the one who called the police."

I glanced to her left and realized I knew the man she

was with. Liam Banks. He'd prosecuted some cases Jayela and I had worked on, and I'd heard just a few days ago that he'd picked up Heath Michaelson's defense case. "Good. It's about time somebody around here did the right thing."

Eve chose that moment to burst through the door, eyes wide and hair wild.

I stared at her, drinking her in, gaze roaming over every inch of her body, making sure none were marked with bullet holes.

She was completely intact.

And pissed as hell.

Her gaze bounced around the club, surveying the damage. But I couldn't stop looking at her. She had a silky robe tied around her waist that was so short it showed off the tops of her bare thighs. The robe gaped open at the top, revealing her perfect cleavage and the hint of deep-cut lace. Lust shot through me hard and fast. Her feet were covered by fluffy slippers, but it did nothing to dampen the need building inside me, or the relief that she wasn't hurt.

Her gaze finally landed on me and Richards, and her lip curled. "Get the hell out of my club, Boston. I've got this."

I narrowed my eyes. I didn't want to hear any more from her, "I'm from Saint View, we don't run by your rules," bullshit. I was still fuming over her not reporting that letter, and I was frankly sick of people changing the rules to suit themselves. Her. The chief. The Reeds. "Your club is now a crime scene, *Evil*. So how about *you* get the hell out. You're holding up my investigation."

At the taunting nickname, Eve shot me a look that

tightened my balls. I was pretty glad I wasn't in kicking distance because she probably would have gone for it.

"I have rights," she seethed.

"You do. Like the right to let me work out what the hell happened here tonight. Don't make me arrest you, Eve. Not again."

More squad cars arrived, and she was forced back behind black-and-yellow crime scene tape. But her gaze followed me while I took statements from Mae and Liam and helped the photographers and crime scene analysts with their jobs. Hours passed, and Eve didn't move. The night air turned chilly, and yet she stood there in the doorway, a complete and utter sex bomb with barely any clothes on.

Every glance I dared to make in her direction was met with fire in her eyes. Hours after I'd first walked through the door, I let out a long sigh. "Eve, go home. You can't do anything here tonight." Or this morning really, as it was well past midnight.

"I'm not leaving. This place needs to be back in order in time for the show tonight."

"There's not a chance. You won't even be able to get back in here for a few more hours, and then there'll be repairs and cleaning..."

"I'm not leaving."

Jesus Christ, she was the most exasperating woman I'd ever met. I stomped into the dressing rooms and, not finding what I was after, changed direction and found myself in a small office.

I instantly recognized the back wall as the one in the video Eve had sent while she'd orgasmed. My dick twitched in my pants at the thought of her doing that here. In that seat. Fuck. I grabbed a blanket from an armchair in the corner and marched back out to where she stood behind the tape. I thrust the blanket at her. "Here."

She eyed it stubbornly.

"Really?" I grumped. "For fuck's sake." I shook the blanket out and put it around her shoulders, tucking it tight beneath her chin. She didn't stop me. She didn't say thank you either. But when I looked down at her and our gazes met, a little of the fire had gone out of hers.

The next few hours were long, but I urged everyone on, pushing them to finish their jobs fast. The fact no one had been injured helped speed things up, and eventually, it was just me and Richards, with Eve watching on.

Richards leaned against the bar top wearily. "Time to go? I'm ready for this shift to be over, and to go home and sleep 'til the next one."

The idea of bed sounded amazing. Our shift was supposed to have finished hours ago, but I hadn't wanted to leave until Eve could get back in. I knew she'd stand out there for days if she had to. I eyed her now and then told Richards to go on without me.

"You sure? You won't have a way of getting back to the station."

"I'll be fine."

He glanced between me and Eve, and maybe he felt the rising tension the same way I did. But he gave me a small nod. "Got it. See you tomorrow."

He ducked beneath the police tape, leaving me and Eve alone in a club full of bullet holes.

She stared at me.

"You can come in now. We're done."

She ripped the tape and let it fall to the ground at her feet. She wandered the main room, inspecting the damage. It was mostly cosmetic. A large broken window, glass shards glittering on the floor. Holes where bullets had entered plasterboard and sent chunks of it flying. Furniture moved out of place so the investigation could take place.

That was our fault. I pushed a table back to where I remembered it from last time I'd been here.

"Thank you," she said quietly.

"It's just a table."

"For hurrying the process along. Don't think I didn't notice. I did." She held up the corner of her blanket. "And for getting this for me."

I stopped what I was doing. "You were cold."

"I was. It's warmer in here." She folded the blanket and put it down on the tabletop. "This place is a mess."

"I'll stay and help."

She shook her head. "I can't ask you to do that. I'll call Augie and the others once it's a reasonable time. They'll come in and give me a hand."

"And until then?"

"Until then, I've got a club to put back together. Glass will have to wait until after nine, but the walls I can fix myself. I've got filler out the back from the last time we painted." She looked up at me. "So like I said. I'll be fine. See you around, Boston."

She lingered for the tiniest of moments, her gaze dipping to my mouth.

My breath hitched.

But then she hardened her gaze and walked away, disappearing into the depths of the club.

I was still standing in exactly the same spot, my lips tingling from her attention on them, when she returned a few minutes later carrying a paint tin, a roller, and an armful of fillers with spatulas.

She dumped them on the table. "You're still here."

"I told you, I want to help."

She held up a tube of something. "Fine. Help then."

I crossed the room and took it from her, picking up a spatula while I was there. Our fingers touched, her skin soft against the callouses on mine. I had the insane urge to wrap my fingers around hers and hold her hand.

She jerked away before I could. "You take this side of the room, and I'll take the other."

"On it."

They'd sprayed up the club good. There were holes everywhere, and plenty of work to be done. I squeezed the thick white paste onto the spatula and slapped it over the first hole, filling it in and smoothing off the excess.

We both worked in complete, stony silence, until it drew out so long I couldn't stand it anymore. "You know we're going to have to talk about this, right? About who might have done it."

"I think we both know there's only one person who has it in for me right now."

I raised an eyebrow. "You think William Reed, middle-aged, church-going Christian and mayoral candidate drove by your club and sprayed it with bullets?"

"You don't?"

"I don't think the man knows one end of a gun from the other."

"Maybe not. But it doesn't take much to pay one of the

Sinners or some other gangbanger to do the job for him, does it?"

She had a point. "We'll be checking cameras. We'll get the plates of whoever did this."

She shook her head. "What cameras? Nobody on the strip can afford surveillance. And even if they could, you think they're going to willingly hand over footage to the cops? You know that's not how things roll around here. If there's even a hint of a gang being involved, any recordings will disappear. Nobody wants that sort of blowback."

My first instinct was to argue with her. To say that going through all the legal channels was the right thing to do, and that we'd take care of any pushback from the gangs. But I stopped mid-sentence, because would we? Would we really be there to support her, day in and day out?

The answer was a big fat no. She'd get shoved to the back of the line, her worries and complaints put into the Saint View basket that was conveniently ignored until someone needed a scapegoat.

I went quiet, silently filling holes, while swearing to do better. If William had even so much as sniffed in her direction, I'd find out about it.

Across the room, Eve filled holes at twice the speed I did. Her spatula slapped and scraped against the wall as she moved from one hole to the next, working with jerky, stiff movements. I couldn't help watching her. She filled them methodically, pulling a chair around with her to stand on when the holes were higher than she could reach by standing on her toes. Every time she lifted her arms, her robe rose as well, flashing me her ass and the lacy panties she wore beneath. Her thighs were smooth and perfect, deeply tanned, and every time I caught a flash of lace, my dick twitched, wanting more of that action.

God, she was so beautiful. No matter what she was doing. I just wanted to storm across the room and run my hands up her legs, familiarizing myself with every inch of them before getting to the treasure at the top. It was a physical ache to keep my feet planted to the floor.

Eve glanced my way from the top of the chair and scowled. "What are you doing? You're taking forever." She inspected my work from her perch. "You're using too much. You need to scrape it right back around the edges otherwise we'll be sanding for hours. Haven't you patched a hole before?"

I looked over the work I'd done and realized she was right. It was lumpy and clumsy. I'd filled plenty of holes with this stuff. I'd flipped a whole house a few years ago with my dad and a couple of old college buddies. My dad would have had a heart attack over the work I'd just completed.

But I'd never had to patch holes with Eve Hawkins across the room. She was all I could think about. The lure to cross the room and kiss her until she shut up became an overwhelming need.

Eve wasn't even giving me a chance to explain. She continued her rant, not letting me get a word in.

"Seriously, Boston. If you aren't going to do it properly, don't bother at all. It just makes more work for me in the long run, and as you can see by the state of this place, I'm in for a very long day. Just stop now if you're not going to try—"

Irritation prickled down my spine. I was trying! She

was just that damn distracting, and the more she told me off, the more I wanted her. "Seriously? I'm here helping you after being awake for twenty-four hours—"

She shoved her hands on her hips, which only made her robe rise higher. "Oh, cry me a river. I never asked for your help—"

My patience snapped. "Eve! For fuck's sake, shut up! I'm doing the best I can, but you're up on a fucking chair, in your goddamn underwear, and I can barely think straight for how bad I want you right now. So take your foot off my balls already!" I slapped another huge chunk of filler onto the wall. Half of it fell straight back off, and I swore beneath my breath while I stooped to pick it up.

Eve's gaze burned my back.

"Boston."

"What?" I snapped, turning around.

She was quiet, all the bossy arrogance from a second ago gone. Our gazes collided. Heat flared in hers, and surprise lit up my chest, forcing my breaths to quicken.

The tension in the air around us thickened, neither of us making a move but something almost tangible sparking to life between us. On feet that seemed to have a mind of their own, I crossed the room, stopping in front of the chair she stood on, and let my gaze travel up her body. Her shapely calves and thighs. The indent of her waist where she had the belt of her robe tied in a bow. It swung in my face, taunting me, tempting me to pull it.

Eve didn't stop me when I did.

Her robe fell open, the belt slipping to the floor as my fingers loosened, and my hungry gaze rolled over her curves. It wasn't panties and a bra. It was an all-in-one piece of lingerie I didn't have a name for. Even if I had, I wouldn't have been able to remember it in that moment, because all the blood had rushed straight from my brain to my dick. The outfit was sheer in parts, the club lights hitting her perfectly, showing off her dark nipples.

Her pussy was right at my face height, covered only by the tiniest scrap of lace.

I put my hand on her hip, drawing her closer, stroking my thumb over the lace and then just below it to touch her skin.

She let out an audible gasp, and I glanced up at her while I fingered the bottom edge of her underwear. Her gaze burned with need, and it called out to the place inside me that wanted her like I wanted my next breath.

Testing her, I dragged my fingers lower, tracing the edge of the garment toward her center, but keeping my fingers to her upper thigh. The scent of her arousal urged me on, as did her breaths when they became ragged. My other hand ran up and down her thigh, squeezing and massaging as I went, while my right hand played with the lace, getting ever closer to the junction of her legs.

She still hadn't stopped me. Hadn't cut me down with sharp words or harsh glares.

Her gaze was molten, her body pliable. Her legs trembled.

"Hold on to something," I murmured.

She pressed her palms to the wall.

I slipped my fingers beneath the lace and ran them over her bare mound, then lower to cup her pussy. She gasped, her thigh muscles clenching. I stared up at her, meeting her gaze and living for the need I found there.

She wanted this.

I pushed one finger between her folds, finding her

wet and needy for me. She mewled at the touch on her clit and she widened her stance as much as the chair would allow.

I should have got her down. Should have put her on the floor, where she would have been safe from falling off. But with her pussy right there at perfect eating height, I couldn't resist.

I pushed aside the lace, holding it tight with my left hand to expose her to me.

I groaned at the arousal shimmering there and explored her folds and clit, running my finger over the tight little bud that made her moan my name.

"Boston..."

Fuck, I loved that. And I'd barely begun.

"Want to taste you, baby. Hold on to me."

I gripped her thighs, keeping her open to me, and my scalp prickled in delight when she thrust her hands into my hair.

I put my mouth to her center, darting a tongue out to taste her. "Fuck, Eve. You taste better than I imagined."

She let out a little moan, rocking her hips in encouragement.

So I did it again.

"You've imagined this?" She massaged my scalp in the same tempo I licked her lower lips. "Oh God. That feels good."

To me, too. My tongue was in fucking heaven, pushing against and around her secret bud. She lit up as I flicked it with the tip, her gentle hold on my hair becoming a push on the back of my head, guiding me to where she wanted it.

"I've been thinking about tasting you for weeks. I

want to watch you come. In person this time, not on video." I pushed two fingers up inside her tight canal, eliciting a cry of pleasure from her.

"Yes," she moaned loudly, the word echoing around the empty room.

My dick strained uncomfortably behind my uniform pants, but I ignored it, my sole focus on getting Eve to come against my tongue.

Her hips rocked, and I picked up the pace, thrusting my fingers deep inside her, hitting her G-spot each time and building her higher.

I felt the change in her even before she called out that she was close. A new flood of arousal coated my tongue. I got my face right between her thighs, licking her from her clit, right back to her tight little hole, and fingering her until she was panting, aching to come.

"Boston," she moaned. "I'm going to come. Oh God, please!"

Her orgasm whipped through her body, clenching down hard around my fingers, then releasing only to do it again. She screamed out, an echoing "Yes!" of ecstasy that had my dick so hard it throbbed. God, I wanted to get inside her. Feel that clench around my bare cock while I kissed the fuck out of her mouth.

But there would be time for that. And right now, I concentrated on riding her orgasm out, her hands pressed to the back of my head, holding me tight to her core where I licked and sucked and worked her until she begged me for mercy.

She stared down at me as I put her underwear back in place, giving it one final rub that had her crying out, then helped her down from the chair.

She sat heavily, completely spent, her cheeks glowing from her orgasm. "I've never had someone go down on me while standing on a chair."

"I've never gone down on someone standing on a chair. But it was the perfect height."

With her sitting and me standing, she was now right at my dick height. She grabbed the outside of my leg and hauled me closer. So close that she spread her legs so I could stand between them. She stared up at me through her dark eyelashes. "Speaking of the perfect height…"

She eyed my cock, bulging behind my fly, and bit her lip. Her fingers fumbled around my button, fitting it through the hole and tugging down the zipper.

"Eve," I groaned.

I wasn't sure whether to stop her or beg her to continue.

But like with everything else, Eve knew her own mind. She tugged my pants down my thighs, and then my boxer briefs followed soon after. I kept my gaze trained on the sweet swell of her breasts that practically fell out of her lingerie, and lower where my mouth had been just moments earlier.

Eve's fingers circled the base of my erection, gripping tight while she slowly dragged it up my length. "It looks even more impressive in person."

I flushed hot, thinking about the video I'd sent her. "I don't know what I was thinking sending you that."

She stared up at me, while she worked my dick in her hands. "It did seem a little out of character for you. I thought you were so by the book."

"I thought I was, too."

"And yet, you filmed yourself jerking off until you

came. And then you sent it to a woman you barely even knew. Nothing very by the book about that. Joshua Boston, gentleman on the streets, freak in the sheets." She chuckled.

I ran my hands through her hair, tugging on her ponytail. She moaned at that, and I felt precum bead at the tip of my erection. "Something like that."

She made a needy little sound at the back of her throat. "Show me."

I groaned, fisting her hair tighter. I pressed my cock to her lips, arousal glittering there like lip gloss.

She opened her full, pink lips, wrapping them around the head. Her fingernails dug into the backs of my thighs, urging me so close my knees hit her chair.

She was warm, and wet, and everything I'd dreamed about from the very first day I'd met her. At her insistence, I thrust inside her mouth, shallowly at first, letting her get used to the size of me. But within moments, she was bobbing her head, taking me deeper and deeper, until the tip of me was hitting the back of her throat. My balls clenched with the need to come, but I fought off the urge, not ready to surrender just yet. Instead, I pulled away, leaning down to capture her mouth with my own. We sank into the kiss. Hot, sweet, and needy. Our tongues tangled without hesitation, and we pawed at each other, fighting to get more, needing to get closer.

I was desperate to get her naked, to rip that flimsy lace from her body, take her somewhere that wasn't covered in glass, and pound inside her. But Eve ran the show, pushing me away.

"I want to taste you."

I couldn't hold back from a request like that. The

chance to have her full lips around my cock when I came was too hot to turn down. She took me deep into her mouth once more, running her tongue along the ridged underside, her hands cupping my balls and working that spot between them and my asshole.

"Eve! I'm going to come." It was a last-ditch effort to warn her. A chance for her to move away.

She didn't take it.

I came hard down her throat, hot spurts pulsing from my tip and marking her in a way that sang out to the alpha male in me.

She took it all, every last drop, swallowing it down until I had nothing left to give.

I slumped back against the wall, unable to do anything but revel in the pleasure of having my mind completely blown.

She stood to kiss me softly, and I enveloped her in my arms, holding her tight and kissing her back.

I would have kissed her all night. All morning. For the days and weeks to come. If I'd had my way, I never would have done anything ever again, except kiss Eve Hawkins.

She pulled away too soon and picked up the putty. "Come on. The sun is coming up, and we've still got a club to fix."

She could have told me to do anything from cleaning toilets to disposing of a body. And in that moment, completely under her spell, I would have done anything Eve Hawkins asked me to.

*B*y the time I called everybody in, I'd found some of Augie's sweats in the locker room and pulled them over the top of my lingerie. I could have done it earlier, but there would have been no fun in that. I'd seen the way Boston had been staring at me. And I knew that every time I reached for something, he caught a glimpse of my bare ass. I'd wanted him to see me. I was so fucking attracted to him, I could barely think straight. And sure, he drove me insane, and half the time I wanted to kill him, but the other half of the time I wanted to straddle his waist, sink down on his erection, and ride him until I screamed for an entirely different reason.

It was such a good-looking erection, too. The video hadn't done him justice. The real thing, pulsing deep in my mouth, was the biggest turn-on. I'd had to make him come so we didn't get carried away and end up fucking on the furniture like rabbits. I had to get my club together in time for the show tonight. There'd be time later to do all sorts of things with Boston. Right now, we'd just needed to take the edge off.

The others all arrived not long after I sent the SOS message out, Phoenix with his truck full of handyman equipment. I thanked him as he walked in with a ladder, and in his quiet way, he nodded and got right to work. Augie was the complete opposite. When he arrived, everybody knew about it. Especially Boston.

He stopped and stared at the two of us talking quietly in the corner. "Is this a thing now? We're friends with the cop?"

I lifted one shoulder, knowing full well I was more than friends with the cop. But Augie didn't need to know that. Augie had the world's biggest mouth, and the second you told him anything, the entire neighborhood would know. Whatever Boston and I were doing wasn't anybody else's business. But I did need Augie to get off Boston's back. "The cop is helping us fix the club. So for today, he's on our team. Got it?"

Augie frowned, but he knew who was boss around here. "You got it. Play nicely with the policeman."

"At least until further notice," I said. "I reserve the right to change my mind."

Boston frowned at me, but Augie seemed pleased by it. "You got it." He wandered off to the back of the club, with me calling after him to sort out the glass repair.

Lyric turned up after dropping Amelia at daycare, and Fawn trailed in moments later. Her eyes went wide as she took in the damage and the work crew I'd already assembled. Her bottom lip trembled, her big eyes filling with tears.

I dropped what I was doing and rushed over. "Hey. What happened?"

She laughed around a teary sob. "Your club got shot up, and you're asking me what happened?"

I let out a sigh of relief. "I thought something happen to you." I waved a hand at the disheveled mess around us. "All of this can be fixed. No one was hurt. That's all that matters."

"How can you be so calm about this?"

I shrugged. Things like this were the story of my life. It wasn't the first shooting I'd been involved in. Growing up in Saint View, you didn't get to eighteen without experiencing gunshots in the middle of the night. Sure, it wasn't normally directed at me personally, and maybe I should have been a little bit more worried than I was, but I was also a believer in karma. And what goes around, comes around. William would get his, eventually. I wasn't going to give him the satisfaction of scaring me. If he thought filling my club with bullets was going to get me to run or back down, he had another think coming.

I was stronger than that. Stronger than him. I'd prove it if I had to.

But Fawn's fingers shook, and a tear dripped down her cheek. She had such a baby face, it was almost like wiping away the tears of my own child. I engulfed her in a hug, holding her tight. "Hey. It's okay. It's nothing a day of elbow grease won't fix, right?"

Her lip trembled, then turned into a full body shake and a complete inability to talk as she broke down in my arms. From the corner of my eye I caught Boston watching us, a worried expression on his face.

"You okay?" he mouthed.

I nodded and held Fawn a little tighter, guiding her toward my office. We found Augie in the hallway, and he took one look at Fawn's tears and lost his shit. "What the hell happened? Was it the cop?" He gripped Fawn by the chin and tilted it up to face him. "Hey. Talk to me."

Fawn just shook her head.

Augie turned to me, true worry making his movements frantic. It hit me then that the big man who almost everybody hated, actually cared deeply for Fawn. I wasn't yet sure if it was in the same way I cared about her, or if his affection was based in something more than friendship.

Either way, he trailed us to the office, shutting the three of us inside.

"I'm so sorry, this is all my fault," Fawn sobbed, sinking into the chair opposite my desk.

Augie knelt on the floor beside her chair and took her hand, squeezing her small fingers between his larger ones. I let him comfort her, taking my regular seat behind my desk. This side of Augie was something I'd never seen before, and it was both startling and tender. If not a little bizarre.

But Augie's words of reassurance did little to dry Fawn's tears. She clutched his fingers tighter, but they just kept coming, as did the blame. "I'll quit," she babbled. "Do you need my resignation in writing? If you just give me a pen, I'll do it now."

I squinted at her. "Slow down. What are you talking about? Why on earth would you quit?"

She stared at me with desperate eyes. "I lied when I came here. Or at least, I didn't tell you the whole truth. I didn't just come to Saint View because I had a friend who lives here. I actually didn't know anybody here at all."

It was the story she'd told me when I'd questioned where she lived. She'd said she was sleeping on a friend's couch, and that was how I eventually came to rent her my apartment.

"Okay," I said slowly. "You wouldn't be the first person who's lied to me. I'm sure you had your reasons."

She nodded hard. "I really am sorry. I hate that I lied. You've been so good to me, coming here was the best thing I ever did."

I waved away her apology, knowing there was something deeper, and more important beneath it.

"I was living in my car," Fawn admitted. "Something happened at home, and one day, I just got in my car and left with nothing but the clothes on my back and a few things shoved in a duffel bag."

I swallowed hard. I'd always suspected that Fawn's life before she came to Saint View Strip wasn't a happy one. But she'd always put on a brave front, and in my opinion, people were allowed their secrets. God knew I had enough things I didn't want to tell anyone. I just figured that if I didn't want people prying into my life, then people probably didn't want me prying into theirs. So I'd done what I could to help her, without asking for details.

I reached for her hand. "Okay, but none of that has anything to do with what happened here last night."

"I don't think you'd be saying that if you knew what I was running from. *Who* I was running from."

"Then tell me."

She took a shuddering breath. "My ex. He's messed up with all sorts of bad shit."

Augie's face went hard. "Did he hurt you? Tell me his name. I'll fucking kill him myself."

His words sent a chill down my spine. I had no doubt he meant it literally.

Fawn seemed to understand that, too. She shook her head. "You can't. You don't know his family. If they've found me, it's over. I've gotta leave. It's the only way."

I shook my head. "Whoa, whoa, slow down. This isn't anything to do with you. Nobody has found you. This is about me. This has William's and Laura's names written all over it."

Fawn pressed her fingernails into my palm. "Because we interrupted his speech the other week? No. No way. This has to be Eddie. He gets off on this shit. Scaring me. Taunting me."

I hated the fear in her eyes. I just wanted to take it away. She was too young. Too sweet and innocent to be that afraid. Fuck this Eddie guy. I'd kill him myself if Augie didn't. But for now, I just wanted the fear in Fawn's eyes to go away. "I'm telling you, this is William and Laura. Laura's been sending threatening letters, trolling me on social media. I went over there the other night, and we got into it. Boston had to break us up. They want me off the strip. But I'm not going. And neither are you."

Augie gripped her chin and twisted it to face him. "Damn right you're not. If your ex wants to show his face around here, I'll deal with it. You hear me?"

"And me," I agreed. Lyric and Phoenix would have our backs as well, once they found out.

Fawn let out a shaky breath. "Do you really think it's William and Laura?"

There wasn't a doubt in my mind. "One hundred percent."

Relief flushed Fawn's face. "Okay. Okay, thank God. Because I don't want to leave. I love it here, with you guys. I've got school and friends and dancing and money and freedom. Freedom most of all."

I hoped the grinding of my teeth wasn't audible. Her ex sounded like a piece of work, and she was too precious and untainted for some asshole to come and try to take that away from her. If he showed up, we'd run the little shit out. "You always have us," I told her. "Nothing comes between the family you choose for yourself. Okay?"

She wiped her tears and stood. That quiet inner strength she hid inside straightened her spine and pulled back her shoulders. "Right then, family. Let's get our home back together."

20

BOSTON

Richards wasn't at his desk in the bullpen, so I hung my jacket up and went searching for him. Over the past week, I'd learned he had a coffee addiction, so there was a good chance he'd be found in the kitchen, brewing up a pot.

He was, and he wasn't alone. Johnson and Stewart sat at the table chatting with him, along with three other officers occupied by cleaning dishes and looking for something in the refrigerator. I tried to keep my face neutral, but it was an effort. I couldn't forget Johnson's expression when he'd dragged Heath Michaelson's unconscious body out of his apartment. Or the sound of him beating the shit out of him on the recording. None of it sat right with me, and though my opinion of the older man had never been high, it had sunk to new lows.

The worst part was that he had a rookie as his partner and was teaching the next generation that his way of policing was the standard.

It was all a giant self-perpetuating circle that made me want to rip my hair out and scream.

"You want a cup?" Richards asked, holding out a mug.

I nodded, taking it from his hand and moving back to the door, not wanting to sit and shoot the shit while Johnson was around.

"You should make him pay you for that coffee, Richards. Since he's making such good coin now."

I stopped in the doorway and glanced over at him. "Did I get a pay rise I didn't know about?"

Johnson stood and took his now empty mug back to Richards for a refill. "Heard you're making a little extra cash on the side from your gangbanger friends."

I froze.

Richards glanced over at me with a frown.

Johnson chuckled, resting a hip on the kitchen countertop while he waited for his second cup. "Don't look so freaked out. It's about time you got down off your high horse and wised up to how things run around here. We don't get paid enough to not take a little on the side when the opportunity arises. Right?"

Stewart grinned, and the guy who'd been putting his lunch away slapped my shoulder as he passed. There was no shock or outrage on his face. The slap felt almost like...support.

My gaze met Richards, but he wouldn't hold it. He put the pot down and walked out of the kitchen without a word to me.

Ignoring Johnson, I followed after Richards, catching him in the empty hallway. "Hey, wait up."

He kept walking until I grabbed his arm and spun him around. "Richards..."

He shook me off.

The look of pure disappointment on his face hit me in the gut.

His expression was near identical to the one Jayela would have given me if she'd still been here.

"I can explain," I promised, but it sounded weak even to my own ears.

"No need. I get how it is, I'm not naïve. I just thought you were different. I've always admired you and Jayela. I didn't think the two of you bought into that shit, and so when...well, you know what happened. I asked to be paired up with you."

I widened my eyes. "You did?" No one had told me that.

He shrugged and kept walking without making eye contact.

Another person I'd let down.

Anger built up inside me. Not at Richards. At the chief for putting me in this position. At myself for allowing it.

I swiveled on my heel, changing direction and storming into the chief's office.

He glanced up from his desk and sighed. "You ever going to learn to knock? When did you stop doing that?"

I ignored his question. "How does everyone else know? Johnson just gave me a virtual high five for taking money from the Sinners. Now the entire floor thinks I'm as crooked as he is!"

"He's not crooked."

"He's not straight!"

Chief sighed heavily. "You're still young. When you've been around as long as Johnson and I have been, you'll see not everything is as black and white as it seems. So many of the laws we swear to uphold just don't work in towns like Saint View. It's not just me who sees that. You know your orders came from above my head."

"I want off that case." It hurt me to say it. Jayela was hell-bent on pinning the Sinners. But it was clear to me that whoever was calling the shots wasn't after them. They were content to let them get away with whatever the hell they wanted in order to catch the bigger fish.

It didn't matter to them that the Sinners might have been running guns or dealing drugs or shooting up Eve's club. They didn't care about gangbangers waging wars out on the streets. There was no glory in bringing down a small-town club. Not for the bigwigs. They wanted the big names. The cartels. The mob bosses. The gangs who would put them on the map.

That wasn't why I'd gotten into policing. I wanted to help people. Unlike them, I did care about the people in Saint View. I wanted kids to feel safe to walk to school, with no chance of them catching a stray bullet from a drive-by shooting. I wanted those same kids to make it to college without a drug habit.

That only happened when there were good cops out there, ones who actually cared about people instead of promotions.

The chief folded his arms across his chest. "Which cases you work isn't your call."

I stared him down. "I don't want to be involved in this, Chief. I can't."

"You can, and you will. Because that's your job. Your contact in the Sinners, DeWitt, landed his dumbass in jail, and now he's running his mouth. I had a call from

Liam Banks, reporting that I had a dirty cop. He called you out by name."

The blood drained from my face. It was bad enough that word had got out internally. But if Liam had heard, that meant that there were probably others. The guards at the prison. Judges maybe. Everyone whispering behind my back. My face flamed hot with shame.

"You need to go down to the jail and talk to DeWitt. Get him to shut his mouth before the whole fucking case unravels."

I shook my head. "No. I'm not doing it."

The chief sat back in his chair, pinning me with a hard glare. "You will. Because the man is also claiming that he ordered a hit on Jayela. And I'm pretty sure you're going to want to talk to him about that."

***

"Well, this is a surprise," DeWitt drawled, led into the room by Rowe Pritchard, one of the prison officers Jayela and I were friendly with. "To what do I owe such a pleasure, Officer Boston?"

Rowe shoved DeWitt into the seat across the table and backed off to the corner of the room. "You good?" he asked me.

"Yeah. I'm fine." I wasn't fine. I was so wired my heart pounded like I'd chugged half a dozen energy drinks.

He nodded and walked out, closing the door behind him.

Dewitt grin was smarmy. Was it the smile of a man who'd put a hit out on a cop? I'd pondered that question over and over again as I'd driven out to the prison.

It took everything I had to sit calmly and study him, counting off the things I knew silently in the back of my mind. DeWitt was my contact within the Saint View Sinners. Exactly where he sat in their hierarchy, I never quite picked up, but the man had enough standing to offer a cop a bribe. At the insistence of my superiors, I'd fed DeWitt the information they wanted him to know.

That had seemed to keep everyone happy. Until DeWitt upset the balance by running his damn mouth.

I curled my fingers around the tabletop, nails pressing hard into the solid wood, trying to hold myself back, while I chose my words carefully. I couldn't just launch into accusing him of ordering a hit. So I went for the smaller of two accusations first, trying to ease myself in, as much as him. My nerves were so frayed, the last few hanging on by a thread, ready to snap at any moment. "Who did you tell that I was on the take?"

DeWitt sat back, crossing his arms across his broad chest. "I've no idea what you're talking about."

I narrowed my eyes. I didn't have the time or the patience for his games. Suspects did this all the time. Played dumb until I laid out the facts in front of them, one by one, proving beyond a doubt that they'd done the crime.

I didn't have any proof this time, though. But my gut instinct told me this guy just liked to talk. My instincts shouted that he was a grunt, and that the Sinners had let him take the fall. After all, he was inside, doing time. And I hadn't heard a whisper about anyone else in the gang going down. Maybe he didn't realize it, but maybe they'd thrown him under the bus. "Don't bullshit a bullshitter. I've just had my chief up my ass about it."

DeWitt grinned slyly. "You ever tried that? You'd probably like it."

I ground my molars. "Who did you tell?" I didn't trust this guy as far as I could throw him. But I wanted to know what he was saying, and to who. I was sick of letting other people run the show. I was sick of being forced into deals I didn't want a part of. I was sick of the chief holding my job over my head.

The rose-colored glasses I'd worn when I joined the police force had been ripped from my face. Then stomped on, over and over, until nothing was left but dust.

DeWitt leaned forward, the smile dropping from his face. "Don't worry about it. I'll deal with it."

I'd become the glasses, pulverized by a boot, kicked and stomped until there was nothing left of me. "I've been letting you deal with it for months. How about you start talking, and I deal with it."

DeWitt drummed his fat fingers on the tabletop. "The new guy. Michaelson. You know, the one you put in here for your bitch partner's murder? You guys fucked up there. There is no way he did it. You and I both know that, though, don't we?"

I froze as his words sank in. I hadn't wanted to listen to the inkling idea in the back of my mind that poked holes in the arrest of Heath Michaelson. I knew that confession had been beaten out of him, but the rest—the fingerprints on the murder weapon, the motive, the opportunity...I'd let all of that push the idea aside. I'd ignored Mae when she'd told me it wasn't Heath.

I launched across the table, grabbing DeWitt by his shirt. I shoved him back against the wall until his head hit the brick, my hands creeping up to circle his throat. "Was it you? Did you kill her?"

DeWitt chuckled, though the sound was choked by the pressure I exerted on his throat. "Wouldn't you like to know?

A hand clamped down on my arm, breaking my hold on DeWitt's neck.

Rowe shoved me away, pushing me to the other side of the room. "What the hell are you doing?" He got right up in my face, going nose to nose with me. "Have you lost your goddamn mind?"

It took a moment for my gaze to refocus. I blinked hard, trying to reel myself in. Shit. What the fuck had I been doing? If left alone, I wasn't entirely sure I would have stopped.

The realization dawned on me thick and fast.

I was no better than Johnson. I'd just done the exact same thing he'd done to Heath Michaelson. Assaulted a prisoner until he told me what I wanted to hear.

My head spun.

Rowe loosened his grip on me. "You good?"

"Yeah. I'm fine."

"You know that was all on tape, don't you?"

"It's not what you're thinking."

Rowe backed off, letting me go. "It doesn't matter what I'm thinking. That's between you and your chief. Ain't got nothing to do with me."

But there was a judgment in his tone, even though his words said otherwise. Shit! Even the prison guards believed I was dirty. And why wouldn't they? Everything I'd done lately made it seem that way.

DeWitt piped up gleefully. "Pritchard probably likes

you better now he knows you're dirty. I get the impression our guard friend here likes a lot of things kinda dirty, right, Pritchard?"

Rowe glared at him over his shoulder. "You want to shut up? Or will I let Boston try to kill you again? Seriously, man. Learn to close your mouth."

I made for the door. I couldn't be here anymore. But I didn't miss the disappointment in Rowe's gaze, and it cut right through me.

"Don't believe his talk." I wasn't even ashamed of the desperate tone to my plea.

Rowe nodded.

That was the best I could hope for. With stiff legs, I pushed past him and out into the corridor.

DeWitt's raspy chuckle floated out behind me "You're as big a liar as he is."

I closed my eyes. We were all liars around here, it seemed. Me most of all.

21

EVE

Fawn, Lyric, and I had been in full-blown hysterics for most of the afternoon. We'd gotten to the club early, blasted some music through the speakers, and cracked a few beers while we set up for the Pin the Penis on the Politician party. I'd had a life-sized cutout of William Reed printed at a place in Providence, where the server had asked if I was part of his campaign. I told them I was his biggest supporter and that I wanted the cutout for my bedroom.

The woman had frowned at me sideways but hadn't commented. I'd just shaken my head, packed the cardboard version of William into my car, and driven back to the strip. Lyric had printed an array of dicks on her home computer, then painstakingly cut them out for the pinning part of the evening. I shifted through them now, creating a neat pile on the table we set up by the cutout. "How many porn websites did you have to open to get this many different-looking dicks?" I questioned. "Oh my God. Is this one even real? It's huge."

Lyric glanced over my shoulder. "Oh, yeah. That's real. I didn't get them from websites. They're my own personal collection of dick pics. That's Eric's."

Fawn squealed. "You printed out dick pics guys have sent you?"

Lyric shrugged. "I finally found a use for them."

Fawn sifted through a couple, wrinkling her nose in disgust. "I always just delete them. I never thought about keeping them. Then again, I never really thought I'd be attending a Pin the Penis on the Politician party either. I wouldn't have minded sticking a pin through a few of them. Nasty-looking things."

I couldn't help but think about the dick pics Boston had sent me. But there was no way I was printing that off to share with a club full of people. His video was for me and only me. Warmth curled through my stomach at the thought, and my gaze wandered to the spot where we'd made each other come. Tingles started low in my belly, and I pulled out my phone, sending off a quick text to him, asking what he was doing tonight.

Because I wouldn't have minded a repeat.

His reply came back almost immediately.

BOSTON

Working at William's fundraising thing.
What about you?

It was followed by several sleeping face emojis.

I wrinkled my nose. I agreed with his emojis. That sounded boring.

EVE

Our penis party is tonight. So I guess I'm working with William, too?

I took a selfie of me and cardboard William and sent it to Boston. I debated over whether to ask him to meet up after my shift. It would be late, but I really wanted to see him. Fuck it. I'd always been the sort of girl who went after the things she wanted.

And right now, Joshua Boston was what I wanted.

EVE

Meet up after we ditch our Williams?

I put the phone away in my purse before I could get obsessive about him answering it. I had a shit ton of work to do anyway.

We decorated the club, going all out with glitter and sparkles and penises. I'd ordered in penis-shaped cookies and suckers, and we decided that for tonight, we'd open up the rooms and have guys and girls together. We were all excited about it, with Augie and Lyric arguing over who was the better dancer and therefore going to get the most tips. Their competitive natures were normally stifled by dancing in different shows each night. Put the two of them together, and it was a recipe for constant ribbing.

Terry turned up at eight, and the line outside was already building. By nine, when we opened, the line was around the block.

Fawn peered out the window and squealed as she let the curtain fall back into place. "I've never seen the line like this. Holy shit. This place is going to be sold out and then some." She shook her boobs in excitement. "We're gonna make some money tonight."

Yes, we were. And we had William to thank for it.

Two minutes before nine, Terry opened the doors. I frowned in his direction. He knew we didn't open early. Not ever. The longer we made people wait outside, the more popular we looked, and the more interest we attracted. If anything, we open five minutes late.

Terry caught my annoyed gaze and raised one eyebrow, not taking any of my attitude in the same way a father wouldn't. "You want me to kick him back out, then?"

Boston stepped through the darkness, and I couldn't help the smile that spread across my face. I fought the urge to run across the club and fling myself at him. I turned back to Terry. "Nah. I think we can make an exception for this one."

Boston grinned and made a beeline in my direction. Without a word, he wrapped his arms around me, holding on tight.

The embrace wasn't expected. It took me completely by surprise, but I wasn't at all opposed to it. I snaked my arms around his waist and hugged him back. "What are you doing here? Doesn't William's thing go until midnight?"

"I called in sick."

I pulled back to study his face, dragging him closer to the light of the bar. "You okay?" His face did seem paler than normal, and a tension frown was etched between his eyebrows. I smoothed it out with my thumb.

He closed his eyes, leaning into my touch. "Yeah. Just had a shit day. This is exactly what I needed."

"A club full of strippers and penises? That's what you needed after a shit day?"

"I meant you. You always make me feel better."

I fought to keep my knees from wobbling. The man always knew exactly what to say. He was actually kind of cute and sweet when he wasn't being an absolute pain in my ass. "Even when you're arresting me?"

He breathed in the scent of my hair, but I could hear the smile in his voice. "Let's just say that while you have the ability to take away my headaches, you're also the cause of some of them."

I slapped him on the biceps, but it was playful. I wished he'd come earlier so we would have had more time to talk. "Tell me about your day after? I've gotta go and get ready."

He nodded, pulling out a seat near the stage. "I'll be here, cheering from the crowd."

"You won't be the only one." With a wink, I sauntered away, letting my hips swing just because I knew he was watching.

Augie was in the women's dressing room, arms folded across his broad, bare chest. The man was built like a Greek god and had a face to match. It was no wonder he made me a great deal of money every time he worked. "So, should we expect your boyfriend to be here every night now?"

I frowned at him. "He's not my boyfriend."

Augie rolled his eyes. "You just hugged the man. You're not a hugger. That makes him your boyfriend."

"One hug does not make a relationship, Augie. Don't push your intimacy issues onto me. I hug people just fine."

He opened his arms.

I held my hand up in a stop motion. "Not a chance. Get out of here, I need to get dressed."

He sniggered and sauntered out to the backstage area, ready to begin his set.

I went to my locker, pulled out my outfit for the night, and stripped out of my day clothes.

Fawn watched me quietly. "He's right, you know. You're different with Boston."

I groaned. "Don't you start as well. I hug you all the time."

She smiled softly. "Yeah. But I'm different. You don't bring guys here. And yet Boston has been here several times now. We were just teasing when we put his name on your dildo, but I like the two of you together. He makes you smile."

I couldn't deny that. "Maybe. He also makes me want to stab him."

"I think you like that, though."

I couldn't deny that she was right. I did like the verbal sparring, and the yelling, and arguing that led to orgasms. He kept me on my toes. I would be no good with a guy who wasn't willing to put me in my place. I didn't want a man I could walk all over. The sort of man I wanted was the one who was waiting out in the club for me.

I smiled to myself as the music picked up, and Lyric, Fawn, and I made our way to the backstage area. Lucinda had pumping beats pouring through the speakers, and Augie was already out there on the stage, riling up the crowd, explaining about our celebration of penises and politicians. He urged everyone to write their name on a dick and then go see Phoenix who was in charge of blindfolding and supervising the party game.

A cheer went up, and I grinned at the other women. "Who knew adults liked kids party games? We should have done this earlier."

Lyric sneaked a glance out from behind the curtain. "There's more bodies out there than I've ever seen in this club, Eve. We should have done this years ago. This has gotta be an annual event. Monthly even!"

The noise of the crowd outside had my heart beating against my chest. "Do you guys mind if I go first tonight? I need to get rid of some of this nervous energy."

Lyric gave me a sidelong glance. "You mean, you want to dance for your man?"

Maybe that was part of it.

I motioned to Lucinda to cue up my song, and when the bass started thumping through the speakers, I let it vibrate through my body. It took over each muscle, and I strutted out on stage like I owned it.

Because I actually did.

My adrenaline high only increased knowing Boston watched me. The last time he'd been here, he was so devastated he barely turned in my direction. He'd spent the night drowning his sorrows in a tumbler full of rum.

But tonight was different. Tonight my gaze slammed into his the second I stepped out on the stage. And though a cheer went up from the crowd, it was him I focused on. Dollar bills floated down around me, but it was Boston I stopped in front of and let my hips sway to the music.

His eyes flared, then his gaze rolled slowly over my body, starting at my head, lingering on my tits, my hips, my thighs. The heat in his stare urged me on, and I grabbed the pole, swaying my body up it suggestively. We lost eye contact when I spun around, and then I needed my concentration to perform the athletic routine I'd spent months perfecting. By the time the song ended and the room broke out into clapping, Boston's gaze was full of unspoken demands.

Demands I wanted to give in to.

I got down off the stage, taking the steps carefully in my heels, and worked my way through the crowd, dancing in time with the beat of Lyric's first song.

I smiled at the men as I passed them and let them stick their money in the sides of my panties and bra. I never got completely naked on stage, but I did normally strip down to a tiny G-string. Today, I'd kept my bra and panties for the time being. This crowd was big, and they'd shell out more money if we teased them a little first.

But I was willing to leave that to the others. Because there was someone in the crowd I wanted to tease more.

I stopped in front of Boston, taking in the baseball cap perched on his head, the plain white T-shirt, and dark denim jeans.

He slouched in his chair, staring up at me from beneath the brim of his hat. "You were amazing."

I grinned. "That was nothing. Just the beginning." I put my hands down on the armrests of his chair and gyrated my body slowly toward him. That move was always a winner with guys who I thought might pay extra for a private room, where I would actually get completely naked. It showed off my best assets—my boobs—and got me close to them without actually making a skin-to-skin connection.

His eyes widened, and he reached toward my face.

I caught his hand. "No. No touching."

I rolled up his body again, letting my long hair form a barrier between us and the rest of the club. He leaned in slightly, so his breath tickled my earlobe. "That's not what you were saying the other night when you were holding my mouth to your pussy."

Holy shit. I pulled back, blinking at him in surprise. And here I was, thinking I was the seductress. I spun around, grinding my ass over his lap instead, just to give myself a break from the intensity of his eyes. The temptation to lean in and kiss him was too strong, and I wouldn't do that here. Not in front of this club full of people. If I broke the rules once and let a man kiss me, then all the others would think it was okay to try their luck. It wasn't. I might let them touch my leg. Or maybe my hip. But every other part of me was off limits. They could look, but they couldn't touch.

Not unless I said so.

And I never said so. Not one man had I ever allowed to touch me intimately while I was working.

But Boston wasn't just any man. "Eve," he groaned from behind me. "You're getting me hard."

More composed, I turned around and took a look at his lap in the dim light. Sure enough, his fly strained, holding back an erection.

I leaned in again. "Good. Hang on to it until after my shift and I'll help you take care of it."

"Have you got private rooms?"

I raised an eyebrow. I hadn't forgotten he was a cop who'd originally come here to prove we were a sex club. Though most of that distrust had disappeared, there was one thing my mama had taught me that I actually did stand by.

Never trust someone with all that you have.

It was good advice.

"For dancing? Yes. It'll cost you, though," I joked, not really willing to charge him for something I wanted to do for free.

But he took me seriously. "I don't care. Take my credit card and charge whatever you want. I just want to be alone with you."

I swallowed hard. Then stood up straight and offered him my hand.

He put his hand in mine, and our palms met, tingles shooting from the place we were joined. I pulled him up and led the way to the back of the club where we had several smaller rooms we saved for private dances.

All three were vacant, though they never stayed that way for long. I took the first one, my favorite, and led the way inside.

"Shut the door behind you." But then a thought popped into my head. "Unless you wanted more than one dancer? Some men like to pay for two."

He kicked the door shut and prowled across the room. "What do you think?" he growled.

I skittered out of the way, wagging a finger in his face. "Nope. Same rules apply in here. No touching, mister." I pointed to a couch set up with fluffy cushions. It sat atop a thick rug, and a lamp to one side let off a dim glow. It was staged to feel like an extravagant living room, designed to make patrons feel like they were at home, and that we danced only for them, and not for money.

There was a pole, though, in case we felt like putting on a show, or in case they requested one.

He eyed the pole as he passed but sank down onto the couch as instructed. These rooms were close to soundproof, and only the barest hint of the beat from the main rooms filtered through. I moved to the corner and hit 'play' on the small stereo we kept there for this purpose exactly.

A sexy beat started up, and I made my way back to Boston, standing in front of him.

His gaze was fire, filled with need, and I rubbed my thighs together, creating the tiniest amount of friction at my core.

"Dance for me, Eve. Just for me."

I closed my eyes, drowning in the possessive growl of his voice. And then I danced. Differently to how I would have out on the stage, differently even to how I danced when I was booked for a private room. Normally I just went through the motions. But the way I moved my body for Boston was a seduction. A striptease in its truest form. I wasn't just shaking my tits and ass, taking off clothes and throwing them around the room to give some random stranger a cheap thrill. The song was slow, and so I moved in the same way, pulling my hair off my neck, only to let it fall down my back. I trailed my fingers across my collarbone, noticing the way Boston followed my every movement with his lusty-eyed gaze. I traced a path between my breasts and then lower over my stomach and the tops of my thighs.

I twirled around, flicking my hair, then searching for his eyes once more.

He sat back against the couch, one arm along the

back, legs spread wide. His erection still tented his jeans, but he made no move to touch himself. Every inch of him was trained on me.

I trailed my fingers back up, hooking them into my bra and undoing it. In one quick movement I stepped up to him, leaning forward. "Take it off."

His breath hitched, but he shifted slightly and drew the straps down my arms, dropping the bra onto the floor at my feet. His gaze lowered, taking in my tits.

My nipples hardened for him, and I had the innate urge to touch myself. To squeeze the tips and roll them, knowing it would feed the sensation building inside me. That wasn't something I did as part of my job, though. So I refrained. I hadn't been lying when I said that this wasn't a sex club.

So I danced some more, trying to push the arousal away. I tried not to look at him, tried to think about all the other dances I'd done in this very room, the nameless, faceless men I didn't care one iota about.

It was impossible. Every time I spun around, Boston was there, watching me with worship in his eyes.

He wasn't like the others. I couldn't pretend he was.

I pushed my fingers into the top of my panties and slid them down my thighs, stepping out so all I wore were my heels.

We'd been here before, with me completely naked and him completely dressed. Last time, he'd been quick to look away and cover me up. This time he groaned audibly, his gaze unashamed in drinking me in. It lowered until it hit the junction of my thighs. I never got turned on while working. Normally I was as dry down there as the Sahara Desert. But tonight, my body had a mind of its own.

My pussy was coated in arousal.

I wanted him to know it.

I dropped down low on my heels, hands on knees, and pushed them wide. I let him see the effect dancing for him had on me.

I wasn't disappointed by his reaction.

His fingers clenched in the back of the couch, as if he were physically holding himself back from launching across the room and grabbing me.

I pushed my ass back and rolled my body up in a wave until I was standing in front of him once more.

The look on his face was everything I wanted it to be.

The man was in agony. Every inch of him stiff, holding himself in check. I leaned forward and put my hands on the back of the couch either side of him, moving my body up his. Normally when I did this, I kept a gap between me and the man. But not with Boston. I pressed my tits to his T-shirt and his hard chest beneath. Though it was against the rules, I ran my mouth ever so lightly up the side of his neck. It wasn't a kiss, more like a drag of flesh on flesh, but Boston's hips jerked up off the couch, unconsciously looking for a place to meet mine.

"You're making it really hard not to throw you down on this couch and fuck you, Eve."

I didn't say anything. Just kept dancing over the top of him, inhaling the scent of his cologne and letting the rasp of his stubble brush over my skin. Every movement designed to turn him on.

Except tonight, it wasn't just him feeling it. My core throbbed with the need to strip him naked and sink down on his thick, hot length. My nipples ached to be inside his mouth. Every ass shake, every grind over his body, every glance at his face and the need there had me wanting to touch myself.

Horny would have been the understatement of the century. The way he looked at me was everything. A sweet, delicious torture that made me wonder how long I could keep this up. Very soon, I was going to have to walk out of this room and go take a very cold shower before I could continue.

Our gazes connected, and this time, when his hand landed on my hip, I didn't stop him. His fingertips pressed into my flesh desperately, holding me to him, unwilling to let me go.

Not that I wanted him to.

The possessive hold urged me on, dancing for him, bouncing over his lap, simulating the sex I wanted desperately. A tiny moan slipped from my mouth, surprising me.

I'd never once moaned while dancing. But Boston's touch had me craving more of it. I couldn't stop thinking about the feel of his mouth at my core, and the orgasm he'd elicited from somewhere deep inside me. That same pressure built now, begging, and desperate for a repeat performance.

His palm traced the indent of my waist, and higher up my side until he stopped, fingers splayed open across my ribs, mere millimeters from my breast. He brought the other hand up to mirror the action, holding me still, until I looked down at him. I stared into beautiful eyes that made my heart thump unevenly.

"I want more."

So did I.

That moan of need escaped again, but that tiny seed of doubt in the back of my mind reared its ugly head. "I meant what I said," I whispered. "I don't have sex for money."

His thumb stroked the underside of my breast in a way that had me wanting to melt into a puddle. "I didn't offer any. I'll pay for the room. And for the dance. But anything else is just us."

His hand moved to cup my breast, and when I pushed into his touch, it was all the okay he needed. With lightning-fast moves, he pushed me down onto my back, the softness of the couch beneath me, and I surrendered to what my body so desperately wanted.

His mouth covered my nipple, hot and wet, and I ran my fingers through his hair as he sucked the tip of me, letting it drag between his teeth, increasing the friction. He took his time, rolling his tongue, flicking at my flesh, and alternating between breasts until I wrapped my legs around his waist, pulling him down on top of me, desperate for the pressure of his body on top of mine.

"You have too many clothes on," I protested, tugging at his shirt.

"And you have none." He fisted the back of his shirt and yanked it over his head. "Fuck, Eve. You're so beautiful like this. You shouldn't be allowed to cover up ever."

I smiled as his mouth lowered to hover over mine. "You'd have to arrest me again. Pretty sure they call that indecent exposure."

"That can be arranged." He pressed into the couch, knees straddled either side of me, and caught my wrists. He brought them together like he was going to arrest me.

"Did you bring your cuffs?" I was only half joking. I knew he hadn't, but if he had, I would have been happy for him to whip them out and put them on me. Being at Boston's mercy had new pulses of sensation tingling at my core.

"Next time."

Some inner kink that liked the idea of him dominating me lit up. And then squealed when he pinned my wrists above my head with one hand and brought his lips to mine.

I closed my eyes and soaked in the feel of his big body over mine. His mouth claimed me, the kiss soft at first, but quickly turning deep with strong, slow strokes of his tongue that reminded me of the way he'd gone down on me. My core gave a happy throb at the memory, and I lifted my hips to meet his, showing exactly what I wanted from him.

"Stay still," he whispered in my ear, the promise of so much more in his voice. "Wait."

I didn't want to. I wanted to shove his jeans down and have his thick cock inside my heat. But Boston wouldn't be rushed. He took his time, kissing me deep and slow, making my head spin, then alternating by sucking my nipples, building them into stiff peaks that loved his attention.

I fought to keep my hips still, but the need gathering inside me was maddening.

"Boston," I gasped, breathing erratic.

He inhaled deeply, sucking in my scent, and then pushed a hand between us. His fingers slid easily between my folds, gathering my arousal as he went, brushing by my clit that sent zings of pleasure throughout my entire body. His fingers found my entrance, and I moved my hips, taking two fingers deep inside.

The relief was near instant and yet quickly not enough. He worked in and out of my core, brushing that spot inside me every time, eliciting moans that became louder and louder as a climax built inside me. I writhed beneath him, taking his fingers, and needing more.

"Fuck, you're so tight. I want you on my dick, Eve."

"Yes!" It was more of a shout than a moan. A demand that he get his goddamn jeans off and fuck me 'til I lost control.

I so desperately needed to lose control.

He pulled out and brought one of my hands down to take over where he left off. I took up the job eagerly, rubbing my clit, while he got up, and undid his belt and jeans. His gaze continued to sweep my body while he took out his wallet.

I froze. "What are you doing?"

He opened his wallet, but instead of getting out cash or a credit card, he produced a condom.

He read the look on my face correctly and leaned down, cupping my face with one hand. "Hey. Relax. Fuck, Eve, I'm not here as a cop. And even if I were, we aren't doing anything wrong. I'm not paying you for sex. I don't think you're anything more than what you say you are. And even if you were, I wouldn't care." His gaze burned into mine. "I just fucking want you, okay?"

I relaxed, body sinking back into the couch as he kissed me. "I want you, too."

He stood, toeing off his Converse, and then shoved his jeans and boxer briefs down over his ass and thighs. My fingers moved between my legs, prolonging the arousal he'd built, keeping me on the edge of orgasm but not quite falling into it.

The anticipation was heaven.

And getting myself off while staring at Boston's naked body was the ultimate turn-on. I'd thought about him while masturbating before. But having him here in person, taking in the chiseled cut of his abs, and the lines that ran either side of his hips was better than anything I could have ever imagined.

His dick was huge and thick, and the tip glistened with the effects of teasing him for the past hour.

All I could think about was getting him inside me. Sinking down and feeling that stretch and the touch of him in places that drove me wild.

I got off the couch and wound myself around him, both of us naked, skin to skin.

Every inch of me lit up like Christmas. I'd never had such a full-body craving for a man. It wasn't just my pussy that wanted him near. Every nerve ending in my entire body called out for him, aching with need and determined to find it's pleasure by pressing tight against him.

His mouth landed on my neck, sucking his way up toward my ear, and I surrendered to it, not caring if he was leaving hickeys in his wake, because the sensation had me so wet I could barely stand it.

"Sit." I pushed him toward the couch, taking back ownership of the show.

He sank down onto the couch, his impressive erection jutting out from between his hips. I plucked the condom from his fingertips, ripped it open, and tossed the package on the floor.

I was no stranger to condoms by this point in my thirties, and always careful, so I rolled it down his length with one hand while I closed my eyes and touched my lips to his once more.

Our tongues met, hot and insistent, while I gripped the base of his shaft and straddled him, lining him up with my entrance.

His palm flattened on my chest, then dragged upward, until he had one hand around my throat, his thumb and forefinger locked around my jaw. He tilted my face to one side so he could growl in my ear. "Ride me."

His other hand squeezed my ass, and fuck if that wasn't all the encouragement I needed to sink straight down on his cock.

There was no controlling the shout of ecstasy and relief that shattered from somewhere deep inside me. It drowned out the soft music floating around us. Hell, my moan was so loud I was sure they'd heard it out in the main room, even above Lucinda's beats.

Boston's cock stretched me wide, but in the most delicious way, my body more than ready and willing to take him in one hard, fast thrust. I threw my head back, lifting my hips, while his surged up to meet them again, and again.

"You're the most beautiful woman I've ever seen," he murmured, his lips seeking mine, his tongue plundering my mouth.

I believed him. His gaze worshipped my body, in the same way his dick, and his fingers, and his tongue did. All of it working together until I was on the verge of orgasm and desperate for it. I rocked my hips over his, feeling every inch the goddess he told me I was. I'd never needed a man for confidence, I owned that myself. But Boston's groan of arousal and words of lust drove me on, getting me to the edge fast and hard and dirty.

I didn't need to tell him what to do. He gripped my hip with one hand, helping to guide my rise and fall, the other finding my clit. We kissed until my moans became jagged pants of need and my movements over his cock turned erratic.

His groans from beneath told me he was close, too.

I rode him harder and faster until I couldn't stand it a moment longer. The first wave of my orgasm swelled and burst against the banks. "Oh God, Boston!" I screamed, ripping away from his mouth and throwing my head back.

His mouth landed on my nipple, and I screamed out in ecstasy again as he sucked me hard, nothing gentle in the way we fucked. We were all tight clutches, nails pressing in, grabbing each other like we couldn't get enough. I lost myself, forgetting the rhythm we'd built amongst the pleasure rocketing through me.

And yet, Boston didn't let up. He took the control, slamming his hips upward to meet mine, while I pulsed and came hard around his dick.

"Fuck!" he yelled with one last thrust. He pressed his face into my chest while he came, his shouts of pleasure muffled by my skin now dampened with a fine coat of sweat.

I held him tight, riding him out, until he was begging for mercy. I gave one last slide and grind on top of him, just to torture him.

He smiled up at me, completely blissed out.

A warm feeling lit up around my heart. Shit. Fawn and Augie were right. I really did like the guy.

With a laugh, he reversed our positions, pushing me back against the plush couch. "Stay there. Do not get dressed."

I raised an eyebrow and glanced down at his dick while he pulled off the condom, tying a knot around one end. "While I admit your cock is very impressive, I don't think even you can get hard again right now."

He tossed the condom in a trash can near the small bar in the corner of the room, then strutted back to me, gloriously naked. I couldn't take my eyes off him. It was like his body had been made for mine. Every inch of him deliciously appealing. My pussy gave a slight throb, pleased with the mind-blowing orgasm but already eager for as much of Boston as she could get.

He kissed me softly. "I'm not even close to done with you, Eve. My dick will catch up. But until then, my tongue wants in on the game. Lie back and open your legs."

With Boston's face between my thighs, I lay back and let him rock my world, over and over again, neither of us coming up for air until well after the club had closed.

22

EVE

The ringing of a phone broke through the darkness. I woke slowly, disoriented for a moment. There was no light peeping in the corners of my blinds, no cat demanding food. There was, however, a heavy arm that tightened beneath my naked breasts when I tried to move. And the most pleasant tingling between my legs that reminded me I'd spent the entire night at the club, having multiple orgasms at the hands of a man who knew how to play my body like a freaking fiddle by the end of it.

I shifted, feeling the delicious ache in every inch of my body, and the leftover arousal still slick at my core. There was no shower in this room, but neither of us had wanted to leave. Somewhere between the second and seventh orgasm, this room had become our own private love nest. I hadn't meant to spend the night here, but obviously we'd passed out at some point, probably from lack of blood to the brain. It had all well and truly congregated in pleasure zones.

"Where you going?" Boston mumbled from behind me, voice still thick with sleep. His bigger body fit perfectly around me on the couch that was too small for us. Yet I'd somehow slept more soundly than I had in years. Maybe it was pure exhaustion after coming so hard.

Or maybe it was the sense of security sleeping in Boston's arms gave me.

"Phone is ringing." I tried to extricate myself from the mess of limbs, but he threw a leg over me, clamping down and nuzzling in even closer. His morning erection prodded against my ass in a way that promised a good time.

"Leave it. I'll make it worth your while."

I twisted in his arms and grinned at him. "I don't think I can handle any more of that just yet. I don't even know if I can walk straight."

"Good," he murmured against my lips. "Then everyone will know what we spent all night doing."

I pushed at his chest. "You like the idea of everyone knowing?"

"Fuck, yes," he growled. "I want everyone knowing you're my girl."

I stilled in his arms.

When I didn't say anything, he finally opened his eyes. "What? Is it my morning breath?"

His morning breath actually wasn't bad at all. "I'm your girl?"

A tiny hint of a blush pinkened his cheeks, and it was all sorts of adorable. He lifted up on one elbow and stared down at me. "I want you to be. So I guess it depends on you."

His gaze was so intensely vulnerable that it broke my stony heart wide open. "You're not embarrassed I'm a stripper?"

His eyebrows knit together. "Are you embarrassed I'm a cop?"

"Of course not. But you're an upstanding citizen. I get arrested on a semi regular basis, and to be honest, I can't promise that'll stop. I don't know if you've noticed, but I'm not very good at playing by the rules. I'm not sure your friends on the force are going to like you dating me."

"Who I date is none of their business. And believe me when I say that being a cop doesn't make you a good person."

"Being a stripper doesn't make you one either."

"Maybe not, but you are, Eve. Don't think I haven't noticed what you're doing here. Running this club and your employees like you're some mother hen, and feeding half the neighborhood. You throw this badass image out to the world with your sassy mouth and give-no-fucks attitude, but I think you're a bit of bleeding heart on the inside. You even gave William Reed's kid a place to come if he needs help. The poor kid probably does, with parents like his."

It took me a second to remember the business card I'd slipped into Dylan Reed's hand. "He told you about that?"

"I noticed it on his desk when I was doing a sweep of their house the other day and asked him about it. The whole thing came tumbling out."

The phone started ringing again from deep within the silent club. "I should get that."

"Not until you answer my question. You gonna be my girl, Evil?"

I couldn't help the grin that spread across my face. I leaned in and kissed him hard. "Yeah, Joshua. I am."

He rolled onto his back and fist pumped the air in victory as I got off the couch and strutted to the door completely buck-ass naked.

"There better be no one out there," he growled.

I winked at him over my shoulder, knowing full well the club would be completely empty at this time of day. My staff knew what they were doing. They would have closed up hours ago. I moved through the main room, noting the sticky floors beneath my feet and making a mental note to mop them after I went home and had a shower. But the phone rang incessantly, and I picked up the pace, hurrying until I was almost running to my office. I grabbed a blanket from the back of the couch and wrapped it around myself before I slid behind the desk and picked up the phone.

An unintelligible babble of words blasted through the speaker, so loud and fast that not only did I not understand a word of it, I held the phone well away from my ear to avoid going deaf. "Mama!" I shouted. I tried bringing the phone back to my ear, only for her to start yelling again.

"I am so embarrassed of you, Eve! How could you do this to me? A penis party?"

I sighed, rolling my eyes, annoyed I'd gotten out of bed with Boston for this. As usual I was a disappointment to my mother. What was new?

"William is a good man! An upstanding member of the community, and you just humiliated him! You stuck penises on the man's face and broadcast it all over the internet! You've brought shame on this family yet again."

All the good feelings Boston had extracted from my body in the past twenty-four hours disappeared into a storm of annoyance. I was so sick of this shit. This was all our conversations boiled down to now. How I was the black sheep. Never the good child. I always did the wrong thing.

"I get it, Mama. You're ashamed of me. But you know what? I can't help that anymore. I can't bring myself to care."

"You will care. You'll show me the respect I deserve as your parent. This isn't how I raised you."

My blood boiled over. "What about the respect I deserve? I'm a grown woman. I'm not a little girl anymore. You're not my superior. Maybe you don't like what I do for a living, but I run a highly successful business. I'm smart, and I'm talented. I know my own worth, and I don't need you trying to bring me down. What I do, or who I stick penises to, is none of your business."

Mama spluttered into the phone, and I could just imagine her pacing up and down her tiny living room. My father argued in the background, but nothing would stop my mother when she was on a rant. And her favorite thing to rant about was me, and how I'd failed at being her only daughter.

Her voice grew high and screechy. "It is my business when you're slandering the name of a good man!"

I threw my hands up in the air. "Who gives a fuck about William Reed? That upstanding man you hero-worship? He tried to have me killed, Mama. How do you feel about him now?"

There was a stunned silence on the other end, but it only lasted a moment. "I don't believe that."

"Believe it. He had a gang member drive past my club and spray it with bullets."

Mama gasped.

There was only the tiniest sense of satisfaction from it. "Now am I getting through to you—"

"No," she yelled. "No! He would never do that, Eve. You're his —"

"I'm his what?" His enemy? That was the only thing I was to William Reed.

My mother's voice went quiet. "Nothing. Never mind."

But I wasn't ready to give up the fight that easy. She'd started it. I was going to end it. "No, what were you going to say? Tell me exactly what I am to William Reed, since you seem to know him so well, Mama. What am I? The thorn in his side? Good. I hope I am."

My father huffed from the background. "You're his daughter."

I froze.

My mother let out a howl and a string of curse words I'd never heard her utter in my entire thirty years. She cussed my father out like a drunken sailor, screaming at him, the slaps of her palm against his skin echoing down the line.

But one by one, amongst the chaos, the pieces fit together. The reason my father had never really paid any attention to me. The reason I didn't look anything like my brothers. The way my mother hero-worshipped a man the rest of this community couldn't stand. "Is that true?" I asked, already knowing what her answer would be.

"Eve..."

"No, Mama! Is it true?"

A sob broke down the line. "I signed a contract never to tell you."

My head spun.

A quiet cough came from the doorway. "Eve."

My head snapped up, gaze clashing with Boston's. He frowned, taking in my appearance, which was likely white as a ghost. He passed me his T-shirt. "There's a swarm of protesters outside, and they're none too happy about the party last night. It's already making the mainstream media."

"What?" I put the landline phone down on my desk, not caring that my mother was probably still blathering away into it. I didn't want to hear anything she had to say anyway. Everything that came out of the woman's mouth was a lie, a deception, or an accusation.

I was done with her. I was done with everything.

I pulled aside the curtain to see the size of the crowd building on the sidewalk outside. I swallowed hard at the sheer number of them, with more coming in both directions. I'd been so focused on my mother, I hadn't even heard them.

Boston's mouth was set into a hard line. "I don't like that we're the only ones here. We're unprotected if they break in. I've called my partner in for backup, but I want to get you out of here now, before they get any more riled up."

I nodded, my chest tight. I already felt like a canned sardine, claustrophobic with the walls caving in on me. The angry faces of William supporters—my father's supporters—lit up in earnest when they saw me at the window. Their yells and chants grew louder, and a rock bounced off the shutter.

I dropped the curtain and picked the phone up, hitting the red cancel button and cutting my mother off completely.

From somewhere outside came the smash of glass breaking. I turned to Boston, feeling more naked and vulnerable than I ever had in this club. My heart pounded against my rib cage, and I wished it were only the protesters outside making me feel that way. The man I'd always known as my father had thrown me under the bus, knowing full well it would send me into a tailspin. He'd done it carelessly, no thought to my feelings. We'd never been close, but it hurt nonetheless. I couldn't even begin to process the revelation of my biological father.

It was all too much.

I went to Boston's side, and silently, without questions, he wrapped me in his arms. Again, I felt his strength and realized how right I felt when we were together. Nobody else did that for me. Nobody else had ever made me feel like their touch was all I needed to get through the worst thing that had ever happened to me.

"We're gonna get out of here, okay?" he mumbled into my hair. "And then we can talk about whatever's going on, or not. Whatever you want. But first we have to leave, we can't be here alone."

I nodded, letting him comfort me. I let him take control. I dropped all my guards, and for the first time in my life, I let a man in.

23

BOSTON

I hustled Eve out the club's back door and into my car before William Reed's groupies out the front could realize we were leaving. I put my foot down, not caring that the back end of the car slid out as I took the turn too quickly with a screech of tires. In the rearview mirror, a few ran after the car, and all I could do was shake my head. Unbelievable. Didn't these people have anything better to do? Richards would move them on quickly once he arrived with backup, but I was annoyed he'd have to bother at all.

Away from the chaos, my focus turned to the silent woman beside me. The color had completely drained from her face, but it had little to do with the mob of protesters. Something on that phone call had rocked her to her very core. I'd never seen Eve without a quick retort, full of fire and passion. But right now, she was completely broken. Small in an oversized hoodie, huddled into the seat.

I didn't try to make her talk. I just drove her on

autopilot back to my place, something deep inside me needing to take care of her. Protect her. She still hadn't said a word when we pulled into my driveway, and I gently let her inside.

I tossed an empty pizza box in the trash as we passed through the kitchen. "Sorry about the mess. I wasn't really expecting to have you here, or I would have cleaned up a bit."

She tried smiling at me, but it didn't reach eyes. "It's fine. It's really not messy at all."

I guided her toward the stairs, and at the top we took a left into the main bathroom. Without even asking, I turned the water on, steaming up the small space quickly with a hot shower.

Eve just watched me, her big brown eyes glistening. Her sadness wrapped around my heart and squeezed. I just wanted to make her feel better. A shower probably wouldn't help much, but until I knew more, it was all I could do. When the water was the perfect temperature, I turned to Eve and gently tugged her out of her clothes. But unlike last night, there was nothing sexual about it. She lifted her arms limply, letting me take off the hoodie. She wore nothing beneath it, and it was a quick job to remove the sweatpants tied tightly around her hips. Her body was just as amazing as it had been a few hours ago, but instead of drinking her in the way that I had then, now my gaze was fixed firmly to her face, my worry overshadowing my attraction to her.

But still, she didn't offer up an explanation.

I put her in the shower, making no attempt to get in with her, and closed the curtain. "There's shampoo and conditioner on the shelf if you want it. I'm going to get you some towels and clothes. I'll leave them on the basin for you."

I paused in the doorway, not wanting to leave, but also wanting to give her the space I thought she needed. When her tiny voice came back with a simple, "Thank you," I knew I'd made the right decision.

I took a quick shower in my en suite, barely long enough to wash off the evidence of everything we'd gotten up to last night before stepping out and pulling on a pair of sweatpants. Then I perched nervously on the edge of the bed, listening to the water fall from the main bathroom. The second the water turned off, I jumped up and paced the hallway, waiting for her to reappear.

When she finally did, she was wearing my clothes, her hair wet and finger-combed, not an ounce of makeup on.

And once again, I was punched in the gut with how stunningly beautiful she was. It didn't matter what she wore, whether she had a full face of makeup or her skin scrubbed clean, Eve Hawkins would never be anything but the woman of my dreams. I wrapped her in my arms once more, and she rested her head against my chest, returning the embrace.

"I'm worried about you," I confessed.

"I know. I'm sorry."

I led her into my bedroom and sat her down on the bed. I sat beside her, threading my fingers between hers. "What happened? Is everything okay? Nobody..."

"Died? No. Everybody is fine. My mother just dropped a bomb on me, that's all. Actually, it was my father. Or... The man I thought was my father."

"What do you mean?"

"Apparently he's not actually my father. But guess who is?"

She didn't give me time to respond.

"William Reed."

I stared at her. "What the fuck?"

She laughed bitterly. "That was my response, too."

"Is that even possible? Is this just some fight your parents are having? Maybe they're just throwing around accusations, trying to hurt each other, and you got caught in the crossfire."

Eve shook her head slowly, her wet hair settling over her shoulders. "I think it's true. My mother can't lie to save a life. I could hear it in her voice. She was more concerned with yelling at my father for telling me, then trying to deny it. I can't even imagine how she would have met William, though? They don't exactly run in the same circles."

"That's probably a story she'll have to tell you. Or he will."

"I doubt he's gonna tell me anything. The man wanted his own daughter dead. Nice!" Her laugh was bitter.

"We still don't know for sure that it was him who organized the drive-by."

"Don't we? Seems even more obvious to me now. I'm a great dirty pimple in his past. All it would take is one inquisitive journalist to dig deep and find out about me and blow his whole campaign out of the water. Maybe he decided running me out of town was the easier option. And maybe the drive-by was more about scaring me. But that just goes to show my own father doesn't know me at all." She rubbed her knuckles across her chest, like she was trying to erase an ache. "Honestly. I'm never having kids. Every parental figure in my life has let me down in one way or another."

There was anger in her tone, but I heard the hurt behind it. Somewhere deep inside her tough bravado was a vulnerable side who had been disappointed over and over again.

Suddenly she let out a laugh that didn't sound strained or fake. She stood and crossed the room, picking something up from the top of my chest of drawers. She spun around with an amused grin, the massive purple dildo with my name on the side clutched in her fingers. "What's this doing here?"

I chuckled. "It was a gift from this crazy girl I arrested."

"I can't believe you kept it. I thought for sure it would have gone straight in the trash."

"It has my name on it. That would have been kind of rude after you went to the trouble of getting it personalized."

She buried her face in her hands. "I really am sorry. That was all Lyric and Fawn." She gave the dildo an experimental wobble. "So, what's it been doing here all this time? Have you used it?" A wicked glint sparkled in her eye, and relief flooded in. The Eve I knew seemed to be bouncing back.

"I haven't been with anyone since I met you."

"Dildos aren't just for women, you know? Perhaps you..."

I realized what she was talking about. "Really?"

She giggled. "Don't pretend like you don't know that some guys love that."

I crossed the room and took it from her hand. "There is something I've been thinking about doing with it."

She looked up, curiosity written all over her face.

I pressed the dildo between her legs. She was still fully clothed, but the gasp she let out made my dick hard. "I kinda want to fuck you with it, Eve."

Her whole body trembled. A head-to-toe shiver, complete with lust lighting up her eyes.

I groaned. "You want that, don't you?"

"God, yes. I started thinking about it the minute I saw that dildo with your name on it."

I pulled her tight, pressing my forehead to hers. "Could you be any more perfect?"

"You don't even know all my secrets yet. So yeah. Maybe I can be. Take my clothes off, I'll show you."

She didn't need to tell me twice. A part of me knew she was using sex as a distraction from what had happened at the club earlier, but I was more than willing to be that for her. She was my girl now, and I was going to do everything in my power to make sure she was happy. If I could take away the last lingering signs of pain by distracting her with orgasms, then I was ready to take up the challenge.

Her clothes were lost in the blink of an eye, and then I was laying her out on my bed. She was almost too stunning to be real, and I went straight for the core of her, spreading her legs wide and plunging my tongue inside her wicked heat.

I'd worked this out last night. I'd tasted her, drowned in her arousal, and brought her to orgasm more times than I could remember. I loved the way her fingers speared into my hair, holding me tight to her pussy, while she ground against my face, completely unashamed about taking her pleasure. My tongue plunged in and out, but I resisted the urge to press my fingers inside her. She palmed her own tits, squeezing her nipples, writhing while I worked her up. When I moved away, she groaned in frustration.

"Don't stop," she panted.

I just chuckled. I loved how eager she was. How she'd been just as needy and desperate for me as I was for her. The phone call with her mother, nor the protesters, had dampened her need for me. And I fully intended to have her screaming my name.

I opened my bedside drawer, pulling out a tube of lubricant. I squeezed a generous amount onto the tip of the dildo, smoothing it down the ridged surface while Eve watched me with her eyes at half-mast. She was already so wet, but I wanted to be doubly sure she could take it. The dildo really was big.

I ran it between her folds, teasing it over her clit and nudging it around her entrance.

"Boston," she groaned. "Quick teasing me and fuck me already."

"God, I love it when you talk like that." I slid the dildo up inside her, watching her cunt stretch to accommodate it.

The moans that echoed around my bedroom found their way straight to my dick, and it was an effort not to come just from watching her. I circled her clit with my thumb, while I thrust the dildo in and out of her.

"More," she moaned. "I need you."

I was still wearing my sweatpants, precum glistening

on the inside. I undid the drawstring and dragged them off, grateful to be free of their restraints.

She took over working the dildo, and when I knelt between her legs, I lifted them over my shoulders, giving me access to every inch of her. My dick eagerly sought her entrance but was forced lower because of the sex toy. I prodded gently against her ass, patiently waiting my turn until she'd had her fill.

Her eyes rolled back, and her eyelids fluttered closed. "Oh God, there."

I was still pressing against her ass.

I almost came at the thought of taking her there, especially with the dildo in her pussy which she was loving. I had to be sure that's what she meant, though. She was so lost to sensation, I wasn't even sure she was completely with me. I slicked my finger with lube and touched it to the puckered star of her asshole. "Here? Tell me where you want it."

"There," she moaned. "Oh God, please, there. I need more."

I groaned hard at the permission. "Have you done that before? I need to know how slow to go with you."

"I'm no virgin, Boston. Not in any way."

Fuck, that was hot. And thank God, because it meant I didn't have to go quite as gently as I would have if she'd never done it before. I took my time, letting her ride the dildo, while I worked beneath it. Her legs trembled around my shoulders, her heels digging into my back as she writhed at my touch. Only when I was one-hundred-percent sure she was ready did I remove the dildo and pressed my dick inside her ass. She was the tightest sort of heaven, but I forced myself to go slowly, inch by inch until I was fully seated inside her.

Through her moans she guided the dildo back and pushed it up inside herself, filling her pussy, too.

I hissed through my teeth and fisted my fingers in the sheets to keep from coming. I'd never felt anything like it, and I was sure I was about to pass out from the sensation. I couldn't move. One thrust and it would all be over.

But that was all Eve seem to need. With her full of me from one angle, and full of the dildo from another, she pumped herself a few times, then fell over the edge, into the abyss of her orgasm, screaming all the way down. She yelled my name, grinding up and down on my dick, the dildo along for the ride.

I held on until I was sure I'd driven out every inch of pleasure, then I allowed myself to fall over the edge, too. I thrust in and out of her, finally able to move now that I knew she was taken care of, until I couldn't take any more. I came hard, moaning out my pleasure against her soft skin.

The dildo slipped from her pussy, my dick from her ass, and I gathered her to me, laying us both down and spooning behind her.

"That was…" I didn't have any words. That had just blown every sexual experience of my entire life, and every porno I'd ever watched, right out of the water.

"I told you I had surprises."

I kissed her hair. "I didn't see that one coming."

"I saw you coming, though." She grinned up at me.

I lay exhausted on the bed, unable to move. "You nearly killed me. I'm not even joking."

She twisted around to kiss me. "Stick with me, Mr. Vanilla. I'll show you all the things."

I didn't even care she was teasing me. I was more than willing to let Eve Hawkins show me anything she damn well pleased.

24

EVE

I was still chuckling over Boston's mind-blown expression when he came out of the shower for the second time, hair slick with water and a white towel tight around his narrow hips. The laughter died on my lips as I rolled my gaze over his perfect body again. "I'm never going to get sick of looking at you naked," I admitted to him. "Just so you know."

He put one knee on the bed where I still lay and kissed my mouth. "Good. Because right back at ya." His kiss lowered to my neck and then landed on my bare breast. "You're making it really hard to go to work today."

I pouted, enjoying the way he sucked my nipple. Despite the fact we'd basically been having sex for the past fourteen or something hours, every time he touched me, my body lit right up for him again. "You people who work while the sun is up are no fun. If you stayed home, I could show you all the other secrets I have..."

"I'll quit today."

I laughed. "No you won't. You love your job."

He drew away from my breasts and shrugged. "Not so sure I do, to be honest."

I frowned. "You do. It's just tough right now after Jayela's murder…"

He nodded stiffly. "It's more than that, though." He forced a smile. "But nothing worth getting into right now when you're naked in my bed. What time are you working tonight?"

"No work. It's family night at the club."

He put on his boxer briefs, and I pouted as his completely perfect cock disappeared inside them. Even more devastating was watching him pull his uniform on, his abs disappearing one by one beneath the buttons.

"Stay here until then? I like knowing you're in my bed naked, even when I'm not home. I'll go down to the club and make sure the protestors have all moved on, but until then, stay. Sleep."

Boston's bed was heavenly comfortable, and sleep was already calling me. I had no desire to leave, and my car wasn't here anyway. "Deal. Meet you at the club later?"

He stopped in the doorway. "For family night? Isn't that a sacred place? You really want me to come?"

He looked so pleased with the notion that I pushed up off the bed and crossed the space between us, wrapping my naked body around his fully clothed one. "Everybody who is important to me is welcome."

"I'm important, huh?"

"Yeah, Joshua. You are."

He claimed my mouth in a searing kiss, grasping my chin and holding me there while he branded me. "Get back into bed. Sleep. I'll see you later." He eyed the dildo we'd left discarded on the sheets. "Don't have too much fun without me." He winked as he walked out of his room.

Cocky. Maybe I'd sleep for a little while, and then Little Boston and I could make a new video for Big Boston. I tucked myself back into the sheets and crashed out with a happy and sated smile on my face.

---

*H*ours later, after sleeping most of the day away, I stepped into the shower off Boston's bedroom and let the water cascade down over me. Every inch of my body was deliciously sore from a night of continual sex, and I was quietly glad the club wasn't open tonight. I wasn't sure I was up for dancing. More sex, perhaps, but grinding up and down a pole while my pussy was still in the after effects of so many orgasms was a recipe for disaster.

My phone was ringing when I stepped out from beneath the spray, Fawn's smiling face flashing on the screen.

"Hey, sweet thing." I put the phone on speaker so I had both hands free to get dressed. "What's up?"

"Everything," she wailed.

"Dramatic much?"

"No! I swear, I'm not. I can't do this. This course is too hard, and I'm just not smart enough for it. Everybody else in my class picks it up the minute the teacher explains it, but I've been reading over this textbook for three hours now and I still don't get it. I'm going to fail and let you down, and waste your money and then I'll have to leave the club because I've disappointed you and—"

"Whoa, whoa. Slow down. Nobody is failing anything or letting anyone down. Take a deep breath. You're struggling with your homework?"

"It's a payroll module, and there's all this stuff about taxes, and I swear, Eve. I've tried to understand it myself, but it's like trying to read Spanish, which I never learned!"

I nodded to myself, pulling on Boston's hoodie and smiling at the fact it smelled exactly like him. "I remember from when I did the course. And I do that stuff all the time when I'm doing payroll at the club. It sucks. It's why I wanted you to do the course so I could hand it all off to you." I chuckled. I didn't mention that Fawn was like the child I was never going to have, and I just wanted to help her better herself in any way possible. Education was important, a fact I'd only realized well after I'd ditched school in favor of stripping. Fawn was smart, but nobody had ever told her that growing up. The woman had no confidence. I believed in her, and this course was not above her capabilities, as long as she got out of her own head. "Listen, I'm at Boston's place—"

She squealed. "You are? Tell me every detail!"

"Nope, not a chance. I'll come over and help you with your homework, and for every question you get right, I'll tell you about one sexual thing we did."

"There's thirty questions."

"Not gonna be a problem."

Fawn burst into laughter. "You Slutty McSlutterson."

"Yeah, yeah. I love you, too. I've gotta get off the phone so I can call an Uber. See you soon."

I hit the 'cancel call' button, then quickly ordered my ride. Downstairs, I found my shoes and purse and a piece of paper. Not wanting to rifle through Boston's kitchen drawers, I fished a pen from my bag and scrawled a note for Boston, telling him I'd had something come up and I'd meet him at the club later.

The Uber arrived quickly, and as we drove through the streets of Saint View, I frowned at the burgeoning darkness. Everyone at the club was used to sleeping for most of the day and eating late, but I was going to have to get a move on if I was going to have food ready for everyone. I probably should have told Fawn I couldn't help her tonight, but I knew what she was like. The longer she stewed over something, the more she'd convince herself she couldn't do it, and then I'd just have a bigger battle when we finally did sit down together to work it out.

No, it was better to just tackle it now, then zoom over to the club and throw together something quick and easy. At least the refrigerator was already full and just waiting for someone to put together a feast.

The Uber dropped me off at the familiar address. It was the very first place I'd bought for myself with my own money after I'd started working. It wasn't anything flashy, and it wasn't on the greatest of streets, but I'd put a bit of money into doing the little cottage-style house up, repairing broken steps and painting the walls a sunny yellow, that actually suited Fawn better than it had ever suited me. I'd bought a bigger, nicer place, still in Saint View but closer to the Providence border when my finances had allowed. This cottage had sat unused until Fawn had come along looking for a place to live. Her rent didn't cover my mortgage, but I didn't care. For Fawn, I was happy to make up the difference myself.

The doors flung open before I even got a foot up the steps.

"Oh, thank God." Fawn reached an arm through the opening and yanked me inside. "I'm ready to throw this stupid thing through the window."

"Let's do it quick then, before any glass gets shattered. Your rent does not cover window repair."

The two of us sat in the dim light of her little kitchen, the table beneath her textbooks covered by a smiley face emoji tablecloth that was just so typically Fawn. She pushed the first book toward me.

I peered at it. "Okay, I remember this. If you get the tax rate from this column..."

I droned on for a little bit, working through the first question with her, and then the second to make sure she really understood what we were doing. The sun outside grew lower and lower with every passing minute, and soon we were in near darkness. "You keep going, I'm getting the light."

Now that Fawn understood the concept, she worked diligently, her tongue sticking out the corner of her mouth while she wrote figures onto a legal pad in precise handwriting.

A flash of pride rolled over me. She really did have this. She just needed somebody to remind her from time to time. Somebody who believed in her.

I flicked the light switch on, but nothing happened. I peered up at the naked bulb. "Is this light blown? Have you got more lightbulbs?"

Fawn darted a look over her shoulder. "Might be the circuit breaker. I only replaced the bulb in that one just the other day. Should be fine."

I walked into the living room and tried the switch in there. Nothing happened either. "I'm going downstairs to check the breaker. You keep going."

"I can go."

I waved away her protests. "I used to live in this house, remember? I know how it plays up sometimes. I'll be back in a minute. I want you up to question ten by the time I get back."

She threw me a mock salute. "Aye, aye, Captain."

I ran down the stairs to the basement, flicking open the flashlight on my phone to look at the fuses. I'd had to change them many a time. They blew regularly, being that the house was old and had stood unloved for a long time before I'd purchased it. But everything appeared intact right now.

My phone buzzed in my hand halfway back up the steps. I paused, leaning against the railing to check the message.

AUGIE

Just got to the club. It's not pretty. There was more hate mail shoved under the door. I'd tell you what it says, but you're a lady, and there's some things ladies shouldn't read.

EVE

No need, I can imagine. I heard the things Reed's supporters were yelling when Boston and I left the club this morning. Just put it all in my office. Boston might want it for evidence or something.

AUGIE

You got it, boss. See you soon.

I tucked my phone away in my pocket. For people who claimed to be good Christians, there wasn't much holy or giving about the way this group treated me and my family. My blood boiled thinking about it. I had an urge to find them and scream in their faces that I was William Reed's daughter, illegitimate at that. Imagine the scandal.

Perhaps, if I hadn't been a better woman than they were, I would have done it. But I didn't want to be associated with William Reed any more than he wanted to be associated with me, so the lot of them could go to Hell.

I stomped back up the stairs, irritation stiffening my limbs. "I think the power might be out on the street," I called to Fawn. "I'm just gonna go outside and check."

Fawn nodded absently, but she didn't look up from the problems she was working through. "Check on Mrs. Soros next door, too, if the power is out. I don't want her falling and breaking her hip again if she's wandering around in the darkness."

I cringed at the thought of my old neighbor laid up in a hospital bed. The woman had to be nearing ninety. "On it."

I opened the front door and walked out onto the driveway to peer over at Mrs. Soros's place, expecting her house to be as dark as Fawn's. But bright lights shone through her living room window, and I could see her propped up in her favorite recliner, probably watching *Wheel of Fortune.* Different colors from the reflection of the TV danced across her weathered face.

Across the road, light spilled around curtains, and farther down the streetlamp flickered annoyingly, like it had ever since I'd bought the place.

I frowned. "Guess it's just us then."

I turned around to go back inside. "Fawn! We might have to call an electrician. Everybody else has—"

A heavy arm clamped around my neck from behind.

The panic was immediate. I tried to scream, but it came out silently, no oxygen to fuel it. I thrashed against the muscled arms that bound my own, holding me tight to his chest. But the choke hold worked fast, and within seconds, darkness danced at the edges of my vision.

The last thing I thought before I went under was that William Reed was never going to stop until I was out of the picture completely.

25

EVE

Faces haunted my dreams. Boston's. Fawn's. William's. But there were other's as well. Shadowed, expressionless profiles I didn't recognize. They swirled menacingly through the darkness, sudden flashes lighting them up, only for them to sink back into the blackness they'd emerged from. I squeezed my eyes tight, trying to block all except Boston's. I held on to his image until it disintegrated into a million tiny pieces that I couldn't gather quick enough to save.

"Hello?"

The voice sounded far away, and I squeezed my eyes tighter again, searching the darkness for my safe place. When that had become Boston, I didn't know. I just knew I needed to get to him. With him by my side, the darkness would go away.

I so desperately wanted the darkness to go away.

"Is somebody there?"

The voice was closer this time, and something about it familiar. I forced my eyes open, fighting against the pull that tried to keep them closed. But the darkness was just as deep and thick with my eyes open, as it had been with them shut. The only difference was that with my eyes open, pain rushed in. A burning ache in my throat that worsened when I tried to swallow. A pounding at my temples that rivaled even the worst migraines I'd ever had. And a dull throb in my arm.

Quietly, I probed the ache with my fingers and winced at the tenderness there. It reminded me of the years my brothers and I had pounded the crap out of each other. A good knuckle right to the fleshy part of a bicep gave off a similar ache, but my fingers glanced over a puncture mark, and my foggy brain concluded I'd been jabbed with something.

Everything came rushing back. Going outside to check the lights. An arm around my neck and feeling like I was suffocating.

"Fawn," I choked out. Oh Jesus. She'd been in the house.

"Eve? Oh my God, where are you?"

There was a scrabbling sound from the corner of the room, and I held my arms out wide in either direction, feeling around in the darkness until my fingertips made contact with her clammy skin.

She immediately burst into a sob, and I pulled her close, wrapping my aching arm around her hunched shoulders. "Shh, it's okay. I got you." It was the automatic instinct I'd always had around her. Comfort and protect. On the outside, I assured Fawn that everything was going to be okay. Inside, I was a mess of panic and wishing somebody would hold me the way I held her.

Not somebody.

Boston.

My heart cracked open with the force of wanting him. A panicked sob of need and burgeoning hysteria clawed its way up my throat, and I swallowed painfully, trying to shove it down. Fawn's shoulders shook while she cried, and we both couldn't fall apart.

It was on me to hold it together. "What happened?"

I felt more than saw her shake her head. "I don't know. I was working on my assignment, and I heard footsteps behind me, but I just assumed it was you. Then there was an arm around my throat, and the next thing I know, I've woken up here."

"Same thing happened to me, but outside.

"I'm so sorry, Eve. I'm so, so sorry. This is all my fault."

"How could it possibly be your fault?"

A fresh round of sobs and shaking took over her body. "Dammit, Eve. It is! I told you! I told you about my ex. I knew he wouldn't stop until he found me. I should have kept running. I shouldn't have stayed in one spot for so long, but you and Lyric and Phoenix and Augie were so good to me, and I like him, and I let my hormones get the better of me. I should have known better. And now I've dragged you into it as well." Her tears soaked my shoulder.

I held her tighter, murmuring quiet denials into her ear. "This isn't you. It's me. This is William and his cult of followers."

"No. He's a businessman. He's an asshole, but he's not dangerous."

"You don't know the whole story. I pose a threat to his career. It was me they wanted. You're just collateral damage." Guilt weighed heavy on my soul, eating away at it bit by bit until the heaviness was almost too much to bear. It wanted to drag me down, but when Fawn squeezed my hand, I knew I couldn't let it. I couldn't just sit here and let this happen.

I had to get angry. I wasn't going to be a victim. "Do you have your phone?"

"No."

"Mine was in my pocket." I patted the side of my thigh and tried to muffle a yelp of delight when there was a phone-shaped bulge still there. I had no idea where our captors were or if they could hear us. I didn't want to advertise that they'd royally fucked up by letting us keep a phone.

I unlocked it with my thumbprint, the phone lighting up the immediate space around me just enough that I could make out Fawn's expression. The fear in her wide eyes was gutting. Pale tracks ran down her dirt-smeared cheeks where her tears had fallen, and bruises already formed around her neck. Judging by how sore mine was, I figured we'd be sporting matching injuries. Not that that mattered now.

"Call nine-one-one. Or Boston," she urged.

I nodded. I went straight for Boston's number, knowing he was at work, and praying I was making the right decision. But there was nobody else I wanted to talk to more than him. I craved the steady, solid timbre of his voice like I craved my next breath. And nobody at 911 was going to care about my whereabouts the way he would.

"Quick, quick," Fawn urged. "Before somebody comes and realizes you've still got it."

I nodded in the darkness, stabbing my finger against

the green 'call' button below Boston's name. I pressed it to my ear desperately, praying he'd pick it up quickly.

There was no ringing.

The phone gave a beep, and when I looked at the screen again, it was flashing the "No cell service" signal.

"No!" I wailed. "I can't get a call out."

A true, chilling fear cut me in two. I couldn't think of anywhere local that would have not even one bar of cell reception.

Fawn came to the same conclusion. "Where the hell are we?"

A terrifying laugh from the other side of the door made me sure I didn't even want to know.

26

———

BOSTON

*R*ichards really wasn't as bad as I'd initially thought. While I still hated that he sat in Jayela's seat, the guy had proved himself of good value. He'd reported to me quickly and factually about what had happened at Eve's club the moment I'd arrived at work and hadn't spared even the smallest of details that I would have normally had to pry out of another officer. He'd moved the crowd on peacefully, though not before some of them shoved their hateful signs and messages beneath the club's door.

"I couldn't do anything about that without breaking in. We could fingerprint them if she wants. Hopefully they won't upset her too much."

"If a drive-by shooting doesn't faze her, then a few bits of paper won't. She's tough." And strong, and sexy, and mind-blowing in every way.

The grin spread wide across my face, and I couldn't remove it even when Richards shot me a knowing smile. I'd hated leaving her earlier, but the memory of her naked in my bed, and the things we'd done in it...fuck.

My personal cell rang toward the end of my shift, sometime after dark when my stomach was rumbling and all I could think about was finishing up and getting back over to the club to help Eve with the food. I pulled my phone out from the pocket of my uniform, excited at the thought it might be Eve.

I frowned at the unknown number but answered it anyway.

"Cop. It's Augie. From Eve's club."

My eyebrows knit together. There was no love lost between the two of us. It was clear he didn't like Eve and me together, but she didn't care, so neither did I. It begged the question as to why the big blond man who looked like he'd just stepped out of a surfing magazine would be calling me. "Yeah, I know who you are. What's up?"

"Is Eve with you?"

"No. I'm on duty. Why?"

There was a prolonged silence for a moment. "She didn't show up for family night. That's not like her. And she's not answering her phone."

"That's weird. She was with me this morning, and we agreed we'd meet there. I thought for sure she'd already be there."

"She's never been late. Not a minute."

"Something probably came up."

"Yeah, maybe. Thing is, Fawn didn't show either. And same deal. Phone isn't on."

A trickle of worry beaded in the form of sweat at my temple. "I'm sure it's no big deal. We had a...uh...late night. I left her sleeping at my place, so I'll run back there now and check on her."

"Let me know." He ended the call without any sort of goodbye.

"Yeah, right. Thanks to you, too." I hung up.

Richards was already heading toward my townhouse, once again proving that he was okay, and maybe working with him wouldn't be so bad. We were a few blocks away, so I called Eve's phone a few times, but every one went straight to voicemail.

"She's probably just got her phone on do not disturb," Richards assured me.

I didn't say anything. At my place, I let us in and immediately headed for the stairs. "Eve?"

There was no reply. I thundered up them, stopping in the doorway and taking in the empty bed, still mussed up from our night together. I stuck a head into the bathroom, but it was empty, too.

"Boston," Richards yelled from downstairs. "I've got a note."

I jogged downstairs, belt jangling with my keys and gun and various other pieces of equipment. Richards offered a white sheet of paper with messy handwriting scrawled across it.

Gone to Fawn's to help with a homework crisis. Can't wait to see you tonight. Don't bother washing the sheets because I'm gonna want to mess them up again.

Eve. xxx.

My worry put a halt to any embarrassment I might have felt over Richards reading that. I looked over the top at him.

He just grinned and shook his head. "So she's at a friend's?"

"Apparently, but neither of them are answering their phones, and they didn't show for dinner at the club. They do it every week, and it's kind of a big deal, so I don't think they'd skip it without a really good reason. You mind if we swing by her friend's house and check it out?"

Richards headed for our squad car with a nod. "You got it. Not like we have anything better to do to ride out the last hour of this shift anyway."

It had been an exceptionally slow night, but uttering those words out loud generally turned the streets into chaos so I hadn't dared. I cringed now, hoping Richards hadn't just opened the floodgates of karma.

27

BOSTON

*A*ugie picked up his phone on the first ring, like he'd had it in his hand, waiting for me to call. "Talk to me."

"I need Fawn's address."

He rattled it off. "I'm already on my way over there. Two minutes out."

We weren't far off either, but an old green sedan was crookedly parked out the front when Richards and I pulled into the concrete driveway. The front door of the cottage was wide open, no lights coming from the interior.

"Augie?" I called from the front step. "Fawn? Eve?"

"They aren't here," Augie called from somewhere inside. "Door was open when I got here."

I walked through the little house until I found him staring at a laptop left open on the small, round kitchen table. "What do you mean by open? Closed but unlocked?"

"No, dumbass. I mean it was wide fucking open for

any asshole to walk in and take whatever they wanted. We're lucky there's anything left." He turned to me, expression stony. "Nobody around here leaves their doors wide open by choice, cop. Fawn's phone is here, and Eve's purse. They didn't just walk out. Not voluntarily, anyway."

A yawning pit of worry opened up. "When did you last speak to either of them?"

"Hours ago. Too many."

It was the same for me. I hadn't spoken to Eve since my shift had started mid-morning. "Fuck. William Reed."

"Or Fawn's ex."

"What's he got to do with it?"

Augie drummed his fingertips on the tabletop. "Fawn thought he was behind the drive-by shooting. She went to Eve about it, but Eve convinced her it was Reed. Fucking Eve! She's so stubborn. She wouldn't listen when Fawn tried to tell her."

I bristled. "Eve's smart. She has her reasons for thinking Reed has it in for her. I'm going over there to talk to him."

Augie shook his head. "You're as stubborn as she is. Open your fucking eyes. Reed is a pussy. He couldn't pull this off if he tried."

"Maybe not. But he's got the money to pay someone who could. And what else do we have to go on? You got a name for Fawn's ex-boyfriend?"

"Eddie...someone. Shit. I don't know if Fawn ever told me his last name."

"Then find someone who does know it and get back to me."

Augie nodded, a determined light in his eye. He looked almost as worried as I felt. Two missing women, neither heard from for hours, was never a good situation. Even worse, when one of those women was somebody I cared about. A new determination fueled my muscles. I wasn't going to panic. I was a cop, trained for this. I could put my feelings for Eve aside long enough to find her.

And finding her started with confronting William Reed.

Richards followed my lead, wordlessly handing over the keys to the cruiser when I made for the driver's side door. He didn't say a word when I put the sirens on, blasting through every light, pedal to the metal until we reached the Reed's place on an affluent street in Providence.

I stormed up the front steps, banging my fist against the door. "Reed! Get out here."

The door opened a crack, and William stuck his head out, eyebrows pinched together. They relaxed once he saw it was me. "Boston? What time is it? What's going on?" He opened the door the rest of the way, coming out onto the front porch in blue silk pajamas, his feet bare. The porch light lit up his silvering hair, messed up like he'd already gone to bed despite the fact it wasn't even nine.

"Do you know where Eve Hawkins is right now?"

"No? Should I?"

I studied him. Trying to determine whether he was for real or a good actor. "She's missing. Her and one of her friends."

I let the silent accusation hang in the air between us.

It took a moment for William's eyes to widen. "You think I had something to do with that?"

"I don't know. You tell me." I fought to keep my impatience in check. If this man had touched a hair on Eve's head, I would kill him myself. But I had no proof. I needed to remain calm and think clearly until I did.

"Why would I do that?"

"Because she's your biological daughter, perhaps? How would that look to all your Christian supporters, if it came out that you had an illegitimate lovechild? One who's a stripper at that."

William shot a panicked look back at his front door, hurrying over to it and closing it. "Shh. Okay, okay. My wife and children don't know about that either, so can you keep it down?"

Disgust for the man dripped from my words. "Did you, or someone you know, target Eve Hawkins and her club? Was it you who organized for someone to spray her place with bullets?"

"What on earth are you talking about?"

But I wasn't done. I inched closer and closer to the older man until I had him cornered against the side of his house. "I'm going ask you one more time. Do you know where Eve Hawkins is right now?"

Reed put his hands up, not daring to touch my chest but trying to keep some distance between the two of us. "I swear. I have no idea where she is. And I had nothing to do with any sort of shooting. I wouldn't even know where to begin hiring someone to do something like that. And even if I did, I wouldn't. Despite what you might think of me, Boston, I am a Christian man. I'm not in the habit of trying to hurt anyone."

"Bullshit!" I lost my patience. "I know all about the threatening letters you've been sending to the club. And your groupies barricading the doors."

"I knew my supporters were protesting outside her club. And I admit, I didn't do anything to stop them. And yes. Eve is my daughter. I know that. Her mother came to me years ago, trying to get me to accept her into my family."

"You couldn't do that, though, could you?"

He at least had the decency to gaze down at his feet. "No. I couldn't. Her mother and I were a one-time thing. A mistake."

Fuck him. "Nothing about Eve Hawkins is a mistake," I growled. "It's your loss. Not hers. You got that?"

The man nodded. "I swear, though, Boston. All the rest, none of that was me. I admit, I did set her up when I told her to come to the house that night and then called you to arrest her. I had to discredit her. Make her look like a common thug so if she and her mother started making claims on me, no one would believe them. But I've never tried to hurt her. God. What must you think of me, to think I'm capable of that?"

"Very little," I admitted.

But I believed him. Goddammit, I believed the man when he said he had nothing to do with the shooting, the threats, and Eve's disappearance.

"What can I do to help?" William asked quietly.

I shook my head. "Nothing."

I spun on my heel, storming back toward the car.

"Please, keep me updated—"

I cut off his fake concern crap by slamming the car door. Richards slid in beside me and waited patiently as I picked up my phone. There was a message from Augie. All it had was the name.

Eddie Sinclair.

I hit one of my speed dial numbers and waited for the chief to answer his phone. "Hell—"

"Chief. Eve Hawkins and another woman are missing, feared abducted from a house. I'm going to need everybody on this immediately."

"Eve Hawkins... From the strip club? What makes you think she's missing?"

I'd already used up all my patience on Reed. "Chief. Just trust me on this. Something is going on."

"She been missing for twenty-four hours?"

"No."

"Then I'm not wasting manpower on this. We're getting reports of a commotion at Saint View Prison. We're on standby to send units there to help. I don't have time to be searching for a stripper girlfriend when truth be told? We all know she's probably...working."

"Working? The club isn't even open tonight."

"You know what I mean."

Shock punched through my gut. "She's not a fucking prostitute."

"All I'm saying is you don't really know the woman. And until she's missing for twenty-four hours, we're not wasting any time looking for her."

"This is bullshit. If I were ringing you right now saying Laura Reed was missing, would that be a different story? Would you take the time then?"

The chief sighed. "Get off your high horse. You need to get back to the station and pick up your riot gear in case we're needed at the prison."

I stared out the windshield, up at Reed's giant mansion. Unspoken words danced over my tongue. I had a burning need to know who'd really killed Jayela. But I couldn't do this anymore.

And she wouldn't want me to.

"No, I don't. I'm not coming back to pick up anything. Because I fucking quit."

I hung up to the chief's spluttering and Richards' wide eyes on me. "Did you mean that? Are you seriously quitting?"

But my path was suddenly clear. I couldn't do this job anymore. Not after everything with Jayela, and now with Eve. I was so disillusioned with the entire system.

I didn't want anything to do with it anymore.

"Yeah. I think I am."

Richards let out a low whistle. "So what now?"

"Get me everything you can find on Eddie Sinclair."

28

EVE

By the time whatever I'd been injected with had completely left my system, I was wishing I had another dose to shoot up with. Because this was not a situation I wanted to be lucid for. It would have been pure bliss and a relief to fuzz right out again and forget that Fawn and I had been huddled together on the floor of an empty room for hours.

The others would be getting to the club by now and wondering where I was. Boston's shift would finish soon, and then he'd go to the club as well. When I didn't show, they'd come looking.

I could just sit tight and wait. But every so often, I glanced over at my phone, clutched in Fawn's fingers while she played a card game on an app I'd downloaded once and then forgotten about. It didn't require internet connection, and I'd thrust it in her direction as a distraction when I was sure she was going to hyperventilate. She'd played round after round ever since, until her breathing evened out.

No corner of this room had any sort of connection to the outside world. I'd left Fawn's side long enough only to search the room by the light of my phone, and determined we were in a basement. There was a single set of stairs, and a water heater that gave off a menacing hiss every so often, but other than that, it was completely empty. The door at the top of the stairs was solid wood, and when I dared to try the handle, nothing had happened. The room was locked tight.

But it wasn't in me to stay down for long. And though I might have yearned for the heavy oblivion the drugs in my system had offered, a bigger part of me knew I was going to have to help myself. It wasn't in me to be a damsel in distress, though I would have welcomed Boston breaking down that door anytime now.

"Screw this," I muttered. We hadn't heard a word from our captors, just the chilling laugh that I knew I'd be hearing in my nightmares for years to come. I was already dreading the therapy bills.

I got to my feet, but Fawn grabbed my leg, fingernails digging in through my sweatpants. "Where are you going?"

"I can't just sit here."

Fawn let out a tiny mewl like a baby kitten being left behind by its mother, but I used that to push me up the stairs. She was my responsibility. I threw the side of my closed fist at the door, banging on it loudly. "Hey!" I yelled as loud as I could.

It felt good after being silent for so long. The thump of my fist against the door gave a place for my coiled-up energy to go, and as that released, so did the anger. I was so sick of people I was biologically related to letting me down. I imagined telling my mother her precious William had kidnapped me and immediately came to the conclusion she'd find a way to blame me. I let the anger swirl and join at my chest, and the words that came out were a bellow of disgust and anger. "Open the door, you piece of shit! What kind of man kidnaps his own daughter? You hear that? Yeah, I know who you are. I wouldn't have told anyone your dirty little secret, Reed! You could have gone on playing the perfect Christian politician, living in your own dream world. All I wanted was my club."

I paused to catch my breath. The rustle of somebody on the other side of the door only increased my frustration. "Fucking open the door and face me, you coward!"

"Shut up, bitch," came the growl from the other side.

Not William. His voice was too deep and gravelly. It only gave me pause for a minute, though. "What's he paying you to kidnap women, huh? A hundred bucks? Fuck, you're probably so stupid you would have done it for a fifty. Is that it?" I pummeled my fist against the door again, both of them this time, one after the other, pounding the wood until my hands screamed for mercy and I let loose with a barrage of language. "Open the door and face me!"

The door flew open, and I stumbled forward, not expecting it.

A meaty hand closed around my throat and slammed me straight up against the doorframe.

I only had a second to take in the man, his eyes a steel blue and as dead as stone, before he leaned in and hissed in my ear, "I said shut up, bitch. Nod if you understand, or I can stay here with my fingers around your throat until you have no breath left to yell."

I couldn't have made a sound even if I wanted to. His fingers choked my air supply, leaving barely enough for me to remain conscious. The only sounds that came out were choked wheezes as I fought in vain to suck in enough oxygen.

From below, Fawn let loose with a scream of her own. She barreled up the stairs, charging for the man. "Get away from her!"

It all played out in sick slow motion. Her reaching the top of the stairs. Him putting one hand out and throwing her straight back down them.

I watched in horror as her body tumbled, her limbs hitting every step, her head cracking against the railing, until she lay sprawled on the cold cement at the bottom.

I couldn't even rasp out her name. She lay deathly still, and through the dim light I couldn't see if her chest moved.

A tear spilled over and ran down my cheek.

The man leaned in and licked it.

My legs went weak, and I started up a new round of thrashing. The feel of his wet tongue against my skin was repulsive and terrifying all at once.

His grip tightened until I stopped.

"You're William Reed's daughter. Nod if you are."

I jerked my head.

"Fuck." His gaze rolled back to Fawn and rested on her lifeless body. For too long, it stayed there, staring at her unmoving body with relentless attention.

His grip on my neck loosened enough for me to speak. "Please help her."

He didn't respond.

"You're not one of William's guys, are you?"

He snapped his head around to stare at me. "What do you think?"

A chill rolled down my spine. "Eddie?"

"She's talked about me, then? What did she say? Fucking slut thought she could leave me, but I told her. I told her she couldn't!" He narrowed his eyes. "You let her do this. You encouraged her."

I shook my head. "No... I just gave her somewhere to live and work."

"You turned her into a ho. Up on that filthy stage, taking her clothes off for men who aren't me. She was pure and innocent until she met you." He shoved me roughly toward the hallway, and though getting out of the room had been my initial goal, I now wanted the complete opposite.

I wouldn't leave Fawn.

"She's hurt," I screamed as he shoved me again. "She needs help. She could die, Eddie! I know that's not what you want."

He got right up in my face, until his breath washed over my mouth. "I'm the only thing she needs, bitch. Not you and your filthy club. You're just a fucking liability. Especially now that I know you're the politician's daughter. I should have just taken you out right then and there, on the porch of that shack she's been living in. It's not fit for her. She deserves better."

He shoved me again, hard enough I couldn't keep my

footing. I met the floor, sharp pain shooting up through my hands and arms which broke my fall. His fingers twisted in my hair and yanked my head back hard.

At the end of the hall, a woman watched TV, completely uninterested in what was happening. But another man watched on silently. He stepped forward, producing a balaclava. All I saw was a flash of his green eyes before he pulled it down over mine, the eye holes not matching up so I couldn't see a thing.

"Stop fighting, bitch," Eddie whispered. "This will all be over soon."

Hysteria rose and choked me worse than his fingers. I thrashed and kicked out, screaming until both male bodies pinned me to the floor and bound my hands behind my back. With my face pressed into the cold tile, and Eddie's wicked voice promising violence, I let the fear consume me.

Had I told Fawn I loved her? What about Lyric and Phoenix? Hell, even Augie... Did they know what they meant to me?

And Boston...

I couldn't breathe, thinking about him and the way he made me feel. Why hadn't I met him sooner? Why had we spent so much time arguing? It all seemed like a tragic waste now.

He was it for me. Something deep in my gut knew it, and I'd been ignoring it since the day we'd met.

Just like the others, I'd never get to tell him what he meant to me.

When I was shoved into the trunk of a car, bound and gagged, that was what plagued me. Not the awkward angle of my limbs or my hot breath, caught by the mask over my face.

With the two men arguing over where to dump my body, I'd go to my death regretting not telling Boston I loved him most of all.

29

EVE

We drove for hours, with music blaring loud enough I could hear it from the trunk. I kicked at the taillights to no avail and screamed until my throat went raw. In between songs, I caught snatches of the two men's conversation. Words like kill, bury, and mine floated back to me until I was so exhausted from the adrenaline pumping through my body that I dozed off.

A car door slammed, and I jerked awake painfully, my restraints cutting into my arms and ankles. I was sure one of my wrists was bleeding.

"Get her out."

Panic broke through the grogginess. No. No, no, no. Suddenly, the trunk seemed like the safest place in the world, and I didn't want to leave it. I'd been dreaming of Boston, but not the Boston I knew now. One who was older. Still hot as hell, but gray flecked his hair, and though I couldn't see myself, I'd felt the wisdom of years I didn't currently possess. I wanted to go back there, to that safe, warm space, that promised a future with him.

The trunk opened, but they didn't say a word.

Their silence told me everything I needed to know.

I wasn't going to get that future with Boston. I wasn't going to get a future at all.

I let out another scream, this one less full of fear and more full of the pain of knowing what was coming.

Strong hands gripped my upper arms and yanked me from the trunk only to throw me on the gravel road. Skin scraped along hard rock, cuts opening up and bleeding, but I barely felt it over the pain of knowing I'd feel nothing soon.

"I love him," I mumbled.

"What was that, bitch?" Eddie's harsh voice taunted.

"I love him," I repeated, louder this time. Stronger.

He was all I'd thought about since this whole thing started. I didn't want my mother. Or my friends, though where Fawn was right now, and whether she was even alive scared the shit out of me. But the person I wanted most was Boston. I yearned for the safety of his arms. For the press of his lips against my hair.

I would have given anything for one last kiss. We hadn't shared enough of them. There hadn't been time. But somehow, I knew, even a whole lifetime of his kisses wouldn't have been enough. "I love him."

The mask was ripped from me, the scratchy material scraping my face as it lifted.

Bright lights shone straight into my eyes, blinding me after being in the darkness for hours.

A gun barrel was pressed to my temple.

I whimpered. "Please," I whispered, shutting my eyes against the glare. Against reality.

"Please what?"

"Don't hurt Fawn. If she's still alive. Do what you want with me, I've done the bad shit to deserve it. But Fawn hasn't. She doesn't deserve this."

"And you do? You deserve to die out here tonight?"

I couldn't answer. A full-body tremble took over, even though the night air was warm.

He pushed the gun harder into my temple, forcing my head to one side.

I waited for it.

The blast of the gun going off and the instant darkness as the bullet took my life.

Eddie leaned down, his lips brushing my cheek. "Not today, bitch. I don't need your daddy searching me down because I offed his little princess. You're not like my girl. Ain't nobody gonna miss her when she's mine and mine alone. But you, you're a thorn in my side that I don't need."

My brain scrambled to keep up, trying to make sense of what he was saying.

"Stay there while I drive away. I'll be watching in the rearview mirror. I see you looking, even so much as twitching in my direction, and it'll be Fawn down on her knees with a gun at her temple. Got me, bitch?"

"Please don't hurt—"

The gun smashed into my cheekbone. "I said, you got me, bitch?"

He screamed in my face until I nodded rapidly, my tears filling my eyes and spilling out from beneath my closed lids. "I got it. I understand."

"Let's go, Zane."

Car doors slammed, while I hunched over, clutching my stomach, trying to ease the nausea threatening to erupt. I sucked in deep lungfuls of air as the crunch of tires on gravel faded into the distance.

Even then, I waited another five minutes to be doubly sure they weren't tricking me into looking.

Finally, I allowed myself to collapse in a ball.

Until the crack of a gun unloading split the night air.

30

BOSTON

Searching for Eve with no information to go on was like searching for a needle in a haystack. The chief had called us back in twice now, and I wasn't even officially a cop anymore, but Richards and I had both ignored the calls. I drove the streets aimlessly, desperately searching for anything out of place, while Richards combed through our databases, social media, and Google for any information we could find on Fawn's ex-boyfriend.

None of the records he found were good.

"Arrested for assault at fifteen. Again at eighteen and twenty-two..." Richards scrolled down the side of his iPad, continuing a progressively worse list of violent crimes. The man had a rap sheet longer than my arm. The thought he might have Eve and Fawn had me gripping the steering wheel so tightly my knuckles turned white.

I wasn't a cop anymore. The promises I'd made when Jayela and I joined the academy no longer applied.

I'd kill him if he'd laid a hand on Eve.

"Richards, Boston." The chief's voice crackled over the radio, followed by a heavy sigh, like he was thoroughly sick of our shit.

I didn't care.

Richards hit the button to reply. "Yeah, boss?"

"Don't know if you've actually been listening to your radio tonight, but everyone has been sent over to deal with the riot at the prison. Since the two of you refuse to obey commands, you're the only ones still out on the beat. We've had a call about a body on a residential street near your location."

My heart stopped. "Male or female?"

"Caller thought female, but she was too scared to go outside in the dark and check. Rather than pull someone from the prison, Richards, it's on you. Since your partner quit, you're in charge."

I clenched my jaw. But it wasn't enough for me to take back my resignation. I knew full well that as soon as I returned to the station, I'd be handing in my badge and gun for the last time.

And oddly, I was okay with that. The weight of everything that was wrong within this police department had lifted the moment I'd uttered those freeing words. I still wholeheartedly believed in protecting those who needed it. But what I'd been forced into doing and the way this department ran went wholly against my moral compass. I couldn't ignore it anymore. Without Jayela, none of it felt right.

Maybe I could have changed precincts. Maybe things would have been different somewhere else, beneath a different leader. But my life was here.

Eve was here.

At least she would be when I got her back.

Over the radio, the chief rattled off an address just a few blocks away, and I turned on my blinker. With a rising sense of dread, I put my foot down on the accelerator, taking corners too fast until the street came into view.

"There." Richards pointed to a lump on the side of the road, a few hundred feet away. It was too dark to make out features, but as I sped down the road, the cruiser's headlights illuminated the woman's body.

A dark-haired woman. In gray sweats that looked familiar because they were mine.

I slammed my foot on the brake and threw open the door without turning the engine off. "Eve!" My boots pounded over the road, and I slipped, nearly going down before righting myself. "Eve!"

I threw myself to the ground, barely noticing the gravel the grazed my thigh even through my work pants.

She was a mess of wild hair that covered her face. I desperately smoothed it out as I hauled her into my lap. "Eve, come on, baby. Talk to me."

She was too pale. Too limp.

I held her to my chest, an agonized scream ripping from somewhere deep inside me. "Jesus, no."

"Boston."

I stopped breathing. I stayed so completely still that there was no other sound, no other movement, except for the slight rise and fall of her chest.

Her big eyes peered up at me, as if she couldn't quite believe I was really there.

A sob of relief choked me. "Fucking hell, Evil. I thought you were dead." I hugged her to me, only now feeling the warmth of her body. My mind whirled with questions, but in the background, Richards called for an ambulance, and everything else paled in comparison. "I love you," I whispered into her hair. "I love you so fucking much."

She clutched me tighter, curling herself into my lap while sobs racked her body. "There were gunshots. Don't let me go," she murmured into my chest. "Please, don't go."

"Not a chance. I'm not going anywhere, you hear me? You're mine, Eve. I've got you."

"I'm going to ask the witnesses about the shots," Richards told me, then left me with my girl.

I couldn't answer him. The ambulance arrived, and when I glanced up, the street was lined with rubberneckers. I hadn't heard any of them, too wrapped up in holding Eve in my arms. The paramedics approached, but Eve buried into my jacket and clutched me tighter.

"I've got her," I told the two women. "I'll get her in."

The two of them frowned, but I'd made a promise, and I wasn't about to break it. When I told Eve I wasn't going anywhere, I meant it. I'd be right here, by her side, until she told me to leave.

The onlookers broke into a round of applause as I picked Eve up from the ground, and she wrapped her arms around my neck. I met Richards' gaze when I passed.

"The gunshot was one of the neighbors, letting off a warning shot into the air. They didn't realize it was a woman or that she needed help." He sighed heavily. "He was very apologetic. You almost can't blame him. There's so much gang activity around here, and the people don't feel safe. Any commotion is treated as a threat."

I understood but I couldn't worry about that now. It was no longer my problem. I paused, pulling my gun and badge from my belt, and passed them to him.

He didn't say anything. Just nodded, and that was enough.

The police were no longer my everything.

The woman in my arms was.

I climbed into the back of the ambulance and sat on a stretcher. One of the paramedics climbed in, closing the door behind her. "I'm Sara," she said calmly, in the way one spoke to a frightened animal. "I need to examine her."

In the front, the other paramedic started the engine and switched on the sirens. With a lurch, we took off in the direction of Saint View Hospital.

Sara watched the two of us with a sympathetic expression, while I smoothed a hand down Eve's back. "Babe, we gotta get you looked at."

"I'm okay," she said, finally lifting her head. "But Fawn..."

Sara turned to me in confusion. "Is there another patient?"

I shook my head. "There was nobody else at the scene."

Eve trembled. "They pushed her down the stairs. It was a basement, somewhere we had no phone reception. It felt like hours away, but I don't know. Maybe we just drove in circles to throw me off? You need to find her, Boston. Please."

For the first time, I noticed the bruising around her

neck. My blood boiled. And for the tiniest of seconds, I regretted my choice. But the chief had already chosen his side. He'd already proven that he didn't see Eve and her friends as worthy of police time and effort.

"We'll find her," I promised. "She's family. We'll do whatever it takes to bring her home. But first, we need to get you to the hospital."

She sank back into my arms, exhaustion taking her once more.

---

*H*ours later, I took my girl home. Just like I had the last time we'd gone back to my place together, I guided her straight up the stairs. In the main bathroom, I sat her on the toilet lid, and she watched while I ran the tub full of hot water. "I'm sorry I don't have any of that nice-smelling stuff," I told her, glancing over at her with a worried frown. "I'll buy some tomorrow."

She didn't smile the way I'd hoped she would. "It's okay. I don't need it."

I still wished I had some. Not that nicely scented water would make any difference to the bruises around her neck or the cuts on her cheek. But the doctors at the hospital had given her a clean bill of health otherwise, and after a drip with a bag of fluids, and a few hours' sleep while they observed her stats, she'd been discharged.

Fawn was still missing. I'd guarded Eve's hospital door while I called Richards and filled him in on everything Eve had told me, not wanting to wake her by talking in her room but unwilling to leave her alone either. I'd checked the bathroom thoroughly before I left, semi-paranoid Fawn's ex might have changed his mind about letting her go.

We'd gotten lucky. Lucky that she was Reed's daughter. Lucky that she hadn't ever been Eddie's intended target. It could have so easily gone the other way, though. Instead of dumping her on the side of the road, he could have put a bullet through her brain first.

I shuddered at the thought.

"Stand up," I said softly, once the water was near the top of the tub. I held a hand out, and she took it, standing on legs that no longer trembled so much they couldn't hold her weight.

She'd had to put the dirty clothes back on to come home, and I peeled them from her body now, slowly shedding each piece to the floor. My uniform followed, until there was a pile of clothes neither of us needed anymore.

I stepped into the almost too-hot water and tugged at Eve's hand to join me. She stepped in gracefully, and the two of us sank deep into the tub, not caring when the water splashed over the sides and onto the tiled floor. I put my back to the porcelain and spread my legs wide, pulling Eve to lie between them, her back to my chest.

As seconds passed, Eve relaxed, her stressed tight muscles slowly unwinding beneath the hot water until she sighed in contentment. She slipped beneath the surface, wetting her hair.

I reached for a bottle of shampoo, squeezed some onto my palm, and then worked it through the lengths falling down her back. With the help of the sudsy lather, I rubbed my fingers across her scalp, massaging her temples until she was as limp as a ragdoll.

"You were all I thought about," she said eventually. "In that basement, and in the car, and on the side of the road. I just wanted you."

"Shh, It's okay. You don't have to talk about it."

"I just...we wasted so much time. I don't want to do that anymore. You said I was yours... You're mine, too, Joshua. You know that, right?" She swiveled to look up at me. "You're mine, and I love you."

My heart roared. I'd felt it in the way she held me. In the connection between us that now somehow felt bone-deep. She'd gotten beneath my skin, and I'd just hoped I was beneath hers.

Hearing her confirm it was everything. *She* was everything.

"I love you, too." I kissed her sweet mouth, reminding myself of her taste when she opened and pressed her tongue against mine. She twisted in the tub, water sloshing again, so we were face-to-face, chest to chest. Her back arched gracefully as she lay on top of me, reaching her arms around my neck, my head cupped in her hands.

"I've never said that to anyone before," she admitted. "Nobody has ever made me want to."

My heart slammed against my chest so hard I was sure she could feel it through hers. I kissed her roughly, unable to get enough before I remembered she was hurt. I pulled back sharply. "Shit. Are you okay?"

She nodded, pressing her lips to mine again. "Don't stop," she murmured between kisses. "Just...touch me. Please. I need it."

I understood that feeling because every part of me called out for her, too. I had no idea how I was ever going to leave her side to find work or get food. But I didn't need any of that right now. I could survive on Eve and Eve alone at least for the next few hours.

So I touched her. I ran my soapy hands over every curve of her body, checking each one, refamiliarizing myself and learning new things about her with every brush of my fingertips. She nuzzled into the side of my neck, flicking over my damp skin with her tongue while I traced the bumps of her spine and dragged my palms lower to cup her ass. Between us, my dick grew hard, nudging against her belly.

"That feels so good," she whispered.

I massaged her ass, sneaking one finger between to prod at her entrance, remembering the way she liked to be touched there. I was rewarded with a hiss of breath as she gasped in pleasure. My dick yearned to get in on the action, but I ignored it.

She found my lips with hers and kissed me deeply, until my balls ached and it was everything I could do not to push my dick between her legs and take her right then and there. But not until I'd made her scream. Not until I'd wiped away the memory of somebody hurting her.

She stood, water dripping from her glistening body, falling from the peaks of her tits and running in rivulets down her stomach and thighs. "Let's go to your bedroom. The water is getting cold."

I hadn't even noticed. I stood to join her, but the lure of her body was too great to ignore. I pushed her up against the tiled wall, stopping only when she squealed.

"Cold tiles!"

But I couldn't wait for the bedroom, a wicked idea forming. I spun her around, and she planted her hands on the wall instead. I reached around her hip and cupped her mound. My mouth at her ear, I whispered, "Arch your back and press your tits to the wall. I want that cold on your nipples."

Her moan of approval went straight to my cock. She did as I'd instructed, sticking her ass back for me to grab, and her breasts against the tile. Her cheek against the wall showed me her profile. Not as good as staring down at her face, but enough that I could see she was enjoying it. There was no squealing this time, and her noises of arousal spurred me on. The water in the tub still sloshed around our calves, annoying, but I wasn't stopping to move now. She needed me. And I needed her.

I found her clit and rubbed one finger against it, before dipping lower to gather her arousal. With my other hand, I massaged the globes of her perfect ass, enjoying the smoothness of her skin and the way she ground back against my finger every time I touched it to her back entrance.

"You like it," I murmured, not really a question, since I already knew the answer.

"It's my favorite," she admitted without opening her eyes. "Just gotta get the right partner for it to be really good."

"That person me?"

The corner of her mouth flicked up. "You looking for compliments? Shut up and fuck me already."

I grinned, partially at what she'd said, and partially in relief. This was the Eve I knew. The things she'd experienced in the last twenty-four hours hadn't stolen her sass, just numbed it for a little while.

I dropped to my knees in the bathtub, lukewarm water splashing around me, and gripped her hips.

She glanced over her shoulder. "What are you doing?"

"Fucking you. With my tongue." With her ass jutting out, she was mine for the taking. I wanted to prove exactly how good I could make it for her. She'd caught me by surprise last time, I wanted to do the same for her this time. Especially knowing it was her favorite.

Keeping one hand on her clit, I used the other to spread her cheeks and dove between them, tongue searching for entry.

"Oh God, yes," she moaned.

A fresh coat of arousal built between her legs, and I drenched my fingers in it, thrusting them up inside her pussy while I tongued her ass until she was mewling, begging for more.

"You're so wet," I murmured between licks and sucks. "God, I want to fuck you bare, Eve. Are you on birth control?"

She nodded frantically, grinding back against me like she hated that I'd stopped to talk. I pressed my tongue against her sweet flesh once more.

"Are you clean?" Her voice was raspy, on the verge of an orgasm I wouldn't let her have.

"As a whistle."

"God yes, do it."

I stood again, enjoying the tremble in her legs as I spread them as wide as the tub would allow. I held her hip and plunged myself deep inside her pussy from behind.

"Oh!"

Her wet warmth wrapped around me like a glove, so much better than wearing a condom. I glided in and out of her tight core, fucking her hard and fast until she was begging me to finish her. I wouldn't. Not yet. Not until I'd wrung every inch of pleasure out of her body and made her forget everything but me, and my cock and the orgasm barreling down on her.

Dripping with her juices, I pulled out and notched myself at her ass, testing her reaction to see if she wanted it.

She ground back against me without any encouragement. I held completely still, letting her run the show as my dick disappeared inside her.

She dropped one hand from the wall, moving it between her legs, stroking her clit as I began a slow roll of my hips, thrusting in and an out, giving her time to adjust.

The view from where I stood was magnificent. I watched the spot we were joined, watched the jerk of her fingers against her sensitive flesh, watched the expression on her face turn from pleasure to ecstasy.

"Harder," she murmured. "Now, Boston."

Her pretty lips begged the words, and I was right where I wanted to be, right where she wanted it. I picked up the pace, dick gliding through her tightness, wrapped in her body like I'd never been with anyone else. Her shoulders shook with the effort of her fingers at her pussy, while I dug my fingers into her hips, slamming my own against hers, our wet flesh slapping in the silent bathroom, her moans echoing off the tiles like music to my ears.

Her breaths came faster, her noises louder, until one final thrust sent us both flying over the edge, my dick deep in her ass, her fingers coated with her own cum. I rode her hard and fast, and she took everything I had, then demanded more. When I was bone-dry, completely emptied out, I spun her around and ate her pussy until she came again.

After she was done, I ran the shower, thoroughly sick of being in the water by now but needing to get us clean again. I wiped her tenderly with a cloth, as if I were handling fine china, but she still moaned every time I touched her sensitive places, aftershocks from both orgasms still coursing through her body.

Turning off the faucet, I took fluffy towels from the rack and wrapped her in one. Her hair hung in damp waves around her face, and she smiled when I picked her up and carried her to my bed.

Naked but dry, we got beneath the covers, snuggled in each other's arms.

It was only then that worry pulled at her expression once more. "I don't deserve this," she whispered quietly. "I'm here, having mind-blowing sex and multiple orgasms while Fawn is out there somewhere...."

I held her tighter, stress gripping me once more, until I reminded myself that she was here. She was with me. And I was never letting her go. I rolled her on her back, and she welcomed me between her legs once more, even though I wasn't hard. We just lay there, drinking each other in, my body weight on top of hers a security that calmed her down. "I love you," I whispered.

She brushed her lips over mine. "I love you, too."

"Richards is looking. We'll find her. I promise."

She turned away, both of us knowing that we'd gotten lucky.

And that maybe Fawn hadn't.

31

EVE

I month later

I stood in the wings of church hall, while William Reed took to the makeshift stage. His campaign posters were everywhere, decorating the wall behind him, along with streamers in blue, red, and white. Confetti littered the floor at his feet, crinkling beneath his overshined black shoes.

"I can't believe he won," Dylan Reed muttered.

I glanced over at my half brother. I would never call William Dad. He wasn't my father, just my sperm donor as far as I was concerned, but in the last few weeks, I had to admit, the man had been trying. I'd thwarted his first few attempts at reaching out to me, ignoring his calls, still too angry even though Boston and the police had explained that they now suspected Eddie of the drive-by shooting and the hate mail we'd received. In the month that had passed, they'd found evidence that Eddie had been hanging around Saint View, stalking Fawn from afar for weeks before he'd actually made his presence known.

None of us had realized. None of us except for Fawn. She'd tried to tell me, and I'd ignored her.

It was a burden I found hard to live with.

Augie, too, was taking it particularly hard, blaming himself for not noticing. He'd taken up drinking until he passed out.

But even though William might not have been trying to kill me, I still harbored ill feelings over too many things for me to just forget about them and play happy families.

Not that Laura would have ever allowed that anyway. My existence as William's daughter was still a sore point for her, especially since he'd made a public announcement about it.

But Dylan wasn't his father, and I liked the kid. He'd been nothing less than thrilled that we were biologically related, and he'd started turning up at the club each week for family night.

But he didn't fill the void, or the fact that Fawn had never come home.

I squeezed Boston's fingers, grateful as always for his solid dependability. The man never faltered. He'd taken his departure from the police force in stride, immediately setting up his own protection company.

Saint View Strip had been his first customer, and he'd joined Terry, the two of them forming our new security staff.

Once upon a time, seeing a guy day in and day out might have been too much. But things with Boston were different. I was happy to live in his pocket, and he in mine. Augie complained constantly about how sickening we were, but we were firmly in the honeymoon stage, and I wasn't planning on leaving it anytime soon.

But my happiness also brought pain. A heavy guilt that I didn't think would ease until the missing piece of my heart returned.

On the stage, William's smile was ear to ear. "What can I say? I'm incredibly honored to be standing in front of you all today. To every person who voted to make this happen, I say thank you. Thank you for your support, and for coming out tonight to celebrate."

A cheer went up from the crowd, accompanied by thunderous applause. I clapped, just a little more limply. I'd really only come around to William when he'd promised to leave the strip alone, including my club. It only took the edge off my dislike for the man, but I could give credit where credit was due. He was trying. Maybe one day, with time, we could be more than we were right now.

William droned on and on with his speech, and beside me, Boston faked a yawn.

Dylan grinned at him. "You thinking about quitting again?"

William had been Boston's second client. He wrinkled his nose adorably. "Nah. Do you know the percentage of new businesses that fail in the first twelve months?"

"That isn't going to happen to you," I assured him. "Best personal protection around."

He wrapped his arms around my waist. "Damn straight. And I haven't missed the bullshit at the station for a minute."

Every time he said that I worried it was bravado, and

that he truly had made a rash decision in the heat of a very emotional moment. But again, I looked into his eyes and saw the truth there. Even though Fawn's whereabouts rested heavily on us all, Boston had been happier these past few weeks than I'd ever seen him. He smiled more. Walked with a bounce in his step. And loved me like nobody else ever had. He was happy.

His smile cracked through my darkness every time. It was why I liked having him around so much.

"My team and I know we have big tasks ahead of us. And we take those responsibilities very seriously. We're here to serve this community. Each and every member of it, from those who live in Providence, to those who live in Saint View. Every person has a voice. And everyone will be heard." He glanced over at me, meeting my gaze. "Nobody gets left behind. As such, I promise to all of you in this crowd tonight..." His eyes burned bright, right into mine. "And to my eldest daughter, that we will find Fawn Conroy, who has been missing for the past four weeks. A task force has been put together by my own personal security and is working in conjunction with the police and other personal investigation services. I'm pledging that whatever it takes, no matter the hours, the manpower, or the money, we will find Fawn and bring her home."

A sob burst from my chest, and Boston gathered me in his arms.

"You knew he was doing this?" I asked him. "Why didn't you say anything?"

"He asked me not to," Boston said into my hair. "If he hadn't been elected, it wouldn't have happened, and he didn't want to disappoint you."

William wrapped up his speech and with a wave to his cheering supporters, he walked off the stage. He stopped in front of me, an arm's length away. "Eve..." he started.

He didn't get to finish.

"Thank you," I said stiffly.

He went to pat me on the arm, but I stepped out of his reach. He might have made a teeny tiny step in the right direction, but I didn't forgive and forget that easily.

He dropped his arm to his side and settled for a, "You're welcome."

"Aw, look at you two getting along. Does this mean you're going to call him Dad now?" Dylan asked with a chuckle.

I shot my younger brother a death stare. But I didn't miss the hope in William's eye.

"Perhaps you could come to dinner sometime." William cleared his throat and tugged at his shirt collar like it was suddenly too tight. "I mean, legitimately this time."

Unlike last time he'd invited me, this time, I could tell he meant it.

"I'll think about it."

32

EVE

"Is the blindfold really necessary?"

Boston grumbled as he tugged me along by the hand. "It is if you actually want to be surprised."

"I don't. I hate surprises."

"You won't hate this one. I promise."

I was doubtful. But he'd been excited about whatever was going on here for the past two days. His enthusiasm was hard not to catch. He'd left me little notes all over the place—at home, and at the club—dropping clues so cryptic that even after half a dozen of them, I still had no idea what we were doing. But seeing his excitement was enough. He wanted me to love whatever this was, and so I would. Because it was from him, and I kinda loved the guy.

I never got sick of saying that.

"Is it much farther?" I asked. "You didn't tell me to dress for a hike." Soft grass was squashed by my new summer sandals, and my long boho style dress swayed around my ankles. I'd assumed we were going to the beach, maybe for a picnic, or a swim, so I'd worn my bikini underneath, but there'd been no scent of salt in the air when we'd gotten out of the car, and no crashing of waves against the shore.

"Just a few more steps and then I'll take the blindfold off."

He stopped and swiveled me into position. "Okay, you ready?"

Despite myself, excitement rose. "This better be good, Boston. You've hyped it up that much."

He chuckled. "It's good. Take your blindfold off."

I pulled the material down and blinked in the harsh midday light. I took in the ugly square building in front of me, with the words, Saint View Dog Rescue scrawled across the side. "What's this? Are we volunteering?"

"Nope. There's somebody here that wants to meet you. She's just over there." Boston pointed to a side door I hadn't noticed.

A woman who stood in the doorway, holding a tiny brown mutt that might have been part chocolate Labrador but only a DNA test would really tell.

I spun around and stared at Boston. "No way. You bought a puppy?"

He grinned. "I bought *you* a puppy."

I opened my mouth to object, but he held up a hand. "Before you say anything, just hear me out. I follow this rescue on Facebook."

I smiled at that. "You're so cute, with your bleeding heart."

"Shut up. Anyway, they put up a photo of that tiny little fluffball and asked for someone to adopt her."

"And you thought that someone should be me?

Why?" I was itching to go snuggle that puppy. She was twisting in the worker's arms, straining to get free, her gaze trained on me.

Boston motioned for the woman to come over, and she smiled as she approached, introducing herself as Lola and handing me the squirming ball of floof.

She came willingly, licking my face and wagging her little tail so rapidly it whipped my hand.

Something inside me clicked.

It felt a lot like my heart opening up once more.

Boston grinned triumphantly at my smile. "I knew you'd love her. You've been so sad, and you can't be sad with a puppy around. Right?"

He peered into my face with such hope. All this man wanted to do was make me smile.

"I did good, right?"

The puppy licked my face. I pressed up on my toes and kissed Boston, while the puppy yelped excitedly and tried to do backflips out of my arms. I caught her and nodded at him. "You did good, babe."

I passed the wriggling puppy to him for snuggles, and my heart damn near burst, watching my man with that tiny baby. It almost made my ovaries ache. The thought of him holding our babies like that one day didn't overwhelm me. In fact, I kinda wanted it. "You'd make a great dad someday, you know."

He glanced up sharply. "I thought you didn't want kids?"

I lifted one shoulder. "A girl can change her mind, can't she?"

He grinned and swept me into his arms once more. "You're going to be an amazing mother. I can just imagine you, with your belly all swollen with my baby—"

"And my ankles twice their normal size, and stretch marks, and—"

"You'll still be the most beautiful woman I've ever seen."

"You'd still want me like that?"

He came in closer and whispered in my ear, "Yes, Eve. I will still want you like that. I will still want you bent over the kitchen counter and screaming my name. I will still want to suck your nipples and rub your clit until you're begging me for more." He darted a glance at the woman walking back to the shelter and grinned at me wickedly. "And I will still want to ride your sweet ass, just because I know you love it."

I didn't blush easily, but I did now. I covered the puppy's floppy ears and shot Boston a stern look. "Stop it! You'll scar her for life!" But we were both laughing.

It felt good to laugh. To really just let go and be happy in the moment with the man I loved.

I kissed the puppy's black nose and took her back from Boston's arms. "You need a name, little one. We can't just call you Puppy."

Boston's expression turned serious once more. "Actually, she already has one. The shelter workers named her and had it up on the Facebook post when they were searching for her forever home."

"Oh, yeah? What is it? I reserve the right to change it if it's awful." I patted her soft fur. "You're too cute to have an awful name."

"Her name is Doe."

My head snapped up. "Doe?"

Boston nodded. "I don't know, maybe it's stupid, but I saw it and I just felt that maybe it was a sign... Doe...Fawn..."

I swallowed hard. "It's perfect. And when Fawn comes home, she's going to love it."

I said it with as much conviction as I could muster. But the wobble in my bottom lip gave me away.

Boston didn't miss it. "We're going to find her, Eve. I promise."

"I know."

But the silent words neither of us wanted to say hung between us, out of place in the happiness we'd created.

When we brought Fawn home, would it be to cheers and hugs...or would it be to tears and a body bag?

EPILOGUE
FAWN

*B*right flashes of light broke through the endless black. I squeezed my eyes shut against it, praying for the darkness to engulf me once more.

Because I remembered everything. Eddie and Eve. Her screams. Him pushing me down the stairs. The pain of slamming into steel steps, the force shuddering through my entire body. The thump on my skull as the world around me cut out entirely.

There was too much pain in my body for me to be in a hospital. If I'd felt nothing, maybe I could have believed that he'd taken pity on me and dumped me in a hospital emergency room. Or maybe I could believe I was dead. Instead, pain curled around every limb, every organ, making it known that I was very much alive and still in the same hellhole.

I had no tears left.

Just hate. I hated him with everything I had. I hated myself for being so stupid and sticking around one place long enough for him to find me.

The flashes went off again. "Eve," I murmured through cracked lips.

There was a long silence and then, "She's not here."

That wasn't Eddie's voice. Somewhere in the back of my pain-riddled mind, I remembered the lower, quieter tone. But for the life of me, I couldn't work out where or why.

I forced one eye open.

Cat-green eyes pierced the darkness, trained intently on me.

There was only one person in the world I knew who had eyes that color. "Zane?"

He didn't say anything.

"Where's Eve?"

"Gone."

Fear knocked at my door, sharp and strong. "What does that mean? Gone where? Is she in another room? Did you take her home?"

An evil cackle of laughter from the other side of the room made me jump. "Do you really think we'd do that, sweet girl?"

A sob crept up my chest. Because that laughter, that cruel, taunting sound had haunted my life and then my nightmares for years. And there was only one person who called me sweet girl. I couldn't even look at him, because if I did, I knew I would break down completely. I focused on Zane because it was all I could do to keep calm. The madness of insanity tried to breach my defenses, tried to invade and force me to shut down. I couldn't. Not yet. Not here.

"Zane, no, what did you do? Tell me."

He didn't respond.

I changed tactics, trying to appeal to the basic sense of human decency that I remembered he'd once had. Zane was just as big as his brother. Just as muscled. Just as strong. If he wanted to, he could get me out of here.

He just had to want to.

I crawled across the dirty floor, agony splintering my chest, making it hard to breathe. I clutched the leg of his pants. "Please. Help me."

Something flickered in his eyes, and hope lit up my chest.

"We were friends once," I blurted out. "You remember? We sat in your room, while you played guitar? Zane, please." My voice broke, and the tears rolled down my face.

"You did what?"

The snarl from Eddie's side of the room was more feral that any animal I'd ever heard.

And anything in Zane's eyes—any part of him that remembered that night—disintegrated along with Eddie's words.

The hope inside me died.

When Eddie's fingers speared into my hair and yanked me away from his brother, I wasn't even surprised. I was too dead inside to feel anything.

"You're mine, you filthy little slut. Mine. You hear me? Not his. Not those maggots at the club you whored yourself out to while you were away from me. Mine."

When his fist slammed into my temple once more, I welcomed the darkness.

It was where I belonged after all.

EVE, BOSTON, AUGIE, LYRIC, FAWN AND PHOENIX'S STORIES CONTINUE IN 'UNHOLY SINS' (SAINT VIEW STRIP #2)

READ ON FOR A SNEAK PEEK AT BOOK 2!

UNHOLY SINS (SAINT VIEW STRIP #2)

PROLOGUE

I could still hear her cries as the girl fell on her knees in the confessional booth.

The agony in her voice as she confessed and repented for being a sexual temptation.

The grinding of my molars, and the crack of my knuckles when I forced myself to remain seated and murmur scripted words of forgiveness.

With my words, I'd forgiven a sin that wasn't hers, but the man who lay sleeping peacefully in his bed in front of me now. Blissfully ignorant of the trauma he'd caused. Completely unaware I watched him with hate in my heart.

She was fourteen years old. Four-fucking-teen.

The room around me was not unlike my own. A cross nailed on the peeling wall above the bed. Rectangular prayer cards depicting saints on the bedside table. A well-used bible with a creased spine and tattered pages within arm's reach on the queen-sized bed. Like he'd been reading it before he fell asleep, filling his head with promises of good, when his soul was black as the night outside.

In and out. His chest rose and fell as he breathed.

In and out for the last time.

I moved silently, my footsteps soft on the carpet until I loomed over him. My fingers itched, knowing what they needed to do.

The church would do nothing if I reported it. They'd sweep it under the rug, like they had so many times before. His unholy sins would go unpunished.

I couldn't let that happen. Not again.

Like he sensed his impending doom, the priest's eyes flew open. He blinked rapidly in the dim light, his vision trying to adjust, clearly attempting to make sense of the hooded, masked figure who stood over him, fingers wrapped lightly around his thick neck.

Panic set in, filling his gaze, then my soul.

I liked it. The confusion in his eyes. The smell of his fear.

I tightened my grip, enough that his fat hands grabbed my wrists in terror, but not so tight he couldn't speak.

"Help!"

It was supposed to be a scream, that much was clear, but it came out a gurgled noise, as pathetic as the man who'd made it.

Anger mixed with the hate. I leaned in closer. "Is that what she said? Did she beg someone to help while you used her? Did she cry, the way you are now?"

Water puddled in his eyes, perhaps tears of fear and regret, or perhaps just a bodily response to me cutting off his airflow. Either way, they had no effect on me. I loosened my grip, playing with my prey, even though I knew I shouldn't.

The scent of piss filled the air.

"Who are you? I've done nothing. Please. Don't—"

Another squeeze as I leaned in, lips to his ear. "Liar, liar, pants on fire." The words were deep. Dark. Deadly. His lame attempt at excuses only fueled the rage that had nowhere else to go except through my fingers pressing against his jugular.

"I never hurt her. She wanted it!"

"Stop. Talking." Squeeze. Wait for him to turn purple. Release.

"I know you..."

He did. I knew him too. And too many others just like him.

I'd joined the priesthood because I didn't want to be like him. I wanted to do good.

And yet here I was, about to commit a mortal sin.

I squeezed one last time. Tight, until he gave up the fight, his body went limp, and the life drained from his watery eyes.

It took all my effort to pry my fingers from the lifeless fuck who'd thought nothing of ruining a young girl's life. Taking his wasn't even close to making amends for the trauma she'd experienced.

As silently as I'd come, I turned and crossed the room, using the sleeve of my black hoodie to open the door so my fingerprints wouldn't be found on it.

I slipped from rectory and started the long walk home.

I waited for it. The guilt. The realization that I'd killed a man.

But when I walked into my own church, up the dark aisle, and dropped to my knees at the altar, the words that came out of my mouth weren't the ones I'd expected.

"Bless me Father for I have sinned...and I don't think I care."

CONTINUE EVE, BOSTON, AUGIE, LYRIC, FAWN, AND PHOENIX'S STORIES IN UNHOLY SINS (SAINT VIEW STRIP, #2)

ALSO BY ELLE THORPE

Saint View High series (Reverse Harem, Bully Romance. Complete)

*Devious Little Liars (Saint View High, #1)

*Dangerous Little Secrets (Saint View High, #2)

*Twisted Little Truths (Saint View High, #3)

Saint View Prison series (Reverse harem, romantic suspense. Complete.)

*Locked Up Liars (Saint View Prison, #1)

*Solitary Sinners (Saint View Prison, #2)

*Fatal Felons (Saint View Prison, #3)

Saint View Psychos series (Reverse harem, romantic suspense. Complete.)

*Start a War (Saint View Psychos, #1)

*Half the Battle (Saint View Psychos, #2)

*It Ends With Violence (Saint View Psychos, #3)

Saint View Rebels (Reverse harem, romantic suspense. Releasing in 2023)

*Book 1

Saint View Strip (Male/Female, romantic suspense standalones. Ongoing.)

*Evil Enemy (Saint View Strip, #1) - March 10, 2023

*Unholy Sins (Saint View Strip, #2) - May 10, 2023

Dirty Cowboy series (complete)

*Talk Dirty, Cowboy (Dirty Cowboy, #1)

*Ride Dirty, Cowboy (Dirty Cowboy, #2)

*Sexy Dirty Cowboy (Dirty Cowboy, #3)

*Dirty Cowboy boxset (books 1-3)

*25 Reasons to Hate Christmas and Cowboys (a Dirty Cowboy bonus novella, set before Talk Dirty, Cowboy but can be read as a standalone, holiday romance)

Buck Cowboys series (Spin off from the Dirty Cowboy series. Complete.)

*Buck Cowboys (Buck Cowboys, #1)

*Buck You! (Buck Cowboys, #2)

*Can't Bucking Wait (Buck Cowboys, #3)

*Mother Bucker (Buck Cowboys, $#4)

The Only You series (Contemporary romance. Complete)

*Only the Positive (Only You, #1) - Reese and Low.

*Only the Perfect (Only You, #2) - Jamison.

*Only the Truth - (Only You, bonus novella) - Bree.

*Only the Negatives (Only You, #3) - Gemma.

*Only the Beginning (Only You, #4) - Bianca and Riley.

*Only You boxset

Add your email address here to be the first to know when new books are available!

www.ellethorpe.com/newsletter

Join Elle Thorpe's readers group on Facebook!

www.facebook.com/groups/ellethorpesdramallamas

ABOUT THE AUTHOR

Elle Thorpe lives in regional Australia with Mr Thorpe and their three kiddos. When she's not at the local cafe writing stories full of kissing, you'll probably find her throwing a ball for her slobbery dog Rollo, or chasing one of the seventy alpacas on the family farm.

You can find her on Facebook or Instagram(@ellethorpebooks or hit the links below!) or at her website www.ellethorpe.com.

If you love Elle's work, please consider joining her Facebook fan group, Elle Thorpe's Drama Llamas or joining her newsletter here. www.ellethorpe.com/newsletter

facebook.com/ellethorpebooks

instagram.com/ellethorpebooks

goodreads.com/ellethorpe